Crime in the Garden

ALSO BY CATHERINE MOLONEY

# CRIME

## IN THE

# GARDEN

## CATHERINE
# MOLONEY

JOFFE
BOOKS

Joffe Books, London
www.joffebooks.com

First published in Great Britain in 2025

Cover art by Dee Dee Book Covers

ISBN: 978-1-80573-211-2

*For Jim and Judy Moriarty*

# PROLOGUE

Whenever he stepped inside the grandly named Hollingrove Park Palm House, Vince Cardew felt a curious thrill, as though he was connecting with a mysterious Palaeolithic landscape that stretched way back into the mists of time.

In truth, the Palm House was really an unassuming, somewhat dilapidated looking conservatory that was home to a variety of rare botanical specimens and a collection of six ancient megaliths known as the Hollingrove Stones.

Generally referred to as 'the greenhouse', Vince's colleagues didn't much care for it, but he was entranced by the tropical atmosphere and eerie primeval vibe. With the strange aqueous half-light, humid air and twisty-turny plant life, it really did feel as if he was stepping back into a world that was as old as time itself.

On this mild Saturday morning in mid-March, he enjoyed his flask of tea sitting on a bench next to the community allotments round the back of the greenhouse, congratulating himself as he often did on having the best job in the world. He was one of the park's team of caretakers personally appointed by Miss Violet Henwood, the last surviving scion of the Henwood family who had owned the estate for generations before it was leased to Bromgrove Council under the management of her nephew, Tony Pardoe, the new CEO. Vince was especially proud seeing as the park boasted the famous Hollingrove Stones as one of its main landmarks. The sandstone blocks (the technical term being menhirs, though strictly speaking these were taller and thinner), had once belonged to a prehistoric burial mound, attracting conservationists, academics and antiquarians who came from all over (strictly by appointment) to study their mysterious spirals and markings. Mr Pardoe scoffed that he had no time at all for 'all that witchcraft and Wicker Man bollocks', but Vince was fascinated by these reminders of an ancient Druid past.

On a mild morning like today's, Vince was content to dismiss metaphysical speculation, inhaling scented garden-fresh air and watching as cottony clouds moved gently across the sky. There was a heady sense of spring touching every nook and cranny and lush greenery blossoming, bursting and blooming all around him. March weather was always variable, so no doubt they hadn't seen the back of high winds and stormy squalls, but, in the meantime, it was a scene to lift the spirits, even if all the competing fragrances made him sneeze. In wintertime when daylight was short, the woodland and copses were dark blotches which lay spider-like across the landscape, almost as if to ward off passers-by by their hostile, gloomy aspect. At such times, the park seemed almost spellbound in a death-like equinoctial trance. With the changing of the seasons, however, and with the earth stirring life of every sort under his feet, the pines and conifers and willows appeared positively homely, even friendly, forming a feathery canopy and melting into a delicate haze that held no trace of shadow.

Reluctantly, Vince heaved himself off the bench. Despite his sinewy build, weather-beaten features and love of the outdoors, he was prone to periodic flareups of arthritis which gave him a cumbrous gait that belied his forty-odd years.

Wincing slightly, he made his way towards the Palm House feeling a familiar tingle of anticipation at the prospect of seeing 'his' stones, for they seemed to belong especially to him as much as to the scholars and academics who came to study them.

Whistling a bar or two, he approached the glass vestibule at the entrance to the greenhouse, only for the tune to die on his lips as he noticed that the doors — usually padlocked — stood wide open.

A chill descended on Vince's carefree mood and he felt unable to stir another step, paralysed before some invisible menace. He tried to call out, but it felt like the sides of his throat were stuck together and his voice seemed to come out of the depths of his overalls in a rasping croak that no one could hear, while his work-worn hands had dampened with sweat. Suddenly, the steamy building with its aquarium-like semi-darkness exuded an evil energy that swelled and surged as though it might at any minute submerge him.

Moving unsteadily towards the inner courtyard and the gravelled sandpit that held the stones, all the "old wives' tales" about their heathenish antecedents seemed to fill the pungent, stagnant air that was overlaid with the whiff of ripe vegetation . . . and another odour . . .

The scent of death.

Tony Pardoe's corpse was lying supine on its back across the tallest of the stones, with the arms flung out almost in an attitude of crucifixion. His sightless eyes stared upwards from a face hideously empurpled and distorted, like one of the ugly little gargoyles in St Mary's Cathedral, Vince thought, aghast, though at least those figurines simulated prayerfulness whereas this was like something out of a nightmare.

Shaking uncontrollably, the groundsman sank to his knees, icy little ripples of horror churning his stomach.

In that moment, the rich, pulsing world of the park beyond the glass windows seemed almost to mock the scene in front of him, as though nature asserted its supremacy and banished pathetic humanity to the shadows.

He knew the Bible taught it was really the woods, hills and flowers that were the shadows in God's sight, since earthly beauties would all perish in time, while human beings were immortal. Looking at the broken body before him, however, there was only the sense of overwhelming revulsion followed by a wave of dread.

Tony Pardoe had mocked the stones.

Now it seemed they had their revenge.

# CHAPTER 1: STIRRINGS

The morning of Sunday 17 March found DI Gilbert ('Gil') Markham deep in thought on a bench in the terraced graveyard of St Chad's Parish Church round the back of Bromgrove Police Station, as was his invariable practice at the start of every new investigation.

Tall with a head of thick dark hair (silvering at the temples) and aquiline features, the detective was an imposing figure, notorious at the station for his reserve and an air of chilly hauteur that enveloped him like chainmail. His courtesy was of the commanding type which kept subordinates at a distance, yet at this early hour the keen grey eyes held a gentle, almost wistful expression as he contemplated the glories of nature and the squirrels frisking energetically round moss-covered graves and monuments.

It was a beautifully mild day — what his partner Olivia Mullen, an English teacher at Hope Academy (popularly known as 'Hopeless'), called 'twiggy' — with earthy smells pervading the graveyard and a rushing, moving, growing feeling in the air. During winter, while nature slumbered, Bromgrove's parks and open spaces had seemed somewhat apologetic, as though asking him to excuse their denuded poverty of aspect, with a sense of discarded clothes in the leaflessness and bareness of trees and shrubs (though the yews and cypresses of St Chad's abided like sentinels over the dead). Now, however, there was an atmosphere of stirring and germination akin to some hidden force preparing to run riot. Olivia's preference was for autumn with the countryside undecorated, stark and stripped down to its bare bones. She said there was honesty in the peeling away of finery and decoration, the stillness and simplicity. For his part, however, there was nothing to beat springtime with its mysterious tingle of anticipation, rooty dampness, chirruping birds and singing life. At such moments, drinking in the tranquil surroundings, he felt himself becoming slowly part of the landscape . . . on the threshold of some sort of nirvana, his brain receptive but at rest and a great peace within and about him.

Despite his benignant mood, grim thoughts of the previous day's call-out eventually forced their way into his mind.

The pathologist Dr Doug 'Dimples' Davidson, a tweedy character with the air of a country vet, had been equally disconcerted by the discovery in Hollingrove Park Palm House, clearing his throat uneasily as they conferred at some distance from the now sheeted corpse, while hovering paramedics waited to transport the body to a waiting ambulance.

'Nasty the way chummy stretched him out . . . like on some kind of heathen altar,' he muttered with an apprehensive eye on the stones.

'Time of death, Doug?'

'Sometime between eight and eleven last night.' Again, the medic looked round warily. 'I don't care for this place,' he muttered. 'Downright eerie if you ask me — devilish . . .'

Dimples wasn't prone to flights of fancy but Markham knew what he meant. For all the swampy heat of the greenhouse, he had felt chilled to the bone at the sight of Tony Pardoe's body in its crucified pose, the richly coloured world of the park outside a mocking contrast to this scene of violent death.

The pathologist lost no time in having the remains removed, he and Markham bowing their heads in respect as the little cavalcade departed for the mortuary. Neither man ever allowed themselves the relief of gallows humour, and the DI was known to be savage if any hapless subordinate displayed a lack of reverence towards the dead, since he regarded the search for justice as amounting almost to a sacred mission. The faces of all his murdered victims were always with him, and it was in punishing those who had snatched them from life that he found the truest satisfaction.

Markham was a lapsed Catholic but now, as he sat in the peaceful graveyard, he recalled a story told by the parish priest of the church he attended as a boy. Fr O'Malley had said the Desert Fathers — those early Christians who lived as hermits and practised fearsome austerities — were so obsessed with thoughts of death that one of them, who worked by spinning wool, adopted the habit every now and then of symbolically letting his spindle drop to the ground and 'putting death before his eyes before he picked it up again'. The DI supposed that this interlude at St Chad's was for him the equivalent of the anchorite's spindle — a chance to remind himself what his job was all about. Markham knew he couldn't change the past or undo the evil that had been committed, but he could at least obtain justice for Tony Pardoe and, in doing so, redeem his memory from the threat of futility and pointlessness. Aware that Easter was just weeks away and swallowing hard at the thought of what others were likely to make of this private ritual, it seemed somehow fitting to offer up a swift silent prayer for the dead man's soul — a hope that it might have emerged from darkness and was even then enjoying a springtime of new beginnings.

*Oh no!*

The clang of the church door along with the sound of voices interrupted Markham's meditation.

Spying the Reverend Simon Duthie, former bank manager and now vicar of St Chad's, he shrank down where he sat, trying to make himself invisible. Luckily for him, Duthie was absorbed in conversation with two female parishioners and sailed out of the churchyard without noticing the detective cringing on his bench.

As Duthie disappeared from view, the DI cautiously exhaled, reflecting that it was a blessing Noakes wasn't with him.

The chiselled features relaxed into a grin as Markham's thoughts turned to George Noakes, former DS turned private eye and his oldest friend. Noakes had been Markham's right-hand man in CID for more years than either of them cared to remember. After retirement, he initially worked as security manager at Rosemount, an upmarket nursing home, before taking the plunge and setting up as a private investigator (*Medway Investigations*) while simultaneously assisting Markham's elite unit as a 'civilian consultant'. After a slow start, the fledgling business was doing well, but Markham was in no doubt his friend missed pursuing 'top end scrotes' as opposed to spying on adulterous couples and the like.

The blunt-spoken Yorkshireman was not popular with the top brass, however. Shortly before his retirement, the then DS Noakes had attended a seminar given by DCI Sidney ('Slimy Sid' to the troops) — who was widely rumoured to hanker after a career in media punditry — on psychological profiling.

'This material has not previously appeared in learned journals,' Sidney intoned.

'Nor ignorant ones either,' muttered his bête noire.

'Every single concept is new,' the DCI continued.

'And most of the married ones,' came from the Greek chorus.

'Shut up, Sarge,' DI Kate Burton had hissed on that occasion, only too well aware of Noakes's propensity for leaving no turn unstoned.

'Well, I ask you, jus' listen to how he's carrying on. Any minute now, he'll be telling us there's a film coming out.' A prediction that reduced his normally po-faced colleague to helpless giggles. 'I tell you, I'm gonna give this chuffin' book of his to everyone I hate for Christmas.' Noakes always had to have the last word.

Fearsomely computer illiterate and regularly humiliated by the dreadful curse "Log Off!" (according to mocking colleagues), it was something of a miracle that the former DS coped with the administrative side of his new business. Equally, he hated battling officialdom on the telephone. 'Wouldn't be surprised if folk passed away waiting,' he groused when regaling Markham with details of his latest ordeal at the hands of the Telecom Madline. Kindly Mr Shah, who owned the takeaway beneath Noakes's minuscule office, strove valiantly to haul his Luddite neighbour into the twenty-first century, but it was a thankless task.

Noakes made no secret of the fact that he considered modern coppers too namby-pamby for words. 'Total snowflakes,' was his withering verdict. 'My old sarn't-major used to say, "Don' send me blokes who've never been knocked down. Send me fellas who know how to keep getting up again."' For all his dithyrambs about declining standards, however, he had an inner kindness that made him a passionate champion of the underdog. The paunchy, uncouth exterior and appalling dress sense also belied a sensitive side to his personality which saw him respond with almost poetic relish to his boss's penchant for 'Big Words' and enthusiasm for the arts, traits that Markham's superiors held against him.

DS colleagues Doyle and Carruthers listened indulgently to the grizzled veteran's salvoes about 'wimps' but on occasion met fire with fire. Like the time he lamented their penchant for occasional forays into Bromgrove's nightlife (pretty tame by metropolitan standards) with the demand 'Don' you know what good clean fun is?' Carruthers had swiftly turned the tables, 'No Sarge, what good is it?'

Olivia was Noakes's number one fan, delighting in his subversive attitude to life and the big heart that lurked behind his gruff exterior and shambolic appearance. She also had a surprising relish for his army stories about 'crap-hats' and 'mess tins' and 'jankers', while he in turn enjoyed her anecdotes from the chalkface, being particularly delighted to hear of one letter from a mother which had read, 'Michael was away last week because I have had a new baby, and it is not his fault.'

The chivalric devotion with which Noakes regarded the guvnor's willowy, ethereal-looking partner was something that irritated his own wife no end. Muriel Noakes, whom Noakes had met (most improbably) on the ballroom dancing circuit, was a snobbish woman and absolute anathema to Olivia, who disliked her archly flirtatious manner towards Markham. The handsome, courteous inspector appealed greatly to Muriel's taste whereas she regarded Olivia as adding a 'neurotic clever clogs and most likely anorexic into the bargain'. The Noakeses' perma-tanned offspring Natalie (apple of Noakes's eye even though she was not his natural daughter) shared her mother's antipathy towards Olivia, though they had mellowed somewhat since Natalie's miscarriage after an unplanned pregnancy. Noakes was a doting husband and father who practically burst with pride when Natalie — a beautician and former doyenne of Bromgrove's nightclubs — obtained her degree in History at the university after studying part-time. Despite a rocky romantic history, she was now engaged to the proprietor of a local fitness centre whose possessive mother had recently (though with very bad grace) allowed the young couple to set a date for their wedding. Since she and Muriel were dedicated social-climbers, the fact that the killing of Pardoe was connected with the Henwood family (i.e. gentry) was at least guaranteed to pique their interest.

DS Roger Carruthers ('Roger the Dodger' as Noakes called him) was also likely to find it an intriguing murder case. Like DI Kate Burton, he was a graduate entrant to the force and had the somewhat desiccated look of an academic with his pallor, slicked back hair and horn-rimmed specs. As the nephew of Superintendent 'Blithering' Bretherton, he possessed an uncanny knack of knowing how to schmooze his superiors. There was a time when Markham suspected

Carruthers of being a mole who had an unhealthily close relationship with various columnists at the *Gazette*, but it appeared his tactic of having Burton drop a heavy hint about undesirable "extracurricular activities" had done the trick. Certainly, there had been no more leaks to worry about. His colleagues had initially been wary of Carruthers due to him being well in with the top brass, but over time the DS had demonstrated that he was his own man, remaining staunchly loyal to Markham and giving as good as he got. Even Noakes — whom Carruthers called 'Sarge' like the rest — had eventually been won over, not least given the fact that Carruthers shared his and DS Doyle's passion for The Beautiful Game. A keen interest in forensic psychology gave him common ground with Burton and he was undeniably ambitious though, like Doyle, he appeared in no hurry to take his inspector's exams, perhaps fearing it would result in a move away from Markham's fabled unit.

DS Doyle — gangling, easy-going and auburn-haired (therefore known as 'the ginger ninja') — was Noakes's protégé and treated him as the oracle in everything from football to affairs of the heart, though now he was happily engaged to teacher girlfriend Kelly, the romantic rollercoaster was a thing of the past. Settled domesticity meant he was less preoccupied with prospects of promotion (despite having gained a degree in criminal law since joining the force), but Markham was hopeful that sensible Kelly would make him see the light.

Then there was DI Kate Burton . . . after Noakes, his most faithful ally.

Like Carruthers, a psychology graduate high-flyer, it had taken a good while before she and Markham's wingman had come to understand each other, not least since she was earnestly as politically correct as the other was proudly 'anti-woke'. Their cast-iron loyalty to Markham and a shared passion for true crime documentaries, however, gradually brought about a rapprochement. There was also the fact that Burton possessed an inner steeliness and was no slouch when it came to sly repartee, proved when she mischievously pointed out that the portly ex-sergeant 'somehow never lost face, as opposed to gaining stomach'. Doyle and Carruthers lamented her culture vulture tendencies and intellectualism, but Markham knew they felt protective towards their school-marmish colleague and were secretly fond of her.

Although engaged to Professor Nathan Finlayson of Bromgrove University's criminal profiling department (nick-named 'Shippers' by Noakes by virtue of his resemblance to the serial killer Harold Shipman), Burton showed no great enthusiasm for "naming the date", a state of affairs which Noakes maintained was due to her carrying a torch for the guvnor. Certainly, Olivia was suspicious of their relationship, and Markham himself knew that there existed some special affinity between them that neither had ever openly acknowl-edged, a tie that he feared might be at the root of her reluc-tance to commit to marriage with Finlayson. His feelings for Kate Burton were a compound of respect, protectiveness and tenderness, together with the sense he always had in her company of a restful homecoming which kept the sordid world at bay. While his passion for Olivia was as strong as ever, 'restful' was not an adjective that could be applied to his spiky, insecure partner. They had been through some rocky patches, including a brief separation when she became involved with a colleague at Hope (a complicated business which ended in tears) and most recently when the longing for a child of her own threatened the life she and Markham had built together.

For all Markham's closeness to Burton, she was not privy to the dark secret in his personal history: the fact that he was the survivor of childhood abuse by his stepfather, a tragedy he had somehow overcome while his brother Jonathan — long lost to drink, drugs and eventually suicide — had not. Only Olivia and Noakes knew about this, and with the latter it was through a process of observation and inference, since the two men rarely spoke about personal matters, their deep-est feelings somehow remaining subterranean and hidden.

Markham knew their triangle was the subject of considerable speculation amongst Bromgrove Police's rank and file, but it was the bedrock of his life and had never expanded to admit another person, not even Burton.

Markham suspected that Burton, who had been hit very hard by the death of her father, was currently meditating some sort of decision, possibly a transfer to Tower Bridge Station in London. He hated the thought of losing her, but was equally reluctant to hold her back. He knew she had the talent and skills to reach the very top — including an emollience in dealing with the top brass that somehow never tipped into sycophancy or servility; he knew also that the current situation was detrimental to her relationship with Finlayson, a wry, laconic man whom he respected. Somehow or other it would have to be resolved. Selfishly, however, he was glad to have her on this case.

DCI Sidney would be decidedly gratified by the fact that this investigation involved the Henwood family, his snobbery the equal of Muriel Noakes's when it came to gradations of class. This would quite possibly be Sidney's swansong before retirement, and Markham was finding him easier to manage since the return of Mrs Sidney (aka 'The Valkyrie') to the marital nest following the Sidneys' brief but acrimonious separation. Sidney had never been a great admirer of the handsome DI whose Oxbridge credentials, culture and exceptional good looks put him in the shade, but they jogged on well enough together these days and the DCI had defended the gang against perennial bouts of sniping by high command. The news of Noakes's involvement was unlikely to be greeted with rapture, but Burton would be able to pour oil on troubled waters, especially once she got Sidney onto the subject of ancient folklore and the history of the Hollingrove Stones, since he was quite the armchair academic and fancied himself as a bit of an antiquarian.

Aware that the gang would be waiting for him in CID, Markham reluctantly got to his feet. The spell of spring was strong upon him and he was loath to exchange it for the stale fug of the station. With a last glance round the picturesque cemetery, sunshine now gilding its masses of sprouting ferns and clumps of violets and primroses, he made his way slowly towards the stone steps which led down to the station car park.

\* \* \*

CID was just as dingy and stuffy as he had feared, but his colleagues' faces were bright and eager as they turned towards him. Casually but smartly attired in chinos and sweatshirts, the two men were dapper as always while Burton's cobalt blue tunic dress over leggings and trendy streaked geometric bob were fashionably edgy and a far cry from her frumpy appearance when she first joined the department. Olivia scornfully described her as a 'field mouse', but the brown, thoughtful eyes revealed gleams of sardonic gaiety from time to time, as now when she watched the two sergeants wolfing down the goodies she had brought in from *Costa*. Noakes had always taken provisioning very seriously and they kept up the custom of 'eats 'n treats' for their team brainstorms. After organizing coffee for Markham and helping him to the last remaining chocolate brownie, she donned her glasses and whipped out a notebook containing details of potential suspects.

'Hollingrove Park belonged to the Henwood family,' she began briskly, before providing a thumbnail sketch of its history and the Hollingrove Stones. After dealing with the background, she continued, 'Miss Violet Henwood leased the estate to Bromgrove Council, but she died a year ago and under the terms of her will the whole shooting match passed to the council with the proviso that her nephew Tony Pardoe was appointed CEO. Mr Pardoe and Miss Henwood's cousin Bernadette Donovan were her only surviving relatives. Mrs Donovan shared Miss Henwood's flat in the mansion house after she was widowed . . . sort of a companion-cum-housekeeper.'

'Weren't the rellies miffed that she left everything to the council and not to them?' Doyle wondered.

'Oh, she was a very wealthy woman,' Burton explained. 'Apparently, she left most of her money to Mr Pardoe, who was a successful businessman in his own right. I've made an appointment with Miss Henwood's solicitors Goldrein Hesketh to go through the financial background.'

As usual, Burton hadn't let the grass grow, Markham thought admiringly.

'Was Pardoe married . . . or in a relationship?' Carruthers was always keen to sniff out anything that smacked of *Cherchez la Femme*.

'There was an on-off girlfriend name of Maureen Slattery . . . and he was close friends with another woman called Loretta Davenport, but that was platonic — almost a brother–sister relationship.'

Since Pardoe's parents were both dead and he was without siblings, there had been no next of kin requiring the dreaded bereavement visit.

'Business rivals?' Markham enquired.

'One Jason Quirk . . . also in digital technology but didn't have the same Midas touch and social connections. By all accounts, he was hopping mad when Pardoe got an OBE while he was left out in the cold.'

'So he had at least one enemy then,' Markham said thoughtfully.

'Oh, I'd say more than one, sir.' Burton was always punctilious about calling him 'Sir' even though they were now the same rank. 'He fired his PA Marion Kirkwood for some reason and she went off to work for Quirk. Then there was Michael Brophy — journalist at the *Gazette* who kept writing snide pieces about Bromgrove's "Ruthless Tech Tycoon". Pardoe had also tangled with Catrina Walsh . . . she's the mansion house's café manager and he wanted to get rid of her — personality clash or something like that.' The DI consulted her notes. 'Plus there's the "old guard", traditionalists who worried that Pardoe didn't care about the estate's history, afraid of him turning the place into a theme park like Alton Towers. The Henwoods can trace their descent from Richard II, and the mansion house has its own museum — the curator Malcolm Devenish is Vice-President of Hollingrove Druid Society . . .'

The two young sergeants exchanged startled looks at this piece of information. 'There's a team of volunteers who run *The Reader Shop* and *Shared Reader Group* . . . and the estate manager and groundsmen,' she concluded.

'That's a lot of people to work through,' Doyle groaned.

'Pardoe was killed on Friday night,' Carruthers pointed out. 'Folk will have been getting a head start on the weekend . . . gone down the pub or out for a meal—'

'Which means they'll be alibied and we can rule them out,' Burton finished crisply. 'The park's closed to the public for now, but the guvnor and I can scope the place out tomorrow while you two start checking people's movements: I've got a list of personnel here, so it's a case of narrowing it down. Hopefully, once I've sorted a venue for interviews, we can do those on Tuesday before the park reopens on Wednesday.' Her eyes gleamed. 'I've arranged for Mr Devenish to give us a private tour of the museum. There's so much history attached to the estate, that it makes sense to check out the background some more.'

'Indeed it does, Kate,' Markham said approvingly, amused to note that Doyle didn't look exactly thrilled at the prospect of an afternoon spent poring over medieval arcana. Carruthers, on the other hand, had brightened up considerably on hearing this.

'What about Sarge?' Doyle wanted to know. 'Is he in on this investigation?'

'Is the Pope a Catholic?' Carruthers quipped.

Markham smiled at Burton's look of resignation.

'I'll be calling on Noakesy tomorrow morning,' he said wryly. 'No doubt he's already heard about the murder, most likely from Doyle, so I anticipate that he'll be eager to make himself available.'

'Wild horses and all that,' Carruthers grinned.

'Quite.'

A short time after the team had dispersed, Markham remained at his desk perusing a pamphlet left by Burton. 'It's a ninety-acre estate and the council did a big promotion drive,' she had told him. 'In addition to the mansion house and museum, there's lots of other attractions . . . café, boating lake, book shop, children's play area along with thousand-year-old oak trees and walled gardens.'

Now he turned to a section on the Hollingrove Stones contributed by Tom Burke (volunteer, *The Reader Shop*) and Suzanne Mackie (*Shared Reader Group*) along with various pen and ink sketches.

It appeared the stones had been part of one of those long hillocks with the earth piled up over stone cells and a passage leading to the outside — a chambered box tucked into the landscape that he vaguely remembered reading about as a child. It wasn't until the 1960s that proper efforts had been made to protect the monuments, elderly locals recalling how they jutted out in the middle of the roundabout on Hollingrove Road before contractors began to widen the highway and made discoveries. Eventually more stones turned up along with some burnt bones, clay burial urns, tools and other artefacts. Even then, however, the stones were simply relocated to the Hollingrove Triangle — a small green space bounded by Hollingrove Avenue and Bramfield Road — where they were enclosed inside tall railings with only a modest plaque to indicate their provenance. Finally, however, in 1964 the stones were transplanted to Hollingrove Park Palm House where they attracted a stream of expert visitors. It had been established that the artefacts were Bronze Age but the monuments themselves were thousands of years older than that, which meant the tomb must have been a sacred site for millennia after it was originally constructed.

It was incredible, Markham reflected in wonderment, to think of generation after generation performing their eerie, secret rituals and burying the dead in a sepulchre that most likely seemed to them as old as the earth itself. According to the little booklet, it was probable that Stone Age people came back to the chamber tomb over and over again to interact with the bones of their ancestors — maybe even remove them and add new ones. Since the tomb (a 'dolmen') would have been positioned towards the top of sloping ground, people most probably used to gaze uphill to where the ancestors were buried as if locating their own special signpost.

Markham liked the idea of this connection between the living and the dead via the sky, hills and horizon. With a wry smile, he supposed such rituals were not so far removed from his own pre-investigation stocktake in St Chad's graveyard.

He went on to read that though the Henwoods were a Catholic family, Miss Henwood had been president of Bromgrove Folklore Society with a profound interest in paganism and the occult. He couldn't see his colleagues — especially Doyle and Carruthers — having much truck with supernaturalism and horned gods . . . Odin and all the rest of it. But personally, he was all in favour of "live and let live", smiling as he recalled Noakes's verdict that 'the Bible said it was a star which guided the Wise Men to Bethlehem, so all that about astrology and soothsayers didn't mean you couldn't be a good Christian.'

Setting the booklet aside, he remained lost in thought. Outside his window, the skies had darkened and the day turned suddenly grey and cold. The glorious riot of spring seemed very far away.

But the case was in motion, the DI told himself.

Whatever evil stirred in Hollingrove Park, he was on its trail.

# CHAPTER 2: RIDING THE DEVIL

The buoyancy Markham had felt over the weekend promptly evaporated on Monday morning as he headed down Medway High Street towards Noakes's office. It was paradoxical that in St Chad's graveyard he had experienced a sense of life beating furiously under the brown earth — a miracle that made his limbs somehow lighter — while this busy thoroughfare felt oppressive and dreary by comparison, as though a large and gracious world had contracted to something much shabbier.

Of course, the weather didn't help, the previous day's mild sunshine and soft breeze having been replaced by a cutting east wind that made his eyes water. Altogether, he was glad when he reached the Tandoori at the entrance to the Medway Centre, its owner Mr Shah renting out the first-floor cubbyhole upstairs to the former DS.

Noakes's quarters were decidedly compact, but despite its dimensions, the office worked reasonably well, a tiny galley kitchen and lavatory having somehow been shoehorned into the space and a fair-sized bay window looking out onto the street below. Olivia had helped 'prettify' the place with tasteful black and white prints of Bromgrove and various pot plants that Noakes was always forgetting to water.

As well as the tasteful cityscapes, there were framed pieces from the *Gazette* citing Noakes's involvement with Markham's 'elite squad' which the DI figured wouldn't do his friend any harm at all. Their most recent case together down at the Tower of London had attracted some very favourable publicity that would no doubt yield dividends in due course — though probably not fast enough for Mrs Noakes's liking! There had been lavish feature spreads in several national newspapers about the successful collaboration between Bromgrove CID and their Tower Bridge counterparts which snared the killer of a female curator while simultaneously laying to rest a tragic cold case involving two missing children and the mystery of 'the Tower prowler'. Sidney had been delighted by the coverage, with Markham careful to stay well in the background and let his superiors bask in the afterglow.

Olivia had insisted that Noakes lived up to his newly burnished profile, overseeing the installation of some decent furniture — an IKEA coffee table plus sofa and armchairs in cheerful patterned fabric, together with a pine desk and shelving unit — so the premises were less dingy than might have been expected from a cursory outside inspection. 'You can have trendy tubular furniture and chrome gizmos galore when you really hit the big time, George,' Olivia had told him kindly. 'But until then, you need to be comfy.'

Even if Noakes ever attained the promised land of elegant décor and executive gadgets, Markham doubted that his friend's appearance would lend itself to an aesthetic overhaul. With his furrowed, pouchy face, piggy eyes and fleshy nose set atop a thick neck and chunky body, this was not exactly a lean, mean crime-fighting machine. His salt and pepper hair never *would* lie down, seeming to sprout in all directions, and sartorially he was a walking disaster, though at least there was no longer a risk of him outraging Sidney's sensibilities on a daily basis. While submitting to his wife's edicts when it came to high days and holidays (i.e. church and Muriel's dinner parties), he was happiest in gansey jumpers of florid hue teamed with flannels or cords, dodgy raincoats and his beloved George boots (indispensable to an alumnus of the Parachute Regiment ). No doubt once out in the field at Hollingrove Park, he would disinter the ancient tweed combo he deemed suitable for 'dealing with poshos'. Certainly Markham could only hope that today's clashing outfit of sludge-coloured crew neck and purple cords was strictly a Working From Home getup.

The contrast between the two men was almost comical. On the one hand, there was Markham immaculate in his pinstripe, the pure contours of his face radiating thoughtfulness, resolution and a certain spiritual fitness. On the other, Noakes with his horribly mismatched attire and air of a disreputable hobo. Yet, somehow, they couldn't do without each other. It was more than the sameness of the goal. In some strange and indefinable way, Markham knew they were brothers under the skin, an alchemy that defied analysis.

It was obvious Noakes was expecting him, sorting tea and chocolate digestives in record time and sitting back in his armchair with an air of eager anticipation. There was no disguising the noticeable odour of Pot Noodle and takeaway, but Markham reckoned this wouldn't necessarily deter the kind of client his friend aimed to attract ('small fry to start with cos where there's muck there's brass', being the Yorkshireman's infallible nostrum).

'D'you want me in with you on this Hollingrove Park jobbie then?' Noakes asked with an elaborate casualness that amused Markham.

'Naturally, Noakesy. I'd say the fact of the park being home to the stones — the whole neolithic angle — is likely to make for a high-profile case.'

'It's proper historical round Bromgrove . . . goes all the way back to when we were joined with Russia . . . covered in tropical vegetation an' half a mile of ice.'

'Really?'

'Yeah, straight up.' A quick slurp and mouthful of biscuit before Noakes continued, 'I saw this documentary about boffins excavating some mound in Old Carton . . . they said it dated from the late plasticine thingy.'

Markham, long familiar with Noakesypropisms — linguistic quirks of dialect that the other had turned into an art form by his vehement sincerity — reminded himself to store this one up for Olivia who was sure to delight in such a rebranding of the Pleistocene Era.

'Hmm,' he chuckled. 'Next thing you'll be telling me they worked that out by carbon dating radioactive black puddings.'

Noakes grinned and slurped some more.

'Kate's arranged for us to have a tour of the mansion house museum once Forensics are done,' Markham continued, 'so we'll doubtless learn more about the park's Druidical antecedents then.'

Noakes scratched his chin. 'D'you reckon that's why this bloke copped it — cos he were mixed up in some sort of *cult* . . . kind of like a human sacrifice?'

'It's more likely to come down to one of the usual motives: Sex, Money or Revenge,' Markham said drily. 'But given where Tony Pardoe's body was found, the pagan dimension *could* be significant.'

'Druids are like the Greens, aren't they?' Noakes ruminated. 'Venerating Mother Earth an' all that crap . . . don' believe in heaven neither . . .' He sounded relieved that he wouldn't be meeting any of said species there. 'Always banging on about spirits living in the landscape an' way-out stuff like that. Our Nat were into it at one time.'

Markham recalled that Natalie Noakes had indeed flirted with new age philosophies during a period when her engagement to Rick Jordan had hit the buffers. This had included a dubious association with the kind of people who promoted bizarre practices such as "self-marriage" ceremonies and betrothals to trees. Muriel Noakes had been in a ferment of anxiety about it.

'Well, Merlin was a Druid,' the DI said finally. 'And plenty of historical figures became involved in magic and mysticism . . . Nicholas II turned to Rasputin, for example—'

'An' jus' look how *that* turned out!'

'Not the best example I could have chosen,' Markham sighed. 'But Henry VII was so obsessed with Merlin and King Arthur that he built his own replica of the Round Table. And there was James I with his interest in witchcraft and Elizabeth I consulting her astrologer Dr Dee.'

'Yeah, Princess Di an' Fergie were into tarot cards an' psychics — not that it did 'em much good! An' didn't Tony Blair get mixed up with some daft bint who claimed she could see stuff in her crystal ball?'

Markham laughed. 'That's right, the Blairs' "lifestyle guru" — a woman called Carole Caplin. She had a dodgy boyfriend in the background, so it all got a bit embarrassing.'

'You couldn't imagine prime ministers like Maggie Thatcher or Churchill bothering with star-gazing an' all that hocus pocus,' Noakes said firmly.

'Sorry to disappoint you, Noakesy, but according to Olivia, Churchill belonged to a Druid association — the Albion Lodge or something like that.' Seeing that the other looked as though the earth was shifting beneath his feet, Markham added hastily, 'I believe Druids *can* be Christians. And, of course, the Romantic poets made nature worship positively respectable, people like Shelley and Keats . . .'

Noakes looked very black at this. 'Might've known *they'd* be mixed up in it somehow,' he muttered.

'*Anyway,*' Markham continued heartily (before his friend could get started on his dislike of 'Sheets and Kelly'), 'the context for this case is certainly highly unusual. As well as the Druid angle, the Henwoods are descended from Richard II. Actually, Violet Henwood — who left Hollingrove Park to the council — belonged to the British Monarchists' Society.'

*That was more like it.* Noakes looked as though he strongly approved, causing Markham to reflect wryly that the late chatelaine and Muriel Noakes would doubtless have got on like a house on fire given Mrs Noakes's enthusiasm for royalty and ardent partisanship of 'the dear King and Queen'.

'Richard II were deposed, though.' Noakes's expression clouded over.

'I believe so,' Markham replied vaguely. 'Kate filled me in on him: Apparently he was rather too keen on the Divine Right of Kings and spent more time with soothsayers and astrologers than working out how to stay on his throne.'

'Should've concentrated on not putting up taxes 'stead of bothering about alignment of the planets an' whatnot.'

Markham smothered a smile. If he knew Burton and Noakes, the two of them would lose no time boning up on the exotic historical side of things, vying with each other to unearth juicy nuggets about wizards and superstitious royals.

In the meantime, though, 'With all the prehistoric and medieval overtones, this case is quite the package,' he remarked. 'As I say, it's likely to stir up all kinds of local interest.'

Noakes grinned wolfishly. 'Slimy Sid won't like it if there's skeletons in the Henwoods' family closet.'

'We'll cross that bridge when we come to it, Noakesy. As things stand, the list of suspects boils down to park employ-ees and associates of Mr Pardoe.'

With that, he went through the previous day's briefing as Noakes listened attentively.

'When I were a lad, I had all kinds of fancies about that park,' the former sergeant said unexpectedly at the conclusion of Markham's recital. 'In the summer when there were moths flitting about — great white glimmering things — I used to imagine they were ghosts. Other times, us kids scared ourselves witless making stuff up about the woods an' them stones.' His expression was reflective as he added, 'I reckon if you spent too much time around them, it might turn you a bit pagan.'

For Markham, the beauties of the park symbolised on the one hand the innocence of God's creation, while on the other hand there were the Hollingrove Stones with their hints of — what was Dimples's word for it? — *devilry*. It made him uneasy.

'So far, there are no obvious Satanists or Wiccans jump-ing out at us,' the DI said heavily. 'But there's definitely something uncanny about the way Mr Pardoe was posed . . . something deeply *unwholesome*.'

His friend was thoughtful. 'Come to think of it, there *were* summat dodgy connected with that greenhouse place back in the seventies.'

'*Oh?*' Markham was instantly alert.

'Yeah . . . a kid went missing from the sandpit or play area or whatever they had for kiddies.' Noakes screwed up his eyes intently then smote his forehead. '*Got it!* Little lass name of Mary Priddy . . . she ended up down the bottom of a hole in the greenhouse.'

'Foul play?'

'Apparently the council had builders in relaying paving slabs or summat. Any road, the coroner ruled it were an accident. A journo at the *Gazette* did some digging, though, an' found out that CID weren't happy . . . said they'd been trying to pin it on the playground supervisor but couldn't make it stick. A couple of cold case johnnies took a look later on, but they didn't come up with anything new.'

'Cheers, Noakesy, that's an interesting coincidence for us to follow up.'

The other knew if there was one thing Markham did not like, it was coincidences.

'What are you up to this arvo then?' he enquired.

'I'm going to take another quick look at the scene with Kate while Doyle and Carruthers check out alibis. We should be able to rule out anyone who was drinking or clubbing on Friday night—'

'As in the young ones.'

'Correct. I'd say we're looking at the names on Kate's list rather than a local madman.'

Markham knew well that DCI Sidney's preferred prime suspect would be the archetypal "bushy haired stranger" as opposed to anyone with a connection to the Henwoods or the park. He might well be on a sticky wicket at any press conference, but they'd get round it somehow.

Noakes must have read his mind. 'How's Sidney these days then?' he asked. 'Still boring on at those godawful "deep dives" an' spouting weirdy psychobabble?'

'*Hashtag Be Kind*, Noakesy.'

His friend merely grunted.

'The DCI wasn't best pleased about that email you sent to Councillor Songhurst over local policing,' Markham said caustically. 'The one where you signed off *Tweet Tweet Tweet!*'

'Songhurst's a dickhead.'

'True, but next time do me a favour and try to remember he's the dickhead who chairs the Parks and Green Spaces Committee.'

Noakes endeavoured to look contrite and failed miserably.

Markham had little hope of Songhurst ever forgetting that civic diversity and inclusion workshop where he had held forth on the subject of Bromgrove's connections with the slave trade only to be interrupted by Noakes who had mischievously heckled: 'We're not the worst. Not when you think of a town like Blackpool which got its name cos of all the escaped slaves who made their way there.'

Time to change the subject.

'Before I forget,' he said. 'I'm to ask you an' Liv over to ours next Saturday . . . kind of a special meal for Easter.' Shyly he added, 'The missus is doing an Easter Tree an' all.'

*An Easter Tree?*

'Splendid.' Olivia would crown him for saying yes, but affection for 'George' would win the day.

'How's Natalie?' he asked politely. 'Not long to go to the wedding — May will be upon us in no time.'

'Oh, she an' Mu have got everything under control,' his friend said solemnly. 'It's all down to spreadsheets, see.'

Markham's lips twitched, even as he felt a pang that Olivia appeared to have set her face against the notion of wedding plans featuring in their own immediate future.

'Have another biscuit,' his friend urged cordially, catching something forlorn in Markham's expression.

'Alas, I'd better make tracks, Noakesy. You're very welcome to come and join us for the recce.'

'I better clear the decks here, seeing as I'm on this park case.'

'Well, I'll text you the venue for Tuesday's interviews just as soon as I know the timetable.'

After some further chit-chat about Noakes's business (apparently Mr Shah's tech-savvy offspring planned to introduce him to the marvels of TikTok and Instagram), Markham took his leave, satisfied that the fledgling outfit was doing as well as could be expected. It was obvious, though, that Noakes had had a bellyful of shadowing errant spouses and tracing missing pets ("bread and butter clients") and was raring to get stuck into another murder case. Sidney would doubtless hum and haw about having his old nemesis on the payroll, but the DI knew he could make a good case for Noakes's inclusion, not least given the gang's impressive solve rate along with his wingman's local knowledge and the keen "inner eye" that made him an invaluable sounding board. If push came to shove, Kate Burton would know how to bring Sidney round. She had an unrivalled knack for propitiating the most prickly senior officers; even had Chief Superintendent Ebury-Clarke ('Toadface') eating out of her hand. Markham dreaded to think how he would manage the likes of Ebury-Clarke without her.

Putting that depressing prospect firmly behind him, the DI quickened his pace. The wind had abated somewhat, so hopefully there'd be time for a quick whiz round the estate before getting the lie of the land back at the mansion house.

* * *

'I'd forgotten how pretty the park is,' Kate Burton declared a short time later after they had done a circuit of the lake and peeked into the Japanese and Old English gardens. 'Everything kind of *glows* . . . the daffodils and tulips . . . *idyllic.*'

The breeze having now picked up again and the skies resolutely grey, they were glad to retreat inside, away from the elements.

Bill Whelan, the estate manager, gave them a whistlestop tour of the greenhouse and mansion house before tactfully leaving them alone in the currently deserted ground floor café.

'He's in the clear, boss,' Burton murmured. 'Wedding anniversary party at *Rossi's* on Friday night. Plenty of witnesses.'

Good, that made one less to worry about. 'This is a delightful place, Kate,' he rejoined as they sipped the excellent coffee and biscuits that Whelan had rustled up.

The mansion house was a restrained neo-classical three-storeyed gem with elegant white-stucco facade. While the frontage dated to the Regency period, the interior was a fascinating hotchpotch of historical styles, the third-floor apartment tenanted by Violet Henwood being papered in crimson flock, raised like braille, while the formal rooms on the floors below merged into a blur of impossibly lofty ceilings, antique rugs, silk-clad walls, fine dark-wood furniture and overflowing bookcases. There were plenty of pre-Raphaelite paintings along with an abundance of carefully preserved family heirlooms: silk Japanese folding screens, old Bohemian glass, eighteenth-century embroidered samplers, antique tea caddies and fans, plus masses of oak in the linen-folded style. All highly quaint and atmospheric.

'I've arranged with Mr Devenish for us to go round the museum on Wednesday, sir,' Burton told him as they enjoyed their refreshments. 'Given the Henwood family's background and the connection with the stones and everything, seems like we need to be on top of the *context*.'

'Absolutely right, Kate,' Markham approved. With a twinkle in his eye he added, 'Noakesy can't wait . . . very much a fan of historical epics.'

'Especially anything starring the great Lancashire Viking Burt de Lancaster,' she shot back deadpan, much to his surprise. But that was the thing about Kate Burton. Despite Olivia's dismissal of her as a dormouse and the DI's undeniable craving for correctness of procedure that irritated her colleagues no end — together with a sense that she was self-imprisoned and always corking up her personal feelings with rigid self-control — she had this habit of suddenly coming out with flashes of wit that revealed glimpses of an intriguing and unexpected hinterland.

He smiled too, the austere features that could wither a subordinate with one scorching glance softening in a way that would have astonished the rank and file.

'Indeed. I imagine he's delving into Iron Age barrows and the rest of it even as we speak.'

'The greenhouse didn't strike me as all that sinister, boss,' she said. 'Just a smell of damp earth, stone and moss — peaty and organic. It might have been happenstance the murder taking place there; just a private, out of the way spot for a meeting.'

He detected a note of doubt.

'You don't think there was any significance in the choice of rendezvous, Kate?'

'Could be, sir. But if we're looking for a killer with some sort of fixation about the ancestors, that's a whole new can of worms.'

He left this supposition hanging in the air as, the drinks finished, they walked over to a sash bay window overlooking trim mown lawns that abutted the park.

Catching sight of swings and slides in the distance behind a low picket fence, he filled Burton in on Noakes's story about the child who wandered off to her death and ended up at the bottom beneath the foundations of the greenhouse.

'I'll arrange an interview with Michael Brophy at the *Gazette* asap,' she said. 'He's on our list of people to speak to, seeing as he enjoyed sticking it to Mr Pardoe on a regular basis.'

'See if you can find out who handled the cold case review, Kate.'

'Will do, sir.' She looked pleased to have a substantive lead, as opposed to more speculative hypotheses. 'I should have somewhere sorted for tomorrow's interviews by close of play . . . okay if I text you the details?'

'Perfect.'

'Forensics will be finished up here by Wednesday. So far, there's nothing of interest from Miss Henwood's flat.' A reluctant grin. 'It's like a time capsule from Victorian times or something — she makes Sarge look like a techno whizzkid.'

Markham pulled a mock comic face. 'I don't suppose there's any chance she was a mad Druidess with followers who were into human sacrifice?'

'By all accounts she was just an old-fashioned Roman Catholic, with a soft spot for notions of Merrie England — maypoles and all that, you know, sir,' she quoted with a hint of cynicism, *"The rich man in his castle, The poor man at his gate—"*

*"God made them, high or lowly, And ordered their estate,"* Markham concluded.

'That's right, sir. A conservative type who liked the idea of the lower orders having a good frisky time in mid-summer but generally knowing their place. Seems she was interested in folklore and such, but not in any subversive sense . . . more libertarian by the sound of it, okay with commoners having their fun so long as it was harmless and didn't threaten the established order. At any rate, the SOCOs haven't turned up anything remotely dodgy.'

'What about Mr Pardoe's residence?'

'Mansion flat in Taggart Mews just off Bromgrove Rise; tastefully neutral, with all the character of an upmarket hotel room. The techies are checking out his laptop and social media contacts, but nothing out of the ordinary so far. Looks like there were a few community groups agitating about his ideas for a revamp of the park, but it was just the usual low-level grumbling, no threats against him or anything like that.'

'Neighbours any use?'

'Nada, boss, looks like he kept himself to himself . . . no fights with girlfriends or anything like that.'

'What innovations did he have in mind for the park?'

'Oh, some kind of fancy walkway to make the stones more accessible — and a shakeup to bring in more "installation art" and young influencers.' With a wry expression, 'Whatever that means.' She paused. 'All pretty standard really for a trendy entrepreneur looking to flex his muscles as CEO . . . might have made the traditionalists bristle but nothing too outrageous. Seems like he wanted to play down the Ricardian stuff and focus more on the environmental side — nature trails, that kind of thing — but nothing worth killing for.'

Markham sighed. A downpour had started outside, sheets of rain rattling the windows and gutters bubbling unchecked. 'Okay, Kate,' he said. 'Let's get back to base and see that everything's set up. Hopefully the other two will have winnowed down the list of suspects so we can see our way forward.'

It struck Markham that his fellow DI appeared somewhat pale and tired. He locked eyes with her for a long moment that seemed to stretch out indefinitely before she self-consciously looked away. He knew she wouldn't thank him for any enquiries about her wellbeing, so said nothing more as, with collars turned up, they hurried out to their cars, thoughts already turning to incident room procedures and protocols.

Behind them, the park dripped damp and dank, inscrutable in the sudden March shower as though hugging secrets to itself.

* * *

That evening, Olivia was intrigued to hear about his experiences as they relaxed in the living room of Markham's apartment at The Sweepstakes, an upmarket complex off Bromgrove Avenue. It was a comfortable space, almost womb-like with its red and gold vintage wallpaper and thick carpet of the same hue. Olivia's ballet prints and figurines proclaimed her devotion to Dance, while Markham's carefully chosen antiques glowed in the soft light from Tiffany lamps and daffodils were artistically arranged in a Waterford crystal vase on the low coffee table. It was still raining heavily outside, but through the French windows, trees in the landscaped gardens were coming into bud and the cherry blossom foamed like a pale vapour.

Markham sat in his favourite wingback armchair next to the windows with Olivia cross-legged at his feet as they reviewed the events of the day.

'Miss Henwood sounds like a woman who was nostalgic for some sort of golden age,' she observed after he had described the mansion house.

'With Druid leanings,' he chuckled. 'By all accounts she was immensely proud that her family were custodians of the Hollingrove Stones.' His gaze wandered to a pile of exercise books atop which sat Thomas Hardy's *Tess of the D'Urbervilles*. Gesturing at it, he said, 'I seem to remember Stonehenge features in that novel. Doesn't the heroine camp out there while she's on the run?'

'That's right. Apparently Hardy was thrilled when he discovered an ancient sarsen stone in his back garden — called it the Druid Stone and wrote a poem about it . . . well actually, it was more about being haunted by the ghost of his first wife—'

'You don't sound too enthused.'

'Oh, don't get me started. I may have to teach him, Gil, but there are times when I see what Henry James meant when he said the only believable things in *Far from the Madding Crowd* were the sheep and the dogs!'

Markham smiled at this.

'And the man was a total *pig* to poor Emma Gifford. I reckon she was spot on when she told a friend that "old Tommy only understood the women he invented and did not have a clue about the rest."'

Her partner chuckled. 'Given that there could be some sort of Druid vibe at work in this case, I may dip into *Tess* for inspiration.'

'Be my guest.' Absently, she twirled strands of long red hair — her most striking feature along with remarkable grey-green eyes — round her fingers. 'D'you *really* reckon what happened to that poor man has something to do with paganism or witchcraft?'

'Well, the positioning of the body seemed quite infernal, as though whoever did this was suggesting that Tony Pardoe was *accursed* or marked by Fate — a sacrificial victim. And then there's the proximity of the Hollingrove Stones; it feels to me as if that's somehow significant, only as yet I don't see how.'

He told her about the Mary Priddy case. 'There were doubts about how that child came to end up in the greenhouse, so Tony Pardoe's death might not be the first murder connected with the stones.' He shivered involuntarily. 'There's something wild and heathen about them which is quite at odds with the trees and flowers and neat gravelled paths. Out in the park, it's very beautiful and you feel as if nature's talking to you and you are talking back to it, uplifting, and all one's worries just drop away.'

Olivia was relieved the conversation had turned away from sacrificial victims and a dead child. Nature felt like an altogether safer topic.

She looked up at him affectionately. 'You remind me of Mole from *Wind in the Willows* . . . all happy and excited when spring arrives.'

She stopped guiltily, as though suddenly aware that he might consider she was being inappropriately flippant. However, he sensed that she was trying to lighten the mood and replied easily, 'I guess Noakesy has to be Mr Toad then — though in *his* case it's a mania for history and the Druids rather than motor cars.'

She giggled. 'Has he got Stonehenge on the brain then?'

'Well, he's decidedly intrigued by the Druidical angle; next thing we know, he'll have come up with a theory about Tony Pardoe's murder being connected with the Spring Equinox or some such.' Seeing her amusement, Markham judged that the moment was propitious. 'By the way, we're expected at Toad Hall for supper on Saturday.'

'*Oh no, Gil!*'

'You won't want to disappoint Noakesy. Apparently Muriel's doing an Easter Tree.'

Olivia had to laugh at this. 'The mind boggles!' She yawned, her eyes wandering reluctantly to the pile of exercise books. 'Suppose I'd better do some marking. Who knows, I may glean some pagan insights to help with the case.'

'Kate's lined up a tour of the mansion house museum for us on Wednesday.'

'How *is* she these days?'

There was a hint of frost in his partner's tone, but he chose to ignore it.

'Looking a bit pale and washed out . . . I get the feeling she's at some sort of crossroads career-wise.'

Olivia tried not to look as though she hoped it was a trajectory that would take Kate Burton far from Bromgrove. 'Maybe she and Nathan are ready for a change of scene,' she said neutrally.

'You could be right,' he agreed quietly.

He sought to recapture their earlier mood of affectionate complicity.

'I wonder which of the *Wind in the Willows* cast list would do for Sidney.'

'Oh that's easy, Gil . . . *He* belongs with the weasels and stoats.' She turned thoughtful, murmuring, 'It was such a tragedy that Kenneth Grahame's son killed himself so young.'

Markham was startled. 'Killed himself?'

'Yes, the poor boy laid down in front of a train when he was up at Oxford.' Softly, she dropped a kiss on his head and headed for their bedroom.

Later, as Markham sat in his study overlooking the neighbouring municipal cemetery — a room almost monastically austere by contrast with the cosy, cluttered living room — those words echoed in his mind.

He thought about Jonathan, memories of his doomed brother revived by the conversation with Olivia.

Finally, with an immense effort of will, he reached for the manila file on his desk and began to read.

## CHAPTER 3: BENEATH THE MASK

The next morning was grey and overcast as Markham collected Noakes from his Medway office and headed across town for the first round of interviews, first checking in with Dimples Davidson who confirmed his original estimate for time of death.

The pathologist and former DS were pleased to see each other, though since their pleasure took the form of friendly insults, a bystander would have been hard pushed to detect any particular regard. Noakes invariably liked to wind Davidson up, as was his wont with medical personnel. It was one reason why the force's occupational health team had experienced a collective shudder when the time came round for the paunchy sergeant's annual health review. Unsurprisingly, his jocular references to the father of the NHS as 'Urinary Bevan' and quips about 'Sputum Cup of the Year Awards' failed to elicit answering mirth, while Doc McPherson didn't appreciate the Noakesian translation of 'stress evacuation' as 'a touch of the trots'. Still less did the dour expatriate Scot — leading light of Bromgrove's Scottish Association — appreciate being chaffed about how Robert the Bruce was 'really half Scotch an' half soda'. Davidson counselled the medic that George Noakes was an acquired taste, but McPherson — along with the station's top brass — had never managed to overcome his antipathy. 'You've got to see past the uncouthness and that Yorkshire bloody-mindedness,' the pathologist insisted. 'George Noakes will fight to his last breath for the guy in the street . . . honest as the day is long.' Even this encomium wasn't enough to convert McPherson, however.

Dimples and Noakes were as one in their reaction to the Hollingrove Stones which they regarded with fascinated repulsion. 'Downright creepy having those things there,' was Dimples's verdict. 'They should be in a history museum or somewhere like that, not smack-bang next to a children's playground.'

'Yeah, creepy's the word, but guess they belong in the park, seeing as it were special to the prehistoric folk, Druids an' them lot,' Noakes demurred. ''Sides, the greenhouse ain't open to jus' *anyone* — you've got to apply an' get a ticket.'

'And there's the fact that Miss Henwood's transfer of the estate included guarantees from the council that the stones would never leave the park,' Markham pointed out, having been thoroughly briefed by Burton.

'She was a nice old lady,' Dimples commented, 'but as for those hobby-horses about ancient Britons and the family tree . . .' He shook his head meaningfully. 'Didn't live in the modern world at all. My wife used to bump into her at the WI . . . said she was always full of talk about genealogies and good times gone by.' Markham suppressed a smile at this, imagining only too well how Mrs Davidson — a brisk, sensible woman with no nonsense about her — would have viewed Violet Henwood's fetish for Saxon and medieval mythology.

Dimples recalled the Mary Priddy case. 'It was 1989 . . . I was a junior doctor when it happened . . . seem to remember there was some finger-pointing which never came to anything.' With a frown he added, 'After that . . . well, they should've moved those bloody sandstone blocks somewhere else.' From which it was clear to Markham that the medic would not be talked out of his dislike of the monument.

Now back in the car, 'Where're we doing the inter-views?' Noakes wanted to know.

'Kate's arranged for us to use a room at Maryvale House.'

'The convent place?'

Markham smiled at the apprehensive tone, well aware that his friend was decidedly superstitious about nuns and inclined to cross the road if he saw one coming.

'It's home to an enclosed order of Carmelites.'

'Why the chuff does Burton want to use a *convent?*'

'Well, for one thing the house is just round the back of Hollingrove Park so our interviewees will be familiar with it. And apparently Kate has an entrée with the Mother Superior.'

*'Yeah, but I ask you . . . a convent!'*

Markham sighed. This was worse than Lady Bracknell's 'Handbag'.

With quiet irony he went on, 'I believe the nuns are exceedingly hospitable, Noakesy. We needn't fear for our . . . creature comforts.'

The other subsided, though muttering under his breath at intervals about 'black crows' and 'statues' and 'smells an' bells' till Markham admonished him. 'Put a sock in it, Martin Luther, they're totally harmless and the convent's convenient.' Privately, he too was curious as to why Kate had fixed on such a venue, but saying so would only provoke more commentary from the Greek chorus at his side.

Maryvale House stood next to the church of St John the Baptist in Woodsorrel Lane on the south side of Hollingrove Park. The church itself was one of those soot-stained horrors that Markham invariably found depressing, but the convent was a modest three-storeyed Georgian structure of brick with stone facings and slate mansard roof. The rows of windows with their glazing bars and wedge lintels gave the building a somewhat barrack-like appearance which was relieved by a quirkily baroque extension of bell tower with pyramid roof.

'It looks like an ordinary house or a boarding school or summat, only I thought you said they're meant to be enclosed . . . locked up,' Noakes burst out with lugubrious relish as they drew up on a circular gravelled driveway where Kate Burton's and various other vehicles were already parked.

Markham had done his research. 'There's an extension at the back with the nuns' cloister and cells. You access their part of the building through that wall over there,' he said, pointing to an arched passageway at the left of the main house, 'though obviously you can only speak to them from behind a grille. Their chapel is built onto St John the Baptist but, again, it's screened off so you can't see them from the main church. Apparently, the front part of the house is used for church functions and there's a guesthouse block next to the nuns' enclosure.'

'S'pose at least that means they're earning their keep,' Noakes admitted grudgingly.

'Well, with the decline in vocations, they have to think commercially,' Markham replied with determined cheerfulness, ignoring the baleful manner in which his friend was eyeing the building's facade, as though he expected a coven of harpies to emerge from its portals in a cloud of incense.

The imposing wooden door of the main building opened to disclose Kate Burton hovering with her characteristic air of shy self-containment.

'Whass with the Quaker getup?' Noakes demanded rudely, taking in her simple black dress with puritan lace collar.

'And good morning to you too, Sarge,' she replied bravely. 'Didn't want to wear anything too flashy . . . out of respect.'

'Oh right, luv, I get it . . . with them all bundled up looking like witches, wouldn't be tactful.'

'See you've made an effort too, Sarge,' she replied politely, having noticed that he wasn't 'rocking his usual bit of scruff', as Doyle was wont to put it.

Noakes looked down complacently at his Harris Tweed jacket, dark pullover, Parachute regiment tie and flannels. 'Well, seeing as we ain't doing undercover stuff, I went for smart casual.'

Judging from the looks Doyle and Carruthers exchanged as they drew up, Noakes's idea of "smart casual" didn't remotely correspond with theirs, the two detectives dapper in Calvin Klein and Hugo Boss. However, they were pleased to see 'Sarge', and after a cordial exchange of greetings Burton ushered the little group through the front door and into a spacious sitting room just off the hallway where a pleasant-featured sister dressed in a brown habit and black veil was bustling around organizing refreshments, clucking in a loud Irish brogue as she directed an aproned teenage assistant.

'This is Sister Renata, one of the extern sisters who liaise between the community and the outside world,' Burton explained hastily, uncomfortably aware that Noakes was looking round for grates and bolts as though after the ultimate vicarious shock-trip.

Markham was surprised by the obvious warmth and easy familiarity that existed between the nun and his fellow DI, becoming even more intrigued when it emerged that Burton was a regular visitor to the convent. There's a story here, he thought to himself as he observed the two women.

There was no time to dwell on the mystery, however, as they were due to begin shortly, Sr Renata explaining that she would send interviewees through in turn from the front parlour. 'There's hot drinks and biscuits next door for them too,' she explained. 'We've done extra for yourselves seeing as it's a long day.'

Noakes thoroughly approved the nun's sense of priorities, eyeing the clingfilmed sandwich platters, sausage rolls and quiches with satisfaction. 'I didn't expect they'd be up to all of this,' he said happily as Sr Renata shooed her assistant out of the room.

Burton caught Markham's eyes self-consciously. 'They're used to catering for guests,' she told him, a faint flush colouring her cheeks.

Noakes was in the mood to be magnanimous. 'Shame they never get a decent feed thesselves . . . being on bread an' water most of the time, y'know, with all the fasting an' stuff.'

Burton looked startled. 'Oh, it's not as bad as all that, Sarge. They do a lot of manual work. Then there's two hours of silent prayer each day and seven services in the chapel, so they have to keep their strength up.'

'You seem to know a lot about it,' Carruthers observed slyly.

Again, that slight blush, but his colleague merely turned to check that everything was ready.

It was a very comfortable space, Markham reflected, like an old-fashioned reading room, the parquet floor redolent of beeswax floor polish and the oak panelling reminiscent of a private club, this impression being enhanced by various portraits of distinguished looking clerics. On one side, a few button back armchairs upholstered in red velvet were arranged in a semi-circle in front of an Adam-style fireplace and bookcases from floor to ceiling covered the wall, their gold-tooled spines all neatly lined up to best effect. A long mahogany reading table and barley twist oak chairs with cushioned backs and seats ran the length of the sashed windows opposite the fireplace, while the beautifully moulded ceiling contributed to an overall impression of light and grace. The setting was altogether pleasanter than the station's interview rooms or, presumably, the mansion house with its reminders of murder. There was no fire — just a decorative arrangement of dried flowers in the hearth — but period style radiators ensured the room was warm despite the unpromising weather, while heavy shutters at the windows (currently drawn back) added a further picturesque touch.

'Right, Kate,' Markham instructed after they had helped themselves to tea and coffee and Noakes had snaffled a couple of custard creams ('to put him on till elevenses'). 'Let's you, me and Noakesy take the side nearest the window. Doyle and Carruthers can move their chairs a little further back; that way they can take notes and check out the body language without looking intimidating . . . yes, that's it . . . okay, who are we scheduled to see?'

Burton consulted her notebook.

'Doyle and Carruthers have whittled things down for us,' she said brightly, with an encouraging smile in the direction of her subordinates who tried not to preen. 'A fair number of park staff are alibied for the time of the murder — out socializing or getting a jump on the weekend. It's mainly the volunteers we're seeing today. Miss Henwood's cousin Bernadette Donovan and Pardoe's girlfriend Maureen Slattery have gone to ground . . . hopefully I'll be able to catch up with them tomorrow. In the meantime, you've got an appointment scheduled at *Medway Logistics* for Thursday afternoon, sir . . . that's the outfit owned by Pardoe's business rival Jason Quirk—'

'The bloke who poached his PA,' Doyle chipped in.

'Well, strictly speaking Pardoe fired Marion Kirkwood,' Burton corrected, 'but yes, that's where she's landed up.'

Burton had briefed her colleagues about the Mary Priddy case and Carruthers now asked eagerly if she knew who had handled it.

'DIs Maxwell and Fellowes,' she replied promptly. 'They're both retired and getting on a bit . . . I've arranged for them to come in to the station Thursday evening.'

'I believe the park's reopening to the staff tomorrow morning, Kate,' Markham said.

'Correct, sir,' she confirmed. 'That's when Mr Devenish is going to give us the museum tour. Then later on, Michael Brophy at the *Gazette* should be available to have a chat about the Priddy case.'

'Excellent.'

'So, today it's just the saddos who were home alone on Friday,' Doyle explained helpfully.

'As in Mr Devenish and volunteers from *The Reader Shop*, along with Mr Pardoe's friend Loretta Davenport and the café manager Catrina Walsh,' Burton amended in chilly reproof. 'Not everyone goes out on the lash come Friday night,' she added acidly.

*I bet you and Shippers don't*, Carruthers thought, grinning. *It's more likely Horlicks and a good book that pass for a fun time round yours*. Catching a flinty look in Burton's eyes, the DS hastily rearranged his features. No doubt she'd be unbearable tomorrow on this museum tour or whatever it was she'd lined up for them. On the other hand, it might be interesting to learn more about the eccentric Henwoods and their ancestor worship. There'd been a piece in the *Gazette* the other day about some company tapping into a new fad for people wanting their ashes stored underground in Iron Age style burial barrows. Obviously you'd be talking about folk with more money than sense — or Sutton Hoo fanatics — but it'd be a nice little earner for someone. Perhaps Tony Pardoe could've done something Stone Age like that, found some way of cashing in on the park's spooky prehistoric monument rather than just leaving it stuck in that greenhouse. That'd give a whole new meaning to the term "barrow boy", he reflected, smirking at the pun.

Markham's voice snapped him back to the present.

'Right, everyone, ready? Let's go, Kate,' the DI instructed. 'Wheel them in.'

In the event, the volunteers came across as a well-meaning little group with an obvious devotion to the Henwoods, though the men were less fulsome about Tony Pardoe.

Malcolm Devenish looked like a throw-back to some previous era. Tall, thin and slightly stooped, he wore an old-fashioned three-piece suit and had a somewhat fussy manner. His receding silver hair was swept back flat on his head and keen grey eyes surveyed the world from behind equally old-fashioned gold-rimmed spectacles. The man had the aura of an Oxbridge don from the last century, so it was a surprise to learn that he was a retired surveyor as opposed to anything more intellectual. A widower 'of private means' who had become friendly with Violet Henwood by virtue of their mutual interest in folklore and Druidism, he drew a modest stipend for looking after the mansion house museum and conducting weekly tours.

In a quiet, clipped accent, he readily admitted that Tony Pardoe had indicated a wish to attract new blood, which would have spelled the end of his role as curator. 'I somehow worked myself into the position over the years,' he told them simply. 'It was always semi-official as nobody else seemed to want to take it on and the council was happy to have me step in. But times change, so it was entirely natural that Mr Pardoe would want to put things on more of a business footing, though we hadn't discussed matters in any depth; he was a new broom, after all.' As to alibi, the curator had been suffering from a heavy cold and stayed at home on Friday night.

'Couldn't imagine him out whooping it up even if he'd been well,' Carruthers opined as the door closed behind him, though Burton pointed out that Devenish looked spry enough and the donnishness went with his antiquarian interests.

'Didn't seem keen to get into any stuff about the Druids,' Doyle observed.

'Well, he's likely going to tell us something about that tomorrow,' Burton commented reasonably. 'I had the feeling he thinks the murder is down to some mentally ill intruder who came over the wall into the park and then blundered across Mr Pardoe by chance.'

A theory doubtless shared by DCI Sidney, Markham thought wryly, but in his own mind he was convinced killer and victim had met by appointment.

Tom Burke, senior volunteer at *The Reader Shop*, exuded the same unworldliness as Devenish. White-haired and short but wiry, with a rather puce and puffy complexion, he too wore gold-rimmed spectacles, but the watery blue eyes had none of Devenish's acuity. A former town planner, the two men had worked on various projects and were good friends, though Markham had the impression Devenish was the stronger character. Being without family and a widower, it was clear the park was very much the centre of Burke's life and he spoke with touching enthusiasm about the little museum where he was assisting Devenish in addition to his responsibilities in the shop. He flushed with pleasure when Markham complimented him on his contribution to the volunteers' guidebook.

'Would you believe, nobody realised what an archaeological gem the town was sitting on with the Hollingrove

Stones,' he rhapsodised. 'Back in the day, local lads even used to carve their names on them.'

Such anecdotes failed to interest Doyle. Still less did he enjoy it when Burke moved on to the subject of Richard II. 'God, I thought he'd never stop yammering about that Wilton wotsit he was all worked up about,' the DS yawned with ill-concealed impatience after the interview.

'It's a very famous diptych in the National Gallery,' Burton said repressively, 'with some very interesting links to the Henwoods' heraldry.'

*FFS, that's what we're in for tomorrow,* Doyle reflected gloomily, having been properly squelched. *Burton in full boffin mode getting off on symbols and badges and all the rest of that bollocks.* Trying not to cast his eyes to heaven, he contented himself by exchanging sardonic glances with Carruthers. Then he remembered how she had been so keen for them to garner their share of glory when the Tower investigation had hit the headlines and reminded himself that Burton really wasn't the worst.

Suzanne Mackie the other senior volunteer and leader of the park's *Shared Reader Group* was a well-preserved woman in her early seventies, with Prue Leith statement spectacles, slightly too much makeup and a nervous habit of patting her Marcel waved ash blonde hair every few minutes. Highly voluble, she was somewhat affected with an arch manner that reminded Markham of Muriel Noakes and wore a busy print dress in a milkmaid style that was too young for her. Amusingly, she took rather a shine to Markham's wingman who drew her out on the history of the Henwoods in a manner that was clearly congenial.

'Though I'm just an *amateur*,' she told them earnestly. 'It's really Mr Devenish and Mr Burke who know it all inside out. They should go on *Mastermind*, they're so well-informed.'

'Blimey, Sarge, she doesn't half run on,' Doyle lamented after the retired teacher left them.

'She's a bit OTT,' Noakes agreed, 'but I thought it were kind of sweet how she hero-worships them Henwoods . . . almost like they're *family* or summat.'

'I guess in a way that's true of all the volunteers,' Burton said thoughtfully. 'As Mrs Mackie said, after losing her husband she needed something she could throw herself into and now it's become her world.'

'She's another one with no alibi for Friday,' Carruthers observed. 'Mind you, fiddling around with that newsletter or whatever she was supposed to be editing sounds kosher. And she was well upset about Pardoe . . . you could tell she thought the sun shone out of his backside.' Devenish and Burke had been distinctly more circumspect when it came to speaking about the dead man, confining themselves to conventional expressions of regret, but with Suzanne Mackie there was genuine emotion. Whereas her fellow volunteers referred merely to his 'energy' and 'business savvy', she spoke of him as being 'one of those men who sweep people along so you feel that anything is possible.'

Likewise, when Loretta Davenport was shown in, it became clear that here was another fan of Tony Pardoe. Tall and attractive, with striking blue-green eyes and sandy blonde hair drawn into a side ponytail that softened a broad forehead and angular jaw, she cut a striking figure in an elegant grey blazer with pristine white t-shirt underneath and matching slim crop trousers. Finished off with grey suede loafers, she appeared effortlessly chic in contrast to Suzanne Mackie's overdone and fiddly look. Markham guessed she was the same generation as Pardoe, i.e. mid to late fifties, but she looked at least a decade younger.

She readily admitted her affection for the dead man. 'But he was no saint,' she added. 'Enjoyed being the centre of attention and stirring things up . . . liked to keep folk guessing, so they were never quite sure of him.' Biting her lip, she said softly, 'He didn't always treat women well either — bit of a "wham, bam, thank you ma'am" merchant.'

'Reminded me of that Sophie Wessex,' Noakes grunted, after Loretta had gone. 'The only one of 'em who don' look like a horse.'

'Unfair to horses,' Carruthers murmured.

'She's the Duchess of Edinburgh now,' Burton pointed out, shooting a cold look at the young sergeant.

'I'm sure I've come across her somewhere before,' Doyle said, sounding bemused.

'Punching above, mate,' Carruthers continued in satirical vein.

Unseen by their superiors, Doyle surreptitiously gave Carruthers the finger.

'She seemed on the level,' Noakes said. 'Didn't sugar-coat Pardoe or owt like that, but you could tell she were dead fond of him.'

'What did she mean about him liking to stir things up?' Doyle mused.

'Presumably she was referring to his plans for modernizing the park,' Burton answered, 'though come to think of it, she was quite vague about all that.'

'P'raps she meant how he treated the on-off girlfriend,' Carruthers suggested, 'though she didn't really get onto his personal life . . . just made him sound like a cheeky chappie—'

'Yeah, bit of a wide boy but a grafter an' no real harm in him,' Noakes agreed.

'She's got no alibi to speak of,' Doyle observed. 'Calling round her brother's won't cut it — family member, so he could be covering for her.'

Loretta Davenport had made a favourable impression on Markham, but the DI knew his own susceptibility to female beauty and determined not to be influenced by it.

Catrina Walsh, manager of the mansion house café, was also striking but her attractiveness was of the brittle variety, a stick thin figure and brunette updo giving her the "lollipop head" look beloved of so many female celebrities. She made no bones about her dislike of Tony Pardoe and seemed genuinely (almost endearingly) indignant about his dismissive attitude to the volunteers and locals 'who put their heart and soul into this place'. She also declared her dislike of being 'micro-managed' and 'picked up over every bloody little thing'. Service was sometimes slow and not as slick as you'd get in a fancy eatery, she told them, but that was part of the charm of the mansion house. It wasn't supposed to be some high-end bistro — 'Miss Henwood would turn in her grave at the very idea'.

'D'you reckon she could've had a thing for Pardoe,' Doyle wondered afterwards, 'but he turned her down and then it got vicious.'

'Bit old for her,' Carruthers demurred.

'Sugar daddy scenario,' Doyle countered.

'She's got a boyfriend,' Burton put in. 'In fact, *he's* her alibi for Friday night.'

'Not worth the paper,' was Doyle's opinion.

Their final interviewee John Sinnott was a softly spoken sixty-something year old who must, Markham thought, have been very striking in his youth. Tall with broad shoulders and thick wavy grey hair, he had strong well-proportioned features and a frank, open manner. Also a volunteer, he had very little to tell them, but it was obvious he was fond of Devenish, Burke and the rest while maintaining a wary reticence about the dead man. 'The volunteers are a great crowd,' he said, 'and very protective about the park . . . tear youngsters off a strip if ever they catch them sniggering about "nutters" or "devil worship".'

'Holding summat back is that one,' Noakes remarked as Sinnott departed.

'Like what?' Doyle challenged.

'Dunno, but there's *summat.*'

Markham too had detected a reticence — something withheld — but the man had been perfectly courteous and composed. Like the rest, his alibi was unsatisfactory, consisting as it did of an elderly mother who retired early to watch TV in her own room.

'Can't really see any of 'em for it,' Doyle concluded. 'Way too nice . . . except maybe the café woman . . .' Realizing how naïve this made him sound, his voice trailed off uncertainly.

Now, as Noakes manfully finished off the remaining comestibles ('It'd be rude not to'), the detectives speculated on the likelihood of the Mary Priddy case turning up anything useful.

'Pretty weird *two* bodies turning up next to the stones,' Doyle said uneasily.

'What if Tony Pardoe had something to do with that kid's death,' Carruthers ruminated, 'and now it's caught up with him.'

Doyle frowned. 'He'd only have been thirteen back then,' the DS objected.

'So what?' Carruthers challenged. 'There've been child killers younger than that . . . remember Mary Bell or the lads who murdered little James Bulger.'

Doyle shook his head. 'I don't see it . . .'

His colleague shrugged. 'You said yourself, it's got to be significant, there being two suspicious deaths in that greenhouse.'

Doyle tried another tack. 'What happened to Mary Priddy could've been an accident — as in Pardoe didn't mean to hurt her — but someone knew about it, or found out, and wanted to make him pay.'

Noakes joined the debate. 'Mebbe some sick twist did for the little lass,' he said through a mouthful of quiche, 'an' then later when they fell out with Pardoe, they fixed on the greenhouse as the place to finish him off cos it were kind of *special*.'

'That's a heck of a stretch, Sarge, seeing as we're looking at forty years between Priddy and Pardoe.' Doyle struggled to get his head round it.

'It's not unheard of for murders to occur years apart,' Burton pointed out with a troubled expression. 'Even with serial killings, there can be "cooling off".'

Fearing that the DI was about to start quoting from her beloved *Diagnostic and Statistical Manual of Mental Disorders*, Doyle said hastily, 'Maybe Pardoe's killer just got off on all the Druid stuff . . . human sacrifice, the occult and all that . . . and decided to top him next to the stones cos they've got a twisted sense of humour. They mightn't have known anything about what happened with Mary Priddy—'

'Or they *were* aware of the case and it added savour to the attack on Mr Pardoe,' Markham finished quietly.

There was a soft knock at the door and Sr Renata appeared.

'Top grub, luv,' Noakes told her.

Clearly victualler nuns constituted an exception to his anti-convent prejudice, Markham thought in amusement.

The homely features beamed. Then the diminutive sister turned to Markham. 'There's been a call from the station, Inspector. Your boss wants you to brief him as soon as possible.' And with that, she made a monastic bow and disappeared.

The DI grimaced. He had turned his mobile off for the interviews, with the added bonus of being uncontactable by Sidney who was now clearly on the warpath.

Burton looked uncomfortable. 'Sorry, guv, I told his PA we'd be over here this morning.'

'No problem at all, Kate,' was the smooth reply. 'No doubt the DCI wants to discuss media queries or some such.'

'More like he wants to say hands off the Henwoods,' Noakes rumbled.

'That too,' Markham acknowledged wearily before adding, 'Kate and I had better head back while you three finish up here. Then you can write up the interviews. Also, see if you can locate Bernadette Donovan and Maureen Slattery; they're practically the nearest Tony Pardoe has to next of kin.' He shot a meaningful glance at his wingman. 'Why don't you bone up on the stones, Noakesy? That way you can dazzle Mr Devenish with your historical knowledge—'

'An' prove we ain't all thick as mince.'

'You took the words right out of my mouth,' Markham said mildly.

Outside, it once more turned blustery and rainy, which perfectly matched Markham's mood.

Whatever hidden evil lurked at Hollingrove Park, their morning's work had brought them no nearer to lifting a murderer's mask.

# CHAPTER 4: THE DANGEROUS DEAD

Wednesday 20 March was the day that Hollingrove Park would reopen to staff and volunteers so that they could prepare to resume business the following day. A private tour of the mansion house museum was planned for the detectives that morning, and the DI wondered what clues it might hold.

As he waited outside Noakes's house for the latter to join him, Markham reflected on his meeting with DCI Sidney the previous day.

Sidney had been fairly benign, due in no small part to the fact that Kate Burton had played a blinder, flogging away at the subject of folklore and the Henwoods' illustrious ancestry in respectful tones designed to soothe and reassure. She hadn't gushed, of course. His fellow had too much self-respect for that. But there was a tacit guarantee of discretion and concern for local sensitivities. By the time she adroitly slipped in a reference to Noakes's involvement, their superior officer was so disarmed that the mention of his bête noire elicited no more than a minor wince akin to a twinge of toothache.

While Burton did her usual PR, Markham's eyes wandered to the Hall of Fame, as the photomontage which took up the whole of one wall of the office and showed Sidney hobnobbing with assorted luminaries was irreverently known. Yes, there was the Duchess of Edinburgh (Sidney's all-time favourite royal) in pole position, with lesser notables pictured in a variety of settings, the DCI cropping up all over the place like some deranged photobomber.

Sidney might have fancied that his buzz cut gave him a passing resemblance to Jason Statham, but the overall effect was somewhat undercut by the little goatee he was once more cultivating, perhaps with a view to counterbalancing any impression of thuggishness or over-muscular policing. Certainly he had the public sector patter that Markham loathed down to a T. Exhortations to 'lean into' a topic, along with references to 'upticks' and 'deep dives' (Noakes's especial hate) were liberally sprinkled through his conversation and made Markham want to grind his teeth, though Burton bore it all with equanimity.

On the plus side, however, the DCI was definitely mellower, the restoration of domestic harmony, his intense pride in eldest son Jake (now a major in the Coldstream Guards) and the approach of retirement making him altogether an easier proposition to deal with. Markham could even envisage a time when he and Sidney might meet on terms of cordiality, once the unspoken element of rivalry was removed from the equation.

In the meantime, the DCI confined himself to unsubtle hints about the necessity of avoiding any cause of offence to 'the local community' (by which he meant the respectable middle-class element) and the Henwoods themselves, though as Burton earnestly pointed out, Tony Pardoe was pretty much the last of that line.

Markham wasn't sure which was worse — Sidney's former jealous competitiveness or the over-hearty jocularity with which he chaffed them on his preference for 'good solid legwork' over 'outlandish theories'. On balance, he thought perhaps the latter.

At least Sidney didn't reject out of hand the idea of a connection between Tony Pardoe's murder and the death of Mary

Priddy. Cynically, the thought occurred to him that the DCI wouldn't exactly object to going out in a blaze of glory should the team solve the two cases at once. Such an outcome should also have the advantage of quashing any mutterings about the unusual remit under which 'Markham's gang' operated.

Now, as Noakes heaved his bulk into the passenger seat of Markham's car, once more clad in his "tweedy" gear, the DI's thoughts turned to the park and what they might expect to learn there. His wingman, adept at hearing the patter of rain on an empty stomach (to quote Carruthers), gloomily forecast a wet day.

'We'll be indoors soaking up all that history, Noakesy,' Markham admonished. 'And who knows what we might discover.'

* * *

Despite their initial apprehension, Noakes, Doyle and Carruthers quite enjoyed wandering through the mansion house's various rooms, taking in their curios and the repro-duction gilt Louis VI sofas and chairs, not to mention a sprinkling of genuine nineteenth-century French gilt mir-rors together with various oils of Henwood magnates striking suitably impressive poses, their haughty gaze seeming almost to challenge any visitor who dared stand too close.

The museum itself was equally fascinating and well laid out, with dramatic prints of bearded wizards and display cases lining the two rooms devoted to Iron Age culture while a little vestibule led to a third room which was devoted to the Henwoods' most illustrious forebear, Richard II.

Noakes peered at the Druids. 'They look like the Jedi with them white robes an' wands.'

Malcolm Devenish chuckled. 'Actually, words were their main weapons, Mr Noakes.'

'Weren't they supposed to be grade A troublemakers?' Doyle, who had recently binge-watched the *Britannia* boxset, piped up. 'Always whipping up rebellions and that kind of thing?'

'Correct,' the curator agreed. 'But they were also custodians of secret knowledge, trained specialists who mediated between ordinary people and the gods.'

Markham could see how the concept of restricting knowledge to the few — casting them as keepers of ancestral tradition and culture — would appeal to a man like Devenish who struck him as instinctively conservative in outlook.

'That's the whole point of priests, isn't it,' Carruthers chipped in. 'The idea that common folk can't talk to the higher being or whatever without getting help.'

Noakes's expression strongly suggested that he found such notions undemocratic to say the least while Markham was struck by the enthusiasm in Devenish's voice when he spoke of secret knowledge and those who mediated between ordinary people and the gods. Was that how the curator saw himself, he wondered — as a privileged expert set apart from the common herd? And did other volunteers share this outlook? If so, was it possible that one of them had become power-drunk to the point that they turned murderer when Tony Pardoe failed to share their vision for the park's future?

'The Druids held enormous sway,' Devenish confirmed. 'Speech, including prophecy and satire, was their number one tool. But they could be utterly ruthless too. One called Mide got into a feud with other Druids and ended by cutting out all their tongues and ritually burning them, presumably because a Druid unable to speak would lose all his power.'

'They were mad keen on bulls an' moon-worship an' crackpot stuff with mistletoe, though?' Noakes asked hopefully, his enquiry eliciting a sniff from Burton who said primly, 'Actually mistletoe is supposed to have great benefits if you've got insomnia or high blood pressure.'

The curator looked from one to the other.

'The bloodthirsty side of their legend was most likely somewhat exaggerated,' Devenish told Noakes.

'What about the human sacrifices an' whatnot?' Markham fancied he heard a wistful note in his friend's voice.

'Historians think it was restricted to times of great crisis. According to Julius Caesar, they preferred to use prisoners of war or criminals, but if none of those were available, they'd use ordinary folk.' Devenish was almost comically apologetic as he tried to let Noakes down gently. Turning (with barely discernible relief) to Burton, the curator continued, 'As for herbal lore, they had their own medicine men, certainly, and there was a shamanistic dimension. Some of the priests would go into ecstatic trances that were possibly aided by hallucinogenics — narcotics were available to Iron Age people and cannabis was found in a tomb in Germany. Archaeologists think some of the strange surreal images in Celtic art could have been produced during drug-induced trances.'

Doyle and Carruthers were visibly delighted at this connection between prehistoric priests and wacky baccy. Burton, meanwhile, turned away to examine a picture which showed a Gandalf lookalike in the foreground leaning on his staff and watching as live victims were crammed into a colossal male figure made out of interwoven branches, with scurrying assistants packing more sufferers in from ladders as others set the structure alight. 'Just like the Wicker Man,' she breathed, staring at the Victorian engraving. 'Yes, that's the dark side of Druidic culture,' Devenish told them soberly as the others crowded round.

'Hey, there's a Bog Man!' Doyle exclaimed delightedly, moving on to a display case further down the room. 'We did 'em at school for GCSE English . . . some Irish poet made a big deal about it. Was that down to the Druids too?'

'Well that one, Lindow Man, or Pete Marsh as the wits call him, had mistletoe pollen in his stomach and there were other indications of ritual — a specially prepared last meal — so it's a fair bet that Druids were involved. Over there,' the curator gestured to another cabinet, 'you've got Tolland Man, a Danish victim who was also garrotted . . . and again, there's evidence of a special meal having been consumed.'

'Mebbe they weren't gifts to the gods or owt special,' Noakes said grimly. 'Mebbe they were jus' local scrotes who got what they deserved.'

'You could be right, Mr Noakes. Certainly the Roman historian Tacitus talks about punitive killings in marshes.'

Markham found Tolland Man almost unbearably moving, struck by something oddly peaceful about the foetally curled body. With its head snuggled into the earth, almost like a child in the womb, it impressed upon him a sense of human vulnerability, in particular that of his victim. In light of the curator's mention of rituals and a 'special meal', he made a mental note to check with Dimples Davidson whether analysis of Tony Pardoe's stomach contents had yielded anything of significance.

'Women suffered too,' the curator continued his commentary. 'Females deposited in bogs might have been offerings to magical forces. Another explanation is that victims of both sexes were punished for having transgressed some kind of code or were marginalised by their communities for being in some way different . . . maybe they had different colouring or some kind of deformity—'

'So Doyle could've copped it for being a ginge,' Noakes interrupted. 'An' a lass like Anne Boleyn might've ended up there cos of having six fingers on her right hand.'

Observing the curator's startled expression, Markham interposed, 'A recent investigation took us to the Tower of London, Mr Devenish; mementoes of Anne Boleyn abounded.'

The other's expression cleared. 'Quite so,' he murmured politely.

Hearing about women victims had set Burton wondering.

'There were female Druids too, weren't there?'

'Indeed there were, Inspector. When the Romans attacked Anglesey, they very nearly turned round and went home because they were so unnerved by hordes of black-robed women on the shore screaming curses at them. The Romans liked to call the Druids barbarians, but they were pretty superstitious themselves, so the imprecations amounted to incredible psychological warfare. There's even a line of thought that says Boudicca was a Druid.'

Markham's head was swirling with all the historical arcana, but at the same time he had the feeling that time spent soaking up the vibes like this was somehow important and would mysteriously prompt memory, reason and intuition to fuse in his brain and produce the key he needed to unlock the riddle of this murder.

Did Tony Pardoe's death have something to do with some hidden unsightliness or deformity that triggered his attacker?

Was this a punishment killing, and if so for what?

Was it connected with ancient ritual? Could an unhinged woman have done it?

The DI perceived that despite their repulsion, his colleagues found these tales of blood sacrifice and black magic curiously compelling; even Burton had fallen under their spell. Could such legends have triggered an unstable personality into committing murder for kicks and, if that was the case, what signs would this individual exhibit?

The questions just kept coming. Doubtless the DCI would scoff at his decision to immerse himself in history, but he and Burton could always sell it as some kind of 'lateral thinking'. Besides, if the process yielded results, Sidney would most likely claim credit for encouraging his officers to conduct a 'deep dive' into the background context!

Noakes had moved on to examine the pictures of ancient passage tombs.

Noting his interest, the curator said, 'Nobody's really sure about the origin of those barrows. Current thinking holds that they were reserved for special people, possibly those who'd started a genealogical line. Radiocarbon dating for some shows they were only used for a very short time after they were constructed and then not used for burials after that, so with them it was more about the landscape having been given a special energy because founding members of the community were deposited there. The really intriguing thing is the way that neolithic people seem to have repeatedly returned to burial sites to interact with the bones of their dead — maybe remove them and add new ones.'

'*Ugh!*' Doyle exclaimed in disgust.

Markham, however, felt that he understood the atavistic compulsion to keep their precious dead close. Could this be instructive in terms of a connection between the Pardoe and Priddy murders, he wondered. Had Tony Pardoe been done to death in the greenhouse that housed the Hollingrove Stones because his killer regarded the place as endowed with a specific sinister aura deriving from an earlier murder? It was well known that murderers liked to return to the scene of the crime, but in this case the DI didn't know whether Pardoe or his assailant had anything to do with Mary Priddy, or even if the child's death *was* in fact unnatural.

As Burton wandered over to examine various astrological charts, Devenish went on, 'The barrows could have had something to do with cosmology and re-inventing the landscape. There'd have been a social aspect too.' With a swift, sideways glance at Noakes, as though the sight of the portly ex-sergeant suggested the idea, he added, 'It'd certainly be a feather in someone's cap to organise the feasting.'

'Kind of like Party Central then,' Carruthers laughed. 'I mean, a place to check out potential partners . . . an Iron Age version of Tinder.'

Burton looked faintly scandalised, but Devenish appeared amused. 'Exactly so, Sergeant.' There might even have been musical activity involved. Apparently the acoustics in some have been found suitable for amplifying a low male voice — personally, I like to imagine Stone Age men whistling to keep their courage up.'

'Sounds like you'd want to keep your courage up in one of them places,' Noakes said, peering into another display case. 'It says here that one in ten folk in them chamber tomb whatsits died from violence . . . arrows or getting clobbered over the head. So it weren't all nature worship an' brotherhood of man.'

'Well, if the tombs were constructed by elite founding families, Noakesy, there were bound to have been fallings-out and dynastic warfare from time to time,' Markham put in mildly.

'It says here they found a body in one tomb that pointed to incest.' Like Noakes, Carruthers was intrigued by the more gruesome aspects of Stone Age culture.

'Inbred,' the older man muttered, 'jus' like them Pharaohs . . . the Ptolemy lot.'

'Well, there are a number of myths about an Irish builder-king who supposedly restarted the solar cycle by sleeping with his sister,' Devenish said deadpan but with a mischievous twinkle in his eye.

'Keeping it in the family,' Doyle sniggered as Carruthers rolled his eyes.

Burton clearly didn't care for this talk of incest. 'It says that later on the focus shifted to stone circles, all part of creating sacred spaces and forging connections with the landscape . . . beautiful really.'

Noakes scowled. 'I remember some dickhead who thought he were a reincarnation of King Arthur — called hisself Arthur Uther Pendragon or summat ridiculous — an' got up a campaign cos he wanted to do some mad dawn ceremony at Stonehenge?'

Noakes could always be counted on to lower the tone! Markham glanced over at Burton who he guessed was having to bite her tongue. Of course, by now his fellow DI was practised at ignoring his friend's outbursts, but she no doubt hoped he wouldn't unduly antagonise their professorial guide.

'I believe it's possible for groups to have access to the monument by special arrangement,' the curator said politely. 'Of course, there are now so many subsets of Druidism — Neo-pagans, Odinists, Wiccans — that it's quite a challenge for the authorities.'

'What's with that picture over there?' Doyle enquired suddenly. 'That one with the urn and freaking tube or pipe or whatever it is?'

'Oh, that's the Caerlean pipe burial,' the curator said happily. 'Anthropologists have decided it was a very particular type of grave which allowed the deceased to be sealed away yet still be provided with sustenance from time to time — a kind of communing between the living and dead.'

'That's what Fred and Rose West did, isn't it?' Doyle rejoined with a shudder. 'Cos nose pipes or rubber tubes or what have you were found protruding out of all that masking tape wrapped round the victims' skulls.'

Devenish was imperturbable. 'We don't think it was meant to have that kind of *macabre* significance,' the curator said carefully. 'More like a rite to *celebrate* the memory of the dead, along the lines of Russian and Greek Orthodox rituals where they gather in graveyards to eat a meal and drink on important anniversaries. I believe they call it "Parents' Day" and set up a table with cake and flowers and shots of vodka to mark the occasion . . . though of course, drinking to excess isn't encouraged,' he added hastily.

'You mean they have a freaking *picnic!*' Doyle sounded revolted.

'It's more about honouring the communion with one's ancestors,' Devenish continued patiently. 'Romano British burial practices incorporated the Roman funerary traditions of feasting, including libations poured onto the grave and offerings of food left there — though apparently it wasn't uncommon for vagrants to help themselves.'

'Fair enough. Sounds like our wakes,' Noakes pointed out, doubtless recalling his participation in innumerable all-you-can-eat funerary buffets and "memorial banquets". 'Or Pancake Day or summat . . .'

A disturbing image flashed into Markham's mind of Tony Pardoe and his killer clinking glasses in that eerie greenhouse. Was it possible that one or both of them had decided on that location as part of some creepy ritual? Or did the killer lull Pardoe into letting down his guard by producing the wherewithal for — what was it Doyle had said — some kind of impromptu *picnic*? Forensics hadn't found any evidence of food but the post mortem might yet reveal if some kind of sedative had been involved.

Again, he noted how comfortable Devenish was discussing pipe burials and funerary practices — the animated manner and the eager flush on his face. But of course that meant nothing, he told himself. The man was a dedicated antiquarian after all.

Noakes was keen to get back to the subject of barrow tombs.

'What went into them mound thingies then?' he demanded half-fearfully, jerking a thumb at the illustrations of various henges.

'We can't really be sure,' Devenish replied evenly. 'Perhaps bodies were exposed and excarnated by vultures — "sky burials" like they have in Tibet — and then the remains moved inside. But there's plenty of evidence for both inhumation and cremation ceremonies. Actually *Yorkshire*,' with a sidelong glance at his burly interlocutor, 'is quite remarkable when it comes to funeral feasts . . . lots of evidence in the form of animal bones and such like. In one case they actually found a rack of ribs with iron meat hook embedded.'

For once in his life, Noakes was silent on the subject of Yorkshire exceptionalism, even the reference to rack of lamb failing to strike an appreciative response. Markham had a feeling that if it came to it, his friend would prefer the idea of a pipe burial to anything more robustly exsanguinatory.

Carruthers, meanwhile, was scrutinizing a disturbing montage headed *Decapitation Burials*.

'*Christ*,' he muttered. 'This lot makes Fred and Rose West look like amateurs.' Aware of Markham's intense dislike of profanity, he hastily added, 'Sorry sir, but it's seriously weird.'

'No one's come to a definitive conclusion about the so-called deviant burials,' the curator said with disconcerting cheeriness.

'*Deviant burials*?' Carruthers repeated uneasily.

'Well, in Gallic culture there was a penchant for cutting off the heads of vanquished enemies — stringing them up from saddles like trophies. And if the opponent was particularly important, the head might even be preserved in oil or kept in a chest and exhibited on special occasions . . . or pickled and preserved like they did with Pompey's. All part of a Cult of the Head.'

*OMG*, Carruthers thought, *it gave a whole new meaning to keeping up with the Joneses.*

'Of course, burials where skulls were placed between skeletons' legs might well have been connected with headhunting rituals,' the curator went on brightly, 'and we shouldn't necessarily decipher decapitated burials in a negative light by viewing them through the prism of our own contemporary understanding or culture. What seems odd or unusual to us might have been perfectly natural to our ancestors. I believe the Ashantis used to deflesh their dead monarchs and put them back together with gold wire. And the Hapsburgs parboiled their royal family prior to repatriation, reducing them down to bones for ease of transport. There might even have been something erotic or fetishistic going on.'

Observing their bleak expressions, Devenish ploughed on gamely. 'Or we could be looking at evidence of executions — punishment of slaves and criminals, that kind of thing. There's a tie-in with prone and other irregular burials.'

*Deviant burials . . . execution . . . punishment . . . something fetishistic . . .*

Again, Markham felt almost dizzy with the possibilities. Were they looking for someone so deeply immersed in all this primeval lore that proximity to the Hollingrove Stones was somehow crucial to the dispatch of Tony Pardoe? Or was the choice of location simply a twisted joke?

Search teams were radiating out from the greenhouse where the body had been discovered, but so far nothing in the nature of pagan or megalithic paraphernalia had been found. He didn't care to imagine Sidney or Ebury-Clarke's likely reaction to discussion of neolithic funerary practices. 'Be your age, Inspector,' would be the probable scathing response. Yet he felt somehow convinced that the murderer was influenced by this strange, uncanny environment . . . *had to have been* . . . and judging from his sergeants' growing absorption in what they had originally anticipated as a boring seminar from an old buffer, it was clear this was a subject that could draw you in.

Doyle, however, looked as though he had had more than enough of disconnected heads for the time being. 'Bloody *sick* whichever way you look at it,' he muttered. Markham could tell the DS found Devenish's enthusiasm for the subject pretty off-putting.

It was almost touching the way the scholarly looking volunteer regarded the young sergeant, as though he was a potential subject ripe for conversion.

'There might have been some kind of superstition about shape-shifters,' he ventured, as though aware that an *Apocalypse Now* narrative was more likely to engage "Yoof".

'How come?' *Now* he had Doyle and Carruthers hooked.

'Where the deceased were viewed as somehow *problematic*, it's possible our prehistoric forebears might have wanted to lay troublesome ghosts.'

Carruthers was quick to catch on.

'You mean, cut their heads off to stop 'em making trouble and stalking folk?' he said.

'Or put them in the ground face down by way of punishment for bad stuff they'd done,' Doyle suggested.

'Exactly so.' The curator was plainly gratified by their interest. 'Actually, there are many ghost stories from the Middle Ages about how to successfully terminate a revenant — what you would call a zombie,' he added, resorting to the vernacular. 'Cognoscenti have been able to establish that necrophiliac medieval superstitions around the dangerous dead derived in part from pre-Christian folklore about unnatural burials.'

Noakes never had much time for *cognoscenti*.

'So *thass* why some depressed Russian blokes go stuffing their faces on "Parents' Day" . . . cos they want to make everything neat an' tidy, check there ain't any nasties lying in wait, draw a line kind of thing.'

'It's really difficult to say for sure what was behind the prehistoric customs that have come down to us, Mr Noakes, and there's probably no end of distortion and exaggeration in the sources. But all the research seems to indicate that there was something incredibly strong at the back of it, whether it be necrophobia or fear of the undead or some kind of brutal personal revenge. If the medievals are anything to go by, then ancient superstitions found their way into our Christian culture. So, who's to say echoes from the past aren't still somehow at work today and haunting the living?'

Markham's attention was caught by the curator's reference to laying troublesome ghosts and the revenge motif in certain prehistoric burial traditions. Could Tony Pardoe's murder have represented some kind of exorcism of a previous wrong, he asked himself . . . perhaps the death of Mary Priddy? As he knew from professional experience, revenge was often a powerful psychological component in homicide cases. It was also one of humanity's most primal urges, which might have been why the murderer chose the Stones — either by way of a deliberate 'statement' or because they were in thrall to an ungovernable instinct as old as humanity itself.

'You're a Druid, right?' Noakes challenged the curator. 'How come you're able to square all this hocus pocus with being a good Christian?'

Burton winced at the bluntness, but Devenish was unperturbed. 'Miss Henwood and I didn't find our folklorist interests to be at odds with churchgoing. Maybe with us, it was to some extent a retreat from the modern world.'

Markham smiled, impressed by the man's honesty. 'If the deities of paganism are the deities of the natural world, then given the current ecological focus on the idea of the planet being disrespected and headed for shipwreck, I'd say you're very much in tune with the mood of the times.'

'That's very kind, Inspector, but I realise there's a strong element of social conservatism in my Druidism — the yearning for an idealised countryside in which everything including the trees know their place!' Catching his fellow inspector's eye, Markham recalled their discussion of Violet Henwood's devotion to the notion of *Merrie England*.

'I suppose most of us volunteers have a streak of escapism in our makeup,' Devenish admitted.

'What about the rest of the volunteers, how many of *them* are Druids?' Carruthers asked, frowning.

'Oh, I'd say most of us have an interest one way or another, Sergeant,' the curator replied with a hint of reserve in his manner. He was being evasive, Markham decided. For some reason, the question made him uncomfortable and the DI asked himself why. The man looked distinctly relieved when he drew him on to talk about neolithic artwork, being genuinely intrigued by the mysterious swirls, zigzags and concentric circles illustrated in a photomontage along one wall.

'Markings on the Hollingrove Stones can now only really be properly deciphered using three-dimensional laser scanning,' Devenish said earnestly, 'but prehistoric people would have viewed them by torchlight. The spiral patterns are the oldest. It's thought they could be topographical markers or perhaps representations of visions seen with the aid of hallucinogens. Or they could be some secret code to speed the dead on their final journey—'

'Happen it were jus' graffiti,' Noakes interrupted. 'Or mebbe the Flintstones were teaching their kids how to carve stone — kind of like neolithic Design an' Technology—'

'Or those lessons in the Juniors when we had to practise our handwriting for hours on end,' Doyle suggested with feeling.

'Why not squares and rectangles . . . or triangles for that matter?' Carruthers wondered. 'Why the obsession with circles?'

'There've always been magical and mystical properties associated with circles,' Devenish answered. 'And, of course, circles were more difficult to do, so there was a kind of kudos in that.' He grinned, suddenly looking far less wizened. 'The theories are endless. Some people even suggest it was all about cattle-worship and the cups and rings represent cow pats.'

Noakes guffawed at this, warming to the curator whom he had initially mentally dismissed as a prissy old git.

Markham was thoughtful, wondering if it was possible the murderer had left any 'calling card' or signature that might offer a clue to their psyche. So far, nothing had materialised.

The little group moved into the next room.

'This is where we keep information about the eccentric antiquarians who popularised the notion that Stonehenge and the megalithic tombs were erected by the Druids, though in fact the Druids came along much later — around 5000 BC — whereas the monuments were created thousands of years earlier.'

'Was it the Druids who did that pervy giant in chalk in Dorset?' Doyle asked as Burton tried to look invisible. 'The one with the massive willy carrying a huge wavy club, with a head like an alien's.'

'Ah, you mean the Cerne Abbas Giant,' Devenish beamed at him. 'That was most probably done by the Anglo-Saxons, but the Druids were certainly keen on landscape markers. There's a tradition that holds they had their own secret method of communication using little marks on sticks and stones called Ogham or the tree language.'

'Pure *Lord of the Rings*,' Carruthers drawled.

'This ain't hobbits, though,' Doyle said, peering at a picture showing a grove with sinister wooden images of gods lurking amongst the trees and skulls in niches. 'More like that haunted burial ground from *Last of the Mohicans*.'

Devenish maintained a polite and interested expression, though it was clear to Markham that the cinematic allusion was lost on him.

Burton came to the rescue with a query about an engraving which depicted a tree festooned in fabrics and items of clothing. 'What's that?' she asked.

'A rag tree in Ireland; the legacy of Druid traditions which regarded groves and woods as holy places possessed by spirits,' came the reply.

As Burton shuddered, Markham's thoughts travelled back once more to the greenhouse which housed the Hollingrove Stones. Was there someone at the park for whom the site of Mary Priddy's death exercised a malign fascination, someone who might see the place as haunted by the spirit of that dead child?

'Were Merlin a Druid?' Noakes wanted to know, squinting at a display cabinet which bore the legend *King Arthur and the Druids*.

Devenish smiled indulgently. 'There's a theory that he was actually a wild Welshman called Mervyn who acquired occult knowledge by living as an animal in the woods.'

'*Mervyn!*' grunted Noakes. 'That don' sound very wizardy . . . More like a used car salesman, if you ask me.'

Devenish chuckled. 'In some traditions, he's the son of the Devil after a plan to create the Antichrist went wrong.'

'Who's his mum then?' Doyle demanded.

'Believe it or not, a nun.'

Burton didn't like where the conversation was headed. 'This is all quite fascinating,' she said repressively, 'but I'd be very interested to see your section on Richard II.'

Carruthers shot a glance at Doyle that said *Spoilsport!*

Suddenly, Catrina Walsh appeared as if from nowhere.

'Bill Whelan said to sort you out with drinks downstairs,' she said. Despite the ungraciousness of her manner, the café manager's expression as she looked at Malcolm Devenish was affectionate.

'Mr Devenish has one more room to show us,' Burton protested stiffly.

Noakes out-manoeuvred her, however. 'Good idea, luv,' he declared expansively. 'Betcha Mr D could do with a break after all that history . . . an' we wouldn't say no to a cuppa.'

Downstairs, the curator joined the estate manager and the other volunteers at a table looking out through French windows onto an attractive outdoor seating area with wooden benches, picnic tables and folded parasols.

The detectives and Noakes were ushered to a table on the other side of the room, Catrina Walsh and a cowed looking teenage girl seeing to drinks and a selection of cakes.

'Nice room,' Doyle observed as they tucked into the lemon drizzle, brownies and flapjacks. 'Judging by the rest of this place, you'd expect it to be all lace tablecloths and fusty knickknacks.'

'They've got to think about attracting younger people,' Carruthers pointed out sagely, looking round at the reclaimed pine flooring, sleek bistro-style fittings and whitewashed walls adorned with framed seasonal park canvas prints.

Burton sipped her oat milk latte and Markham his black coffee as the other three demolished the cake stand.

'That Devenish knows his stuff alright,' Noakes said eventually, coming up for air.

'Yes, very impressive,' Burton agreed warmly. She looked over thoughtfully to the other table, where Whelan and the volunteers had been joined by the café manager. Judging from their animated chat, it appeared there was some good-natured ribbing at the curator's expense, even slow-spoken John Sinnott joining in the laughter.

Carruthers followed her gaze. 'They seem an okay bunch,' he commented. 'Even Miss Sulky Boots Walsh seems to gel with the rest of them.'

'You don't think Devenish is a bit, well, *intense?*' Doyle mused. 'I mean all that Bamber Gascoigne stuff about Druids, not to mention the creepy stuff he's got up there. Isn't it OTT for a family day out, right?'

'It's obviously a passion with him,' Markham answered. 'But he presents as well-adjusted, if a little precious and old-fashioned.'

Noakes nodded vigorously. 'Yeah, that were upfront what he said about him an' old Vi preferring Cathbad looka-likes on account of thinking the olden days were better than here an' now.'

Burton frowned. '*Cathbad?* I don't remember him mentioning that name.'

Noakes regarded her pityingly. 'Figure of speech, luv . . . You could tell they had a soft spot for weirdy Druid types called Caradoc an' Willy Bach — y'know, the kind who swap stories about King Arthur an' get off their faces "all through the night".' The romantic associations of Eisteddfods had evidently passed him by.

'Oh, I'm with you now, Sarge,' Burton said faintly. 'Yes, I can see the nostalgic appeal of all that.'

Burton's tone suggested she was unlikely to share Noakes's suspicion that modern-day Druids were most probably unregenerate sex maniacs, pacifists, nudists and other dubious revolutionaries. At that moment, her mobile sang out and, with evident relief, she got up to take the call.

As the DI disappeared into the corridor, there was a slight kerfuffle across the room and Loretta Davenport joined the volunteers. Snatches of conversation floated across to Markham from which he deduced she had somehow blagged her way past the uniforms posted at the park entrance. Hardly surprising, he reflected, given her air of authority and friendship with Tony Pardoe. At all events, the others seemed glad to see her.

Suddenly, Markham realised why the woman's face seemed vaguely familiar and Doyle had thought he recognised her . . . she was one of the more photogenic subjects featured in the DCI's Hall of Fame. Interesting that Sidney hadn't mentioned it, though it was of course possible that he hadn't connected her with Tony Pardoe.

Doyle's voice cut across his reflections. 'So, what's next then?'

'Back to Devenish's time machine for a quick decco at Richard II,' Carruthers told him.

'Big yawn to that,' the other muttered.

'On the contrary, Sergeant,' Markham said inexorably. 'Understanding the Henwoods' pedigree could provide a way in to this investigation.' Trying to ignore his subordinates' sceptical expressions, the DI asked himself why it was he felt the Ricardian dimension could be significant. He really couldn't give a reason . . . there was just that prickle between the shoulder blades he had felt upstairs in Devenish's strange repository of historical curios, as if something was crying out to be noticed. He tried not to think about what Sidney would make of this trip back into the distant past, being well aware that the DCI regularly disparaged the team's historical interests as 'Markham's talking shop'. Mind you, he reminded himself fiercely, context had proved to be *everything* in their Tower of London investigation where a deranged killer was indeed proved to have been in thrall to echoes from the past.

Burton was back.

She nodded at the sergeants. 'Good work leaving all those messages with the neighbours,' she told them. 'Apparently Bernadette Donovan's arrived back home, so we can interview her tomorrow morning.'

'Oh right, the companion . . . Where'd she get to then?' Carruthers asked.

'Away visiting a friend in Clacton-on-Sea . . . doesn't have a mobile. According to the people next door, she was shocked to hear about Mr Pardoe's death.'

'What about Friday night?' Doyle.

'I've no idea of her alibi status as yet,' was the crisp response. 'If she was taking a morning train on Saturday, maybe she decided to turn in early.'

'What about the other woman, Pardoe's girlfriend?' enquired Carruthers.

'Doing a digital detox at Old Carton Retreat Centre.'

'*You what?*'

Markham had the impression Burton rather enjoyed Noakes's slack-jawed bewilderment.

'One of those breaks where you ditch all your technology so you can focus on mindfulness and holistic therapies,' she said smoothly.

'Sounds a right Rip-off Com Dot,' Noakes muttered.

Doyle grinned. 'Dot Com, Sarge.'

Noakes scowled. 'Whatever.' Beadily, he pressed Burton, 'So when did she head off for the mud baths an' brushing with twigs an' all the rest of it?'

The DI sighed. 'Apparently she drove over to her girl-friend's in Old Carton at around half ten on Friday night. They booked in to the centre together on Saturday morning.'

'That means another one with no bleeding alibi,' Noakes growled.

'We'll know more tomorrow,' Burton said wearily. 'At the moment she's "in shock".'

'*Ahem.*'

Malcolm Devenish and Tom Burke had materialised next to their table.

'Is this an inconvenient time, Inspector?' the curator asked diffidently.

'Not at all,' Markham told him. Smiling at them, he said, 'I take it Mr Burke is joining us for this session.'

'Well, Tom's collated most of the Ricardian material, so it's only right that he shows you our treasures.'

The other man glowed, his slightly protruding, glaucous eyes shining behind his spectacles. Clearly he was cut from the same cloth as Devenish, Markham thought, noticing the same old-fashioned demeanour and the somewhat pained expression that crossed his face as Suzanne Mackie cackled loudly on the far side of the room at something one of the volunteers had said.

The team got to their feet, Burke leading the way upstairs with undisguised eagerness to share his insights. Noakes lagged behind, however, apparently in no hurry for part two of the tour, ambling across to where Loretta Davenport and the volunteers were sitting. It was some twenty minutes or so before he found his way back to the little museum where Burke was visibly champing at the bit to get started.

'Miss Henwood's uncle was a nineteenth-generation nephew of Richard II,' he told them. 'That's why the Henwoods' coat of arms features the white hart, which was Richard's personal emblem.'

'Can they even trace that far back?' Doyle enquired wonderingly.

'Don't forget that a team of genealogists turned up a cabinet maker whose mother was related to Richard III,' Burke told them. 'His DNA was a match for the body they found under the car park in Leicester. It *is* possible to research family trees a long way back.' With a twinkle, he added, 'Malcolm and I worked out that we're Violet's fifteenth cousins twice removed or something like that . . . Not that we ever tried to capitalise on the family connection.'

'Ricky II were the Black Prince's son,' Noakes said as Burton smiled approvingly. Her smile congealed, however, as he added, 'But the Black Prince died of the trots.'

Burke merely chuckled. 'Yes, he had dysentery after years of campaigning in France. Richard became king on the death of his grandfather Edward III and reigned for more than twenty years.'

'How come he didn't end up snuffing it?' Noakes asked curiously. 'I mean, boy kings meant big trouble back then . . . thass why old Crookback — Ricky III — made a move . . . cos his nephews were jus' kids.'

'And because he was a thoroughgoing psycho,' Carruthers muttered. Markham was amused to note Noakes's scowl at this. His friend would never be persuaded that a fellow Yorkshireman was *all* bad.

'Richard II had a powerful uncle in his corner,' Burke told them hastily, picking up on the whiff of tension. 'John of Gaunt, Duke of Lancaster. So that helped. And the nobles were onside for a while; everyone stuck together, which is how they managed to put down the Peasants' Revolt. But then later on, factions developed. The big guns didn't like the way Richard had favourites and eventually they mounted a sort of coup which ended with his friends being exiled or executed. It took him five or six years to come back from that, take his revenge — kind of a slow burn — and get back to where he was before. But then conflict broke out again and he exiled John of Gaunt's son, Henry, for life before seizing his inheritance.'

Noakes shook his dead. 'Bad decision,' he opined, 'doing the dirty on family.'

'Oh, he could be ruthless,' Burke told them. 'Most likely had one of his uncles murdered . . . Those were the times, you see. *Anyway,*' sensing Burton's impatience that he should finish the story, 'Richard went off to deal with Ireland because they were giving trouble over there.' Same as usual, Noakes's expression seemed to say. 'And that's when cousin Henry invaded and deposed Richard to become Henry IV . . . most likely starved him to death in Pontefract Castle.'

Burton frowned. 'Isn't Richard buried in Westminster Abbey?' she asked.

'Henry IV stuck him in an obscure friary, but Henry V arranged to have him reinterred in the abbey alongside his wife, in the tomb he had commissioned for them both.' Burke made a deferential little bow to Noakes. 'Henry V had been knighted by Richard when he was a boy, so at least *one* of them showed some proper family feeling.'

'Quite the roller coaster of a reign then,' Markham remarked.

Factions, coups, counter-coups and favourites, he mused. Not unlike the complicated set-up at Hollingrove Park, although at this stage he couldn't be sure who exactly might have had Tony Pardoe's ear.

'Richard was a dramatic and glamorous figure,' Burke said solemnly. 'And diehard monarchists admire how he defended the royal prerogative and the divine right of kings.'

After that, Devenish and Burke took the group round various display cases and cabinets, with the curator taking over as tour guide.

'Richard had an almost pathological need to assert his own power and royal antecedents — absolutely obsessed with the royal arms and heraldry.'

'Isn't that typical of medieval kings, though?' Carruthers demurred. 'Wanting to make sure everyone knew they were top dog.'

'Yes, but it might be said that Richard was relentless when it came to projecting and manipulating his image,' Devenish pointed out. 'He certainly flaunted this idealised godlike vision of himself in sculpture, painting and writing.'

Doyle peered at the copy of Richard's portrait from Westminster Abbey which showed him crowned and holding an orb and sceptre, staring out frontally almost like an icon of Christ. 'Looks a bit girly to me,' was his verdict. '*Hey, isn't that the picture you see on posh Christmas cards!*' he continued as his eyes roamed the exhibits. 'Over there . . . the one with all the angels.'

'That's a reproduction of the Wilton Diptych,' Burke told them. 'The left-hand panel shows Richard with various saints, including John the Baptist, while the Virgin and Child are on the right-hand side giving the king a blessing.'

'What's with that white banner and red cross?' Carruthers wanted to know.

'Most likely it's meant to be symbolic of Christ's Redemption . . . or perhaps connected with the idea of Richard being prepared to go on crusade.' Noakes grunted approvingly at the reference to soldiering, which was more in line with his conception of kingly values.

'Still looks weedy,' Doyle insisted.

Noakes was scrutinizing a wall display. 'This is all about his "favourites" and how folk said he "indulged hisself in unmentionable ways", so don' that mean he were gay?'

'Appearances are misleading,' Burke retorted with a prim little cough. 'A contemporary chronicler called the Monk of Evesham described him as fair-haired with a pale complexion and a rounded, feminine face, while others described him as having "beauty" and being "the flower of boys" with also possibly a stammer. On the other hand, when his tomb was opened in 1871, his skeleton was found to be six foot. Furthermore, he loved hunting and hawking and was transparently devoted to his wife, Anne of Bohemia — utterly devastated when she died — so much so, that he wouldn't go into any room that she'd been in and ordered the manor house where she had died to be pulled down. He was also kind to his second wife, Isabella, who was only six when they were betrothed.' (Noakes snorted noisily at this). 'So all in all, a very complex character who's suffered from misinterpretation.'

'He probably developed a neurosis from being compared to the Black Prince who was this great warrior with an international reputation,' Devenish pointed out. 'You see, Richard inherited the throne as a child and all his life he was tortured by being unable to reconcile his ambitions to the physical reality.'

'How come Miss Henwood didn't mind all the stuff about Richard maybe being gay or bi?' Carruthers asked stubbornly, thinking of that TV play where David Tennant played him all droopy and long-haired, like some sort of hippy. 'Surely a woman of that age and background wouldn't care for details like that coming out,' he added. 'It's not an issue for most people nowadays, but her generation might see it differently.'

The curator was unfazed. 'She might have been a bit of a snob,' he said, 'but she was quite broadminded.'

Markham observed that Noakes appeared sour at hearing this. No doubt he was unimpressed by Miss Henwood's indulgent attitude towards royalty.

'Did Richard and Anne of Bohemia have any children?' Burton enquired.

'No. It's likely they were infertile. And the second marriage held no prospect of children, what with Isabella being a child when they married.'

At this reference to the monarch's predicament, Markham's thoughts wandered to his own personal circumstances . . . He had recently come to believe that Olivia's inability to have a child lay behind her snip-snapping, biting humour and spikiness. Hers was a brittle, highly burnished carapace which harboured deeply personal darkness, as though something serpentine lay coiled within her that vented itself in sudden shafts of caustic malice. The whole topic of children was now a no-go area between them, and he was somewhat ashamed at being relieved that this was so. He supposed that, like Richard, the two of them were in their different ways vulnerable and damaged.

'Maybe Richard had a hang-up about not having kids because he thought people would cast aspersions on his manliness,' Carruthers speculated with his customary interest in psychological kinks.

'That's quite possible, Sergeant,' Devenish agreed. 'Together with the fact of his being physically puny, that might well have set up a neurosis, possibly even become pathological.'

As they canvassed the likely effect of childlessness on Richard's character, Burke moved across to where Burton was examining illustrations of medieval nobility with their accompanying descriptions of court ceremonies. From the fussy way the volunteer was clearing his throat and fiddling with his tie, it appeared he wasn't entirely comfortable with the discussion about sexuality and infertility, and it occurred to Markham that he might have felt such talk to be prurient or somehow in bad taste. He recalled what John Sinnott had said about the volunteers' protectiveness towards Hollingrove Park and the Henwoods and remembered, too, Suzanne Mackie's almost reverential air when she spoke of the family's heritage. In some ways, the older volunteers had given their lives to it, so it would behove the team to avoid trampling on their sensitivities — a fine line to tread, especially given the gulf between their attitudes and those of young officers like Doyle and Carruthers.

Possibly something similar had occurred to Devenish, because he dropped the subject of the Plantagenets' personal lives, steering the group over to join his friend and Burton.

'Richard was really fussy about protocol and how he was addressed — "'most excellent and powerful prince'" rather than "'rightful and gracious lord'",' he continued. 'He held regular crown-wearing ceremonies, too, where he sat in silence watching everyone and if his eye fell on someone, they had to kneel and pay homage.'

Doyle grinned at the idea of this medieval version of Grandma's Footsteps.

'I remember the missus telling me about that book Princess Di's butler wrote,' Noakes mused. 'It had all this stuff about the servants at Buck House having to flatten thesselves against the walls if they met royal folk.'

'Well, it's all about preserving mystique, isn't it,' Burke said, after digesting this salvo. 'And, of course, Richard identified kingship with the godhead. So if you think of it in that way, it's logical.'

'But if he had, er, "favourites", doesn't that mean he was a bit of a playboy?' Doyle countered. 'I mean, hanging out with the lads ain't exactly *regal*.'

'That was the confusing, theatrical side to him,' Devenish answered, seeing that his friend was rather flummoxed by Doyle's observation. 'Plus, he was quite an insecure personality due to a lonely and unsettled childhood, then later on being brought to heel by his nobility in a coup, so a lot of the self-dramatisation was most likely a defence against feelings of inadequacy and vulnerability. He was a real bundle of contradictions.'

'It sounds as though you feel sorry for him,' Carruthers pointed out shrewdly.

Devenish considered this. 'I think he was probably narcissistic — had to have this idea of being semi-divine and superior to other people, because otherwise he felt worthless and empty. Although he put a good face on it after the nobles — the Appellants as they were called — staged their coup. They forced him to knuckle under so he never really forgave them for destroying that omnipotent self-image. He bided his time until he was in a position to take his revenge ten years later. Narcissists are vindictive if their self-image is threatened, so I think that was why he became increasingly authoritarian and aggressive. He held it together pretty well until his cousin and other disaffected nobles started challenging him . . . That's when all the old insecurities he suffered during the coup surged up and triggered an extreme

— almost insane — obsession with notions of superiority and "regality".'

The allusions to theatricality, narcissistic grandiosity and self-dramatisation set Markham to wondering again. Surely there *was* something more than a touch histrionic and ostentatious about deciding to kill Tony Pardoe next to the Hollingrove Stones . . . as though the *mise-en-scène* mattered. And yet, so far, no one in their pool of suspects had come across as unbalanced or exhibitionistic. They were just your average bunch of well-meaning, community-minded individuals who, allowing for natural differences of age and temperament, all seemed to get along pretty well. If their killer was like Richard — hollow inside with a fragile self-image constructed to conceal seething insecurities — then they had camouflaged it very well.

The talk of plots and counter-plots — medieval strikes left, right and centre — led the DI to speculate afresh about the power structure at Hollingrove Park. When interviewed, Devenish had spoken of Tony Pardoe being a 'new broom', and there had been friction with Catrina Walsh over the café. Not only that, but Michael Brophy had labelled the CEO 'ruthless' in the *Gazette* and his PA Marion Kirkwood had ended up in a rival camp. Perhaps the prospect of everything they cherished being swept away had proved unbearable to someone in the Hollingrove "family" and, just like Richard's long-suffering royal cousin, the worm had finally turned . . .

'So, you reckon self-worship was the key to Richard then?' Carruthers pressed, surprised to find this medieval ruler curiously modern in terms of his mental health problems.

'I think it's why he became increasingly detached from reality and his subjects towards the end of his reign. The loss of Anne probably accelerated the process . . . certainly it was eerie how he began investing buildings and objects that celebrated kingship with a life of their own. The self-dramatisation was another symptom, if you like. Let's face it, all leaders are narcissistic at a level . . . even characters as far apart as Hitler and Churchill.'

Noakes looked as though he didn't care for the comparison, and Markham observed Burton hastily directing the group's attention to another wall display of illustrated prayer books and psalters. No doubt she didn't want her colleague delivering an encomium to Churchill by way of pushback against the suggestion that his hero might be some sort of narcissist.

'Richard might have been interested in alternative, anti-clerical religious beliefs — the Black Prince and his mother were fairly radical in that respect — but he became much more orthodox as he grew older,' Devenish told them, 'most likely because he came to associate heresy with popular unrest. In any event, he was seriously into saints and relics — had one of the largest relic collections in Europe and really cherished his relations with the saints. He was born on the feast of John the Baptist, so that was a particular favourite. He acquired the dish on which the Baptist's head had lain and also managed to get hold of a tooth of the Baptist.'

Doyle turned to Carruthers. 'Blimey, that's just like *Blackadder*,' he sniggered. 'Y'know, the episode with Jesus's nose and St Peter's and—'

'*Thank you, Sergeant*,' Burton interrupted him, aware of their guides' affronted expressions.

'Richard's personal piety was very cultish hence the fixation with relics,' Devenish said somewhat stiffly.

'Sounds downright unbalanced,' Noakes observed.

'Well, he came to identify very strongly with the sufferings of Christ on the Cross — almost felt them as his own — which fed into a certain embattled paranoia. He presented as quite the peace-lover and never all that keen on fighting the French—'

Noakes frowned at this.

'But temperamentally and given his experiences with the nobility,' Devenish continued, 'there was this part of him that was inwardly longing for a fight.'

'What's that?' Doyle pointed to what looked like an astrological chart.

'A medieval horoscope,' came the reply. 'Richard took prophecies and omens very seriously.'

'I thought you said he was religious,' Carruthers frowned.

'In those days, the two weren't mutually exclusive,' the curator explained. 'Orthodox lay piety often existed alongside superstition.'

Markham had the feeling that buried amidst all this history was *something*, some clue, vitally important to the investigation. As he watched Devenish and Burke chatting with the other three, he had an unnerving sense of the Devil breathing down his neck, only he couldn't pinpoint the source of his sudden acute unease. All kinds of thoughts started to crawl out of the woodwork of his mind, although to a casual observer the DI was his usual calm self, surveying the exhibits and display cases with every appearance of detached interest.

Did Tony Pardoe's death in fact have nothing to do with neolithic or medieval history, despite all these unsettling echoes from the past? Wasn't it more likely that the murder was some sort of revenge for past wrongdoing — the Priddy case, for example? Markham's brain buzzed with possibilities.

'Bernadette Donovan's made quite a study of the Henwoods' Ricardian heritage,' Burke said, bridling in a way that suggested he was intensely gratified at sharing a common interest with the lady of the manor's cousin. Some might have found this pathetic but to Markham it was rather poignant, the natural desire of an older man to remain relevant.

'I believe Maureen Slattery was interested too,' Devenish informed them. 'She mentioned something about how it would make a wonderful school project . . . but,' now he looked vaguely embarrassed, 'it came to nothing in the end.'

'How come?' Doyle wanted to know.

'Mr Pardoe wasn't keen for some reason,' he said, his embarrassment visibly increasing. Hesitantly he added, 'Ms Davenport probably advised against it . . . didn't seem to think it was such a good idea in light of the Plantagenets' more *controversial* aspects . . . She was quite protective about the family's good name — wanted to keep all the Ricardian stuff in-house rather than attract the wrong kind of publicity.'

This cast an interesting light on Loretta Davenport's character, Markham thought, wondering to what extent she might have alienated Tony Pardoe's cousin and girlfriend by her watchfulness. It struck him suddenly that such an attitude might well have jarred with Pardoe himself if he preferred to be his own man and chafed at outside interference.

'Bernadette and Maureen spent quite a lot of time in the museum,' Devenish assured him, clearly anxious to dispel any impression of disharmony. 'Loretta certainly had no objection to *that*.'

As they stood clustered round a cabinet containing replicas of medieval astrolabes, Catrina Walsh unexpectedly appeared in their midst looking annoyed. 'Sorry to interrupt, gents,' she said, clearly anxious not to rain on the volunteers' parade, 'but I seem to have lost one of my helpers.' Apologetically, she added to Devenish and Burke, 'It's Cathy Price . . . nice kid but a terrible habit of going walkabout just when I need her! I don't suppose she came wandering up here.'

Assured that they hadn't encountered her assistant, the manager disappeared with a set expression which boded ill for the young lady in question.

Her brisk purposefulness made Markham conscious that others in CID might regard this visit to the museum as self-indulgent wool-gathering. Though outwardly cool as a cucumber, he felt sweat prick the skin beneath his collar. Sidney and Ebury-Clarke would never stand for any theorizing about echoes from the past, whether it be Druidical antecedents or medieval monarchs. The mere sighting of what they called 'one of Markham's hobby-horses' was usually enough to set them off, though in the wake of all the publicity about the Tower of London investigation the higher echelons had considered the possibility that Bromgrove might pilot a Heritage Crime Unit, 'seeing as your cases generally involve some kind of time travel, Inspector,' Ebury-Clarke had snidely conceded.

Of course, it was possible that he was allowing the atmosphere of this strange little universe to affect him. Undoubtedly, there was something in this tour that made him feel the key to their investigation lay hidden somewhere within the quaint museum.

If only he could pinpoint what it was . . .

'Have you ever had any break-ins here?' he asked Devenish, seeing that the two volunteers were making tactful noises about leaving the police in peace. 'Or any signs of unauthorised interference with the exhibits?'

'Interesting that you should ask that,' Devenish said slowly. 'Once or twice I thought items might have been moved or disturbed but,' with an awkward smile, 'it was most likely what they call a "senior moment" and I got distracted . . . forgot to lock up properly.'

Markham noticed the curator's clouded brow and had the impression that this question was curiously unwelcome for some reason. Of course, he told himself, a character as conscientious and punctilious as Devenish would likely be embarrassed by any lapse in security due to absent-mindedness, so it would be as well to leave it there for now.

Eventually the two volunteers withdrew, leaving the team to mull over their impressions in a cosy book-lined room across the landing from the museum. Wandering across to a bay window with far-reaching views across the park, Markham took stock as his colleagues collapsed gratefully into armchairs on either side of a baroque mantelpiece above which hung a fine art oleograph of the pre-Raphaelite variety, with nymphs and shepherds cavorting across a pastoral landscape. Turning back to the others, he sank into an armchair a little apart, crossing long legs and bringing his elegant hands together, the fingertips touching.

'Any thoughts?' he asked lightly.

Noakes weighed in. 'Well, the Iron Age stuff's spooky all right. If someone got into all that pagan malarkey, you could see 'em luring Pardoe to the stones an' finishing him off there.'

'If it was punishment for something, then like Devenish said about that deviant burial stuff, they could've been trying to get even, draw a line under the past,' Doyle suggested.

'Punishment for Mary Priddy?' Burton asked. Then, proceeding to answer her own question, 'Devenish talked about the landscape having a sort of mnemonic quality—'

'*You what?*' Noakes demanded.

Markham could not help being amused , having listened on many occasions to his friend's outrage at 'needing a bleeding thesaurus to understand Burton', even though he suspected Noakes took a vicarious delight in his own reputation for using 'Big Words'.

'As in ancient monuments acting like reminders, *signposts* to where important people were buried,' she explained patiently. 'Maybe it's like that for our killer, and the Hollingrove Stones are a marker for some sort of secret knowledge—'

'Knowledge about that kid's death,' Carruthers finished. 'The problem being,' he added caustically, 'that none of them back there exactly comes across as the kind of nut who gets off on the idea of pagan rituals.'

'What did you make of Miss Henwood's Ricardian interests?' Markham enquired. 'Anything there to shed light on our murderer?'

'Again, it's all quite bloodthirsty stuff,' Doyle mused, 'plus there's plenty of stuff about superstition and omens.'

'Yeah, them medievals were worse than the Druids for that,' Noakes said with relish. 'Burke said Frederick the something of Saxony was a massive collector of relics. Kind of a way of getting to heaven — go and pay your respects to a collection of relics an' get time knocked off Purgatory. Old Freddy claimed he had a thorn from the Crown of Thorns Jesus wore on the cross an' a twig from the burning bush an' some of Mary's hair. Plus he had thousands of bits of saints' bones an' if you went to see 'em on special days you wouldn't go to Hell.'

Noakes was looking more and more Protestant by the minute during this recital, Markham observed with amusement, thinking that if it came to the crunch, his friend was likely to favour Druids over Papists.

'Richard II sounded a bit of a head case,' Doyle surmised. Maybe if you were around all that stuff for too long, it might send someone a bit screwy . . . kind of into magical thinking and all that. But like Carruthers says, nobody we've seen jumps out as being paranoid or — what was it Devenish said — "spoiling for a fight".'

*Unless they're doing a damned good job of concealing their true persona from us*, Markham thought with a cold trickle of discomfort at the base of his spine as he recalled the weals on Tony Pardoe's neck and those bulging eyes.

Aloud, he said, 'Noakes and I will go and see what Michael Brophy at the *Gazette* has to say for himself. In the meantime, Kate, I'd like you to liaise with Dimples and check what's shown up on the tox screen while Doyle and Carruthers find out from forensics if there was any sign of interference with the stones themselves or any indication in the greenhouse that could point to ritual enactment. It would also be useful to ascertain *discreetly* from Bill Whelan if anyone showed excessive interest in the museum and its artefacts.'

Outside, the rain had held off but the sunshine was weak and the sky streaked with billowing clouds that suggested a downpour was in the offing.

The strange sense of evil that had oppressed him earlier had lifted, but he would be glad to get out into the open air.

*Far away from the park.*

The sound of pounding feet and shouting suddenly interrupted Markham's reverie. With one bound, he was out of his chair and racing for the stairs. The team followed, jolted out of their debate about motives, ways and means.

A white-faced Bill Whelan met them in the ground floor café.

'It's Cathy Price, one of our waitresses,' he said. 'Catrina was looking everywhere for her and asked me to check the basement. When I got down there, well—' he gestured towards a door behind the cold food display counter at the back of the room, 'go and see for yourselves.'

They found her lying in a crumpled heap at the far end of the cellar wedged between stainless steel racks filled with supplies and catering equipment, her face purplish with ugly contusions and blood pooling around her long black hair. Markham recognised the nervous teenager who had been helping the café manager just a short time earlier. There was something hideously poignant about the clumpy Doc Martens, the last 'fashion statement' the dead girl would ever make.

Careful not to touch anything, Noakes squatted down next to her. 'Looks like the poor lass took a right clobbering,' he said quietly, taking in the bruised eyes that were swollen shut. Straightening up, he rejoined the others, but Markham noticed the fists clenching and unclenching as if Sarge badly wanted to vent his own impotent fury.

Burton looked round at the rows of stainless steel racks filled with supplies and catering equipment. 'I'll get SOCOs down here right away, sir,' she murmured. 'Most likely the weapon came from here.'

'Hell, we saw her less than an hour ago,' Doyle said in stunned disbelief. 'She's just a kid. Why would anyone want to kill her?'

'It's got to be one of the staff,' Carruthers pointed out grimly, 'seeing as the place doesn't open to visitors till tomorrow.'

'Have everywhere sealed off and get Dimples over here asap,' Markham instructed Burton. 'Speak to Whelan about all potential access points so we can be sure of ruling out an intruder.' He turned to the two sergeants. 'I want you to take statements from all the park personnel — everyone who's been on the premises. We need to account for their movements.'

As the team scurried to do his bidding, he turned to Noakes. 'We'll take the next of kin, Noakesy.'

Everyone in CID dreaded undertaking bereavement visits, but Markham never pulled rank to avoid such assignments.

'Whoever attacked the lass had to have got blood on them,' Noakes said thoughtfully.

'There's a sink over by the door,' Markham said, 'so they could've mopped themselves up in a matter of minutes.' He looked round the gloomy space consideringly. 'I don't believe this was premeditated. Something happened which made them lash out.'

'You reckon it's the same nutter who whacked Pardoe?'

'I think it's got to be, Noakesy, given the proximity in terms of time and location.'

'Mebbe it were a stalker or some random whack job who got in somehow an' then followed her down here.'

'We can't rule it out,' the DI replied calmly, though the prospect of a crazed sex attacker and mad paganist on the loose in the park at the same time sent chills down his spine.

The two men took a final look at the dead teenager. Almost tenderly, Noakes remarked, 'She's gotta be all of sixteen. Poor kid never even had the chance of a bit of life.'

Markham knew the other was thinking of his own daughter.

'Which is why we need to catch whoever did this,' he said quietly.

Noakes shivered. Despite the heat of the day and the electric lighting, the basement was cold and gloomy. 'It's well spooky down here,' he said. With his massive head cocked on one side and sniffing the air like a scent hound, he added, 'I c'n *feel* 'em,' he added. 'Like they've left an evil trail behind or summat.'

Markham sighed, knowing all too well that any kind of forensic trail would be so heavily contaminated as to be almost worthless. Metaphorically, however, he knew what Noakes meant.

'Let's be on our way, Noakesy, and leave the field clear for when the SOCOs arrive,' the DI urged. 'We need to inform Cathy's family before word gets out. And then it's on to see Michael Brophy at the *Gazette*. Kate can handle the crime scene here and brief us on developments later after she's interviewed Bernadette Donovan and Maureen Slattery.'

As Noakes barrelled his way back up the stairs, Markham unobtrusively crossed himself and said a silent prayer for

Cathy Price's soul. If asked, he couldn't really have explained why this felt somehow essential for him on such occasions. He only knew that it helped to remind him of the inestimable value of his murdered victims and the huge void their absence left in the lives of those who had loved them. He was surprised by the words that sprang to his lips. Where had they come from? How was he even able to say them? They seemed to well up inside him without any input on his part. All he knew was that this intensely private ritual worked, mysteriously enabling him to find for victims that "eternity" which rescued them from nothingness and insignificance. At such moments, he seemed to defy the negative reality of death and transform it into something better, something that wasn't limited by time and space but rather an in-between to another dimension. He was well aware Sidney and the other apparatchiks had little time for 'mystical claptrap' but could never disavow this sense of a special thread which connected him to the murdered dead, a vital tie that wove itself into the fabric of his professional life.

Wrenching his thoughts back to present reality, he told himself that for now he needed to remain focused on the fact that Cathy Price's short existence had been brought to a fatal conclusion.

Dead before she had begun to live.

# CHAPTER 5: DEAD ENDS

Later that day saw Markham and Noakes heading for the *Gazette*'s offices in the town centre after their harrowing visit to Cathy Price's parents. Her mother had been ominously calm and the father grim-faced but her older brother, summoned home from work, did his best with cups of tea and broken words of comfort.

'They'll be alright,' the FLO Carolyn Holder told Markham, though in truth they both knew nothing would ever be alright again.

Carolyn had appeared surprised at seeing the DI accompanied by his civilian consultant rather than another member of his team, but Markham regarded his friend's "common touch" as invaluable on such occasions. When it came to newspaper hacks, Noakes's presence was also invariably useful for the sense of menace he managed to convey, his stormy history with reporter Gavin Conors having become the stuff of legend over the years.

Now, as if by tacit consent, the two men put the latest tragedy to one side and mulled over their impressions of the museum tour and the park's volunteers.

'It seemed to me you quite enjoyed going round the exhibits,' Markham ventured.

'Devenish ain't the worst,' his friend conceded (high praise coming from Noakes). 'When I went over for a chat in the canteen, he told me not all them Druids were wimpy types. There were this Irish fella tied hisself to a tree when he knew he were going to die cos he wanted to remain standing and not give the other lot the satisfaction of falling down in front of 'em.'

Markham smiled to himself. Clearly the curator had intuited that this particular ex-serviceman and proud alumnus of 'P' Company was far keener on warrior priests than namby-pamby tree-huggers or earth-worshippers. He had overheard Noakes tell Devenish his favourite parade-ground story about RSM Desmond Lynch of the Irish Guards who, at the passing-out Queen's Parade at Sandhurst, berated Officer Cadet King Hussein of Jordan with the immortal words, 'Stand still, you idle little Monarch!' The curator had enjoyed that, though Markham felt sure his friend was embellishing the facts. Far funnier in the DI's opinion was Noakes's insistence that some unnamed Tim Nice-But-Dim had told him, 'It's a true story. And would you believe it, the Queen never flinched!'

The traffic moved forward sluggishly, but now Noakes's spirits seemed to be reviving after the awful discovery in the café basement. 'I thought Devenish were a bit drippy to start with, but *ackshually* he's quite interesting once you get used to that prissy voice . . . told me about some doctor in the seventeenth century who later became a vicar — name of William Stukeley. Anyway, he changed his name to summat exotic an' made folk call him the Arch-Druid. Turned his garden into some sort of creepy grove, even had a pagan burial service there for one of his kids who died. Mad as a box of frogs but did all sorts of research on Stonehenge an' ancient monuments.'

'How did he square his, er, extracurricular interests with being a vicar?'

'Oh, he came up with tons of links between the Druids an' Old Testament prophets an' Jesus. Some of it were totally bats, like him saying the Druids had a thing about the number three being sacred an' that showed they believed in the

Trinity. Plus he went round preaching "vegetable sermons" to show how the Druids an' vegetables an' natural religion were all linked to Christianity. Yeah, Devenish is a mine of information.' He sniggered. 'Burton wouldn't have liked hearing him tell about the old Roman cemetery down in Winchester where they found a pile of women with their heads cut off an' left down by their feet—'

'Not too sure I like the sound of it myself, Noakesy.'

'But that ain't the best bit, guv.'

'*Oh?*'

'Their jaws had been taken out an' spindle thingies buried next to the bodies.'

'*Spindles?*'

'Yeah, cos the spindles symbolised Fate an' Destiny, an' witches could kill someone by snapping the thread.'

'Hmm.'

'Devenish said their jaws were removed to stop 'em casting spells an' making trouble after they were dead.'

The DI felt a sudden chill but said lightly, 'Very *Hammer Horror*. I'm glad Kate wasn't treated to a full recital.'

'Being a feminist, she'd have got off on all the stuff about prophetesses,' Noakes said cheerfully. 'There were one who had locked herself away in a tower an' got her rellies to pass on messages an' offerings . . . had a nice little business going,' he added admiringly, for all the world as though it was some kind of Iron Age startup, Markham thought, trying not to laugh.

His wingman turned confidential. 'I thought Burton were looking a bit peaky, to tell you the truth.'

'Well, the museum *was* rather claustrophobic,' Markham replied. 'And some of the exhibits struck me as being on the gruesome side, at least in the Iron Age section.'

'The whole house is OTT,' Noakes agreed. 'Like summat out of *The Woman in Black*. I mean, you could tell from her flat that old Vi must've been a hoarder, all them animal figures an' miniature tea sets an' tiles an' bits of old glass an' whatnot.'

Markham was thoughtful. 'Did anyone else join in with this discussion of crazed Arch-Druids and spindles?'

'Well the whole lot of 'em were sitting there an' seemed to know all about it,' Noakes replied.

'Did anyone strike you as being noticeably affected by what Devenish was saying?' the DI pressed. 'Anyone appear unusually animated or intense?'

'Can't say I really noticed,' came the laconic answer. 'It looked like they were all in for it . . . Mebbe the catering woman an' Sinnott were a bit bored an' Davenport copped a quick yawn but they'll have heard the spiel umpteen times, seeing as it's Devenish's hobby horse.'

Returning to the subject of Markham's fellow DI, Noakes continued, 'I don' think it were jus' that creepy house getting Burton down, though.'

'*Oh?*'

'She looked well down in the dumps . . . *Trouble At Mill*,' his friend intoned lugubriously. 'Shippers told me at home she goes round spouting religious guff all the time an' rabbiting about the afterlife . . . not to mention reading dodgy types like CS Lewis an' some depressed Russian writer.'

Clearly in his friend's opinion, Dostoevsky was the thin end of the wedge. 'Any road, they've had a few rows about it.'

It darted through Markham, with the speed of an arrow, that this was somehow connected with Burton's visits to Maryvale House.

'What kind of religious "guff" are we talking about?'

'Oh, about everything being artificial an' fake an' how we need to look for a deeper meaning . . . go *behind the veil*, stuff like that.'

*Behind the veil.* The words struck him with a sensation of uneasiness.

'Shippers reckons it's all tied up with losing her dad. The other night she tore him off a strip for talking like he were out of the way an' didn't count for owt anymore.'

'The rhythms of bereavement are different for everyone,' Markham replied slowly. 'Being a psychologist, I'm sure Nathan understands that. A universe without one's parent seems somehow inconceivable,' he said haltingly, 'makes one question all the old realities.'

'Sounds as if she needs a break. Kind of like, *Stop the World: I Need to Get Off*,' Noakes observed sympathetically.

'A break from *policing?*' Markham asked with a sick dread, before reproaching himself for the selfishness that lay behind his question.

'Happen the lass jus' needs a change of scene,' came the reply. Noakes shot the DI a surprisingly shrewd look. 'If she's confused — *mebbe pulled in different directions* — a move'll help clear her head.'

Markham heard the unspoken message: *She needs to sort out her feelings for you too, guv.*

He slid away from the implications, parking the problem for now.

'Once this case is behind us, I'll sit down with Kate and work something out,' he said neutrally. 'But in the meantime, things are coming into perspective with this investigation.'

'You might wanna tell your face then,' Noakes said laconically.

Markham caught sight of his pale, set expression in the rear-view mirror and became aware he was gripping the steering wheel as if his life depended upon it.

He forced a smile. 'We may not have uncovered a swashbuckling, blood-drenched Druidic narrative that points to a likely killer, Noakesy, but I'm increasingly certain there's a link between Tony Pardoe's murder and the Priddy case. Let's see what Michael Brophy has for us.'

'Brophy's a suspect too,' Noakes cautioned, 'seeing how he liked having a go at Pardoe. You're always saying "the pen is mightier than the sword", so this Biro Platoon merchant's *gotta* be in the picture.'

\* \* \*

Michael Brophy, the *Gazette*'s Features Editor, was a rather haggard forty-something with receding dark hair and the unnaturally pale complexion of someone who spent too much time hunched over a computer monitor. His minuscule cubicle was even staler and more meanly furnished than Markham's own hutch in CID and absolutely stank of nicotine, despite the newspaper offices being a smoke-free zone. Sartorially, too, he was something of a mess, so that Noakes appeared almost elegant by comparison.

Squinting at the detectives from across a paper-strewn desk on which it appeared almost impossible that he could find anything, the reporter responded politely enough to their questions.

No, he told them in a gentle Irish brogue, he had no alibi for Friday, having decided to turn in early (with a bottle of Johnnie Walker by the look of him, Noakes thought acidly). Yes, he had run various pieces on Tony Pardoe, but they were more along the lines of *Is this Bromgrove's answer to Alan Sugar?* Than anything scabrous.

'He wouldn't give you an exclusive then?' Noakes asked perspicaciously.

Brophy didn't appear rattled. 'True, but he didn't give interviews to the *Bromgrove Echo* either.'

'Did you have anything to do with him socially?' Markham asked.

'We crossed paths at the odd civic bunfight, but us reptiles were kept well away from the celebrities.' The tone was rueful and humorous, with no discernible resentment. Altogether, Brophy appeared like a man with nothing to hide, though Markham knew better than to rely on first impressions. How often did he think he'd got someone all figured out only to discover they were an entirely different individual — in some cases possessing several layers of personality, layer upon layer of masks. He knew from bitter experience that it didn't pay to make assumptions.

'I came across his friend Loretta Davenport now and again,' the journalist continued easily, 'but she's what they call a "lady who lunches", while as you can see,' he gestured wearily round at his untidy office, 'I'm just a humble hack.'

Markham thought he detected a hint of regret behind the self-deprecation.

'Did she ever have a job?' Noakes asked curiously.

'I believe she qualified as a solicitor but didn't practise for long. After that, there were relationships with various wealthy men who showed their appreciation in the usual way.'

An image of Sidney with Loretta flashed across the DI's mind. Surely not, he told himself firmly.

There was no condemnation in Brophy's voice as he continued. 'She gets on with all her exes and women seem to like her too. Doesn't suffer fools gladly; got a social conscience; does quite a bit for charity.'

'She wasn't romantically involved with Mr Pardoe at any time?' Markham asked.

'Not that I was aware. By all accounts, they were just good friends.'

The DI changed direction. 'Were you aware of any controversy regarding Mr Pardoe's planned shakeup at Hollingrove Park?'

The other smiled thinly. 'We'd heard rumours about it and there were some anonymous letters in the postbag — *Outraged of Bromgrove* kind of thing . . . nothing serious, so we just chucked them out.'

Markham decided to take a risk. 'I'd like the next part of this conversation to remain confidential,' he said as the man opposite raised his eyebrows. 'If it comes to anything, then maybe there's a scoop in it for you, but in the meantime . . .'

There was a pregnant pause before Brophy answered. 'I'm listening.'

'Do you remember hearing anything about the death of a little girl called Mary Priddy?' the DI continued. 'This was in 1979, well before your time here obviously.'

Trawling through digital archives, Burton had been unable to find anything concrete in the *Gazette*'s back numbers other than cryptic references to a local man having been ruled out of the police's enquiries, but Markham knew journalists had their own hotlines to local gossip.

'It's funny you should mention that,' Brophy said slowly.

'How so?'

'Well, by a strange coincidence I'd heard a rumour your lot were thinking of reopening the Priddy case . . .'

Markham's expression was flinty as he asked, 'May I enquire where this rumour originated?'

'D'you know, I'm genuinely not sure how it started,' Brophy said easily. Despite his casual manner, the lean features were watchful. 'I think it was just one of those throwaway comments — once news came in about Tony Pardoe's murder, people were raking up anything to do with the park. It's been pretty much a scandal-free zone over the years, so the news desk's been scrambling around to put a nose on the story.'

'Anyone ever in the frame for it?' Noakes asked idly.

'Oh, you'd know more about that than me,' Brophy replied equally casually, but his eyes were wary.

'Of course, we'll be liaising with our cold case team,' Markham said levelly, 'but I'd be interested to know if *you'd* heard anything.'

The other's gaze flickered. 'Not as yet, Inspector, but it's still early days.'

Afterwards, Noakes said, 'Slippery git. An' you could tell he fancied having a crack at that Laura. Talk about punching above.'

'Loretta.'

'*Shifty*,' Noakes repeated emphatically. 'I reckon he were jealous . . . had a big fat chip on his shoulder about Pardoe being a sleb with folk running after him while he's just this lowlife reporter stuck in a crummy office that smells of sweaty feet.'

Markham laughed at that. 'There was a distinct whiff of something unpleasant,' he agreed before turning serious. 'Yes, I think you're right about Brophy holding something back . . . On the other hand, the *Gazette*'s sailed close to the wind in the past so won't be naming names any time soon in case they land themselves in legal hot water.'

'*Putting a nose on the story!*' his friend exclaimed wrathfully. 'Sniffing out dirt more like.'

It sounded as though Noakes wouldn't have minded landing a punch on Brophy's own nose, as had happened on one infamous occasion with Gavin Conors. All in all, Markham wasn't sorry to leave the *Gazette*'s offices behind as they headed towards the town centre.

They had arranged to meet up with Kate Burton in Waterstones whose first-floor café was virtually deserted when they arrived. Markham liked the fact that the eatery was in the middle of all the bookcases, though Noakes looked round suspiciously as if expecting the likes of CS Lewis to be lurking nearby, waiting to pounce. He relaxed, however, once they were settled in surprisingly comfortable red leather moon chairs with drinks and pastries on the low table in front of them, Burton having been quick to take the hint when Noakes grumbled that the *Gazette*'s hospitality fell way short of the mark.

She lost no time in relaying developments at the park.

'The basement's fire escape door was left open for some reason,' she informed them. 'Bill Whelan wasn't able to say when he first noticed it.'

'So, someone could've broken in from outside,' Markham's wingman mumbled through a mouthful of chocolate twist.

'We had the perimeter secured, but I suppose technically it's possible someone got through the cordon even though the uniforms on duty said no way.' She frowned. 'Far easier for one of the staff or volunteers to follow Cathy down there.'

'But *why?*' Noakes demanded in bafflement. 'I mean, it don' make any sense murdering a kid like that.'

'Were people able to account for their movements, Kate?' Markham wanted to know.

This enquiry met with another frown. 'Well, after drinks and snacks in the café they drifted off . . . went to the loo or pottered about in the shop or grounds, doing whatever is they do. They didn't stick together and nobody had any reason to notice what other folk were up to.'

The DI suppressed a groan.

'Murder weapon?' he asked.

'Dimples reckons a kitchen ladle or something similar — Catrina Walsh did an inventory and there appears to be one missing. It wouldn't have been difficult to hide it under a coat or in a bag.'

'Do we know what Cathy Price was doing down in the basement?'

'Apparently, she had a habit of sloping off to make calls on her mobile; it was nice and private down there, so she was unlikely to be caught skiving.' Burton's face was compassionate. 'The boyfriend is devastated. He was out on a plumbing job so there's no chance it was him.'

'How's Sidders taking it?' Noakes demanded.

She pulled a face. 'Keen that we shouldn't rule out the possibility of a random attacker rather than linking it to Tony Pardoe.'

'That chuffing figures.'

'The park's a law unto itself,' Burton said slowly. 'I'm having all the official entrances and exits rechecked, but there's most likely ways in and out that only people connected with the place for donkey's years know about.'

Noakes moved on to the subject of Burton's other assignments. 'What were the old biddy an' Pardoe's fancy piece like?'

Markham suspected his fellow DI was inwardly raising her eyes to heaven, but she managed not to wince.

'Bernadette Donovan's all there, Sarge. Sharp as a tack. When I said something about it being sad that Mr Pardoe had no family, she told me, "I suppose in my case the next of kin is the budgie."'

Noakes guffawed heartily at this gem. 'What did she think of Tone getting all Vi's dosh?'

'I don't think she felt short-changed. There was a decent bequest of five thousand left to her. Besides which, she benefited from living with Miss Henwood rent-free.'

Noakes pulled a face. 'At her beck an' call all day long, though,' he pointed out. 'Like some sort of skivvy.'

'I had the impression the arrangement suited them both,' Burton replied. 'She's well-spoken and very striking looking . . . tall and graceful with lots of silvery hair piled up in a chignon.' Judging from her portrait, Violet Henwood had been short, homely and beaky-featured, so it sounded as though her cousin had received the better genetic inheritance, Markham reflected.

'Bernadette worked in the civil service,' Burton continued. 'Has a house on Bromgrove Rise and a decent pension, so it wasn't as if she was some kind of put-upon dependent. It seemed like she was genuinely fond of Violet for all her idiosyncrasies.'

'How about Tone?' Noakes wanted to know. 'What did Bernadette think of *him?*'

'Hard to tell,' Burton answered. 'It didn't sound as though he wasted too much time on her . . . focused his energies on charming Violet. What you might call an operator, but very attentive apparently and humoured her when she rambled on about the Henwood family tree or folk customs. It was obvious he really couldn't be doing with all the hoo-ha about the stones, but she said he tried to show an interest.'

'Waiting for the old bat to pop her clogs so he could turn the place into a theme park,' Noakes declared cynically.

'Bernadette said the volunteers were up in arms about that, but she thought they'd have come round in the end. She had the feeling Mr Pardoe would have tried to woo them — use Loretta Davenport as a go-between to make them see things his way.'

'Did she say anything about Mr Pardoe's private life?' Markham asked.

'No . . . apart from telling me she thought he was a bachelor at heart; liked his freedom and didn't want to be tied down. With him — and I quote — work came first, his sporting interests second and women a poor third.'

'Alibi?' Markham asked, though without much hope.

Burton grimaced. 'Early night on account of getting the eight o'clock train to her friend's.' The DI thought for a moment. 'She came across as a decent, well-adjusted woman . . . definitely had Tony Pardoe's number but was quite philosophical about him being CEO and all that . . . Didn't seem at all resentful that he couldn't really have cared less about Richard II or his heritage.'

Noakes was eyeing a cinnamon Danish.

'Go on, Sarge,' she urged kindly. 'It'll make up for Mr Brophy being stingy.'

He needed no second invitation. 'Ta, luv. Reckon I'm eating your share.'

'I'm not hungry,' the DI told him. Aware of Markham's eyes on her, she continued hastily, 'Did Mr Brophy have anything for you?'

'Nada,' Noakes replied glumly. 'But he seemed to know we were looking at Priddy again. The crafty bugger were ever so vague about where he got it from.'

'D'you think the leak came from CID, Kate?' Markham asked. 'Carruthers perhaps?'

'Him an' Kim have split up, you know,' Noakes confided.

Markham was concerned. 'No, I didn't,' he said. 'When did that happen?'

'A while back but the lad wanted it kept quiet. I'm only telling you now cos you might want to cut him some slack.'

During their bridal boutique investigation, the team had warmed to Carruthers after he confided in them about the bullying experienced by his girlfriend after she had put on weight and been subjected to some "mean girl" unkindness. It had shown another more appealing side of his character and helped ameliorate the off-putting impression created by his occasional superciliousness.

'Doyle thinks he's living on the never-never right now,' Noakes went on. 'Went a bit mad splashing the cash after he got dumped.'

'I don't want to throw accusations around,' Markham said consideringly, 'particularly not if he's going through a bad time. But you might drop another gentle hint, Kate; it's curtains for his career if he's found to be on the *Gazette*'s payroll.'

'Will do, sir.'

'And see if you can encourage him to speak to me about his personal issues . . . without hurting his pride.'

She nodded assent.

'What's Pardoe's girlfriend like?' Noakes demanded, his thoughts turning to Burton's other interviewee.

'I was expecting Maureen Slattery to be hard-boiled and ultra-chic,' Burton admitted, 'but she's nothing like that. Very gentle and fresh-faced, long chestnut hair tied back from her face, almost schoolgirlish.'

'Were she and Mr Pardoe "on" or "off" when he died?' Markham wanted to know.

'"On a break from each other" apparently.' A tiny pucker creased Burton's forehead. 'She was very self-contained talking about him . . . said he was much nicer than he cared to let on and a lot of the bombast was just a front.'

Noakes was puzzled. 'She don' sound like the sort he'd go for.'

'There was something quite soothing about her,' Burton replied. 'I can see how he might have found her restful to be with.'

It was funny, Markham thought, but that was exactly how he felt about Burton herself.

'Did she mention him having other women?' Noakes asked hopefully. 'Dolly bird types?'

Burton laughed. 'She called him a serial monogamist — said he wouldn't have it in him to run more than one woman at a time.'

The uxorious Noakes looked thoroughly disapproving at hearing this. As far as he was concerned, working one's way through a conveyor belt of women was bad form. You mated for life and that was that.

'She didn't bat an eyelid when I brought up Loretta Davenport, said Pardoe needed his mother hen,' Burton continued.

An interesting choice of words, thought Markham. And even more interesting that the woman didn't seem fazed by "three in the relationship".

'Did she have much to do with the Hollingrove Park crowd?' Noakes asked.

'She called them Miss Henwood's lame ducks, but not in an unkind way; more like she found them all a bit eccentric.'

'What does she do for a living?' Markham asked.

'History teacher at Medway High.'

'*A History teacher!*' Clearly it was the last thing Noakes expected to hear. Recovering his sangfroid, he added, 'I c'n see how you an' her would get on then . . . birds of a feather an' all that.'

She laughed. 'I'm flattered, Sarge, but we weren't swapping book recommendations.'

Noakes looked unconvinced. He was willing to bet that boffin talk had featured at some point . . . maybe even the dreaded 'Sheets and Kelly'.

'Maureen's a *suspect* just as much as the rest of them,' Burton insisted. 'She didn't arrive at her girlfriend's till half ten, so there was time for her to have met up with Mr Pardoe beforehand.'

Markham recalled what they had learned at the museum. 'Did she say anything about wanting to do a school project on the Henwoods, Kate?'

'Only that she backed off when Pardoe didn't go for the idea. She was quite casual about it . . . Looked surprised when I asked if his decision had anything to do with Loretta and said he just thought it would be too much faff.'

Markham's thoughts turned to Pardoe's PM. 'Did Dimples's tox screen flag up anything?'

'Pardoe's BAC was 0.10 per cent.'

'So him an' the killer could've had a drink together in that greenhouse,' Noakes mused.

'Dimples thinks it's a strong possibility.'

'Which presumably means he knew them and had no reason to be fearful,' Markham concluded.

'Could a woman have done it?' Noakes wondered.

'Assuming Pardoe and the killer sat down to chat on that window seat which runs round the inside of the greenhouse,'

Burton theorised, 'then with him properly tipsy and letting his guard down, an attack would've caught him totally unawares.'

'He were fit, though,' Noakes objected. 'One of them silver fox types like Paul Hollywood; worked out an' looked after hisself. You're not telling me some lass would be able to bring him down.'

'According to Dimples, the murder weapon was a wire garotte,' Burton pointed out. 'This wasn't manual strangulation. With the advantage of surprise, a woman could've done it. Heck,' she laughed, 'there's sites on You Tube demonstrating how to make your own DIY strangle kit.'

A long silence followed her words. Then Markham looked at his watch. 'Time to check out Mr Pardoe's business rival at *Medway Logistics*,' he said.

'An' the pissed off PA,' his wingman added.

'Indeed. So if you've quite finished noshing, Noakesy . . .'

Burton looked aghast as the other scooped up a chocolate muffin and wrapped it in his none too clean hankie. Catching Markham's eye, however, she managed a weak smile.

Some things never changed!

* * *

*Medway Logistics* was housed in an unprepossessing cinder block at the far end of Medway Innovation Park, a site where Lego-like offices sat cheek by jowl with retail outlets. The location suggested that Jason Quirk was not exactly in the Richard Branson league of entrepreneurs, Markham thought, as a sulky bottle-blonde receptionist at the front desk directed them to a suite on the first floor which looked like a call centre, with desks separated by blue felt screen dividers and two glassed-in offices at either end.

Quirk was a stocky sandy-haired man with a prize-fighter's build and truculent expression to match. Unlike Pardoe, he could hardly be described as a silver fox or Paul Hollywood lookalike, though piercing blue eyes did something to redeem his otherwise nondescript appearance.

Somewhat to Markham's surprise, he waxed eloquent about the Hollingrove Stones and advances in technology that offered the possibility of uncovering their secrets. 'I studied Archaeology at uni,' he said gruffly. 'Local history's a bit of an obsession with me.'

How much of an obsession, Markham asked himself.

The DI wondered if Quirk had hoped for a share of the action when it came to preserving and researching the stones. Certainly, it sounded as though the businessman possessed the right credentials.

'Pardoe was a real dog in the manger,' he said in answer to a question from Burton about 'shared opportunities' with reference to the park. 'Made it clear there was no room for anyone else — always one to hog the glory. I don't think he gave a flying fajita about the monument, but he was possessive about everything to do with the Henwood estate.' His lip curled. 'Enjoyed playing the local squire even though he was just CEO.'

Unlike Mark Brophy, the man's jealousy was overt. In terms of alibi, though, his (for a marvel) appeared to be watertight. 'I was working late on an order till eleven that night,' he told them belligerently. 'The office manager'll confirm it.'

Duly summoned, Clive Hooper provided chapter and verse, though Markham had a hunch he would swear blind that black was white if required to do so. Glancing across at Noakes and Burton during Hooper's pedantic recital, he could tell they felt the same.

Markham noted the way Quirk sneered about 'Bromgrove's boy wonder' and made little effort to conceal his antipathy. 'Undercut me all along the line and did me down every chance he got. Brownnosed his way to the top, that's how he ended up with an OBE. Those poor sods of volunteers would all have been out on their ear once he'd decided the best way to get shot of them.'

Marion Kirkwood turned out to be a simpering middle-aged blonde who was inclined to gush. Pressed as to why Tony Pardoe had dispensed with her services, she told them, 'He got it into his head that I was spying, talking to people about him.'

'Why would you want to do that?' Noakes asked disingenuously. 'I mean, ain't a PA *supposed* to take messages, arrange the diary an' that kind of thing?'

'Act as a gatekeeper?' Burton prompted.

Her plump hands fluttered helplessly, though Markham noticed how her eyes were trained on Quirk.

'*That's just it!*' she exclaimed. 'He was totally *paranoid!* Didn't like his friends talking to me, though I could hardly have given them the brush-off. After all,' she sounded genuinely nettled now, 'like you say, I'm a highly trained personal assistant and not just some typist.' With a petulant inflexion, she concluded, 'It was hardly *my fault* if people liked me.'

'Of course she were spying on him,' Noakes said afterwards. 'Seemed the nosey type. Probl'y having it away with Quirk an' all.'

Burton looked as though she didn't much care for the image that conjured up.

'Clive Hooper vouched for her too,' she pointed out.

Noakes snorted. 'Hooper's scared stiff of Quirk,' he said. 'Them alibis ain't worth diddly squat.'

Burton thought about what the PA had said. 'If Marion's right about Pardoe being "paranoid", it begs the question — what did he have to hide?'

'Business secrets?' Markham suggested. 'His plans for the park?'

'Mebbe summat in his private life,' Noakes speculated. With a self-conscious clearing of his throat, he continued, 'An okay-looking bloke like that; happen he were batting for both sides.'

Markham thought about the picture of Tony Pardoe pinned to a noticeboard in his office back at the station (now doubling as an incident room). Their victim had undoubtedly been an attractive specimen — albeit something of a 'Ken doll' (Noakes) — with a certain charisma that jumped out at one. It wasn't difficult to imagine that he might have appealed to both sexes. Indeed, this was something that had occurred to the DI when listening to the stories of Richard II and his favourites during that tour of the museum. However, if the man was leading a secret double life, they had yet to uncover any evidence.

'Or p'raps it were connected with Priddy,' Noakes cogitated. 'Some deep dark secret about how that little lass ended up in the slurry pit. Mebbe he were being blackmailed about it.'

'There was no reaction from Quirk or Kirkwood when we mentioned Mary Priddy,' Burton demurred.

'Could've been an act,' Noakes pointed out. 'They've both lived here all their lives and were around when it happened.'

'They were definitely ill at ease about *something*,' Markham said. 'But there could be any number of reasons for that, especially if Quirk operates on the shady side of the street.' He sighed, frustrated that, so far, they didn't appear to have got a handle on *any* of their suspects.

Burton glanced at her watch.

'Maxwell and Fellowes should be arriving at the station shortly,' she said. 'Hopefully they'll have something for us.'

'Are you up for this, Noakesy?' Markham enquired, knowing it was pretty much a rhetorical question since there was no way his wingman would pass up the chance to meet the duo.

'*You betcha!*' was the enthusiastic response.

Heading to Markham's car, his friend reminded the DI (not for the first time) of a huge St Bernard happy to be "off the leash" and ranging at will. He could only hope that the two retirees would have something to re-energise himself and the rest of the team.

* * *

Back at the station, Markham glanced up at the darkening sky. It looked like being a typical English spring of alternate sunshine, keen blasts and sudden squalls — not dissimilar to the fluctuation of moods during a challenging murder investigation. As matters stood, the outlook on all fronts was not especially promising.

Maxwell and Fellowes were already waiting in his office when they arrived, Burton promptly disappearing to fetch more chairs.

'This place could do with a makeover,' Maxwell said once they were all squeezed in and the two men had declined the offer of refreshments, somewhat to Noakes's incredulity.

'Management's too busy chucking money at *Inclusion* an' *Diversity*,' Noakes grunted. Jerking a thumb upwards, he added, 'Stanley Tucci up there kept promising all sorts.' He mimicked Sidney's adenoidal honk: '*A New Environment for a New Era*' before concluding with a ferocious scowl, 'New environment my backside.'

Fellowes chuckled at the sarcastic comparison of Sidney to the world's "sexiest bald man", as the Hollywood actor had recently been described.

The two retired detectives were a study in contrasts, Maxwell being tall, spindly and stork-like with white hair, creased schoolmasterish features and a stoop, whereas Fellowes was shorter, with smooth face and forehead and a placid air. Balding on top, with a fringe of grey hair at sides and back, he had an almost childishly guileless face while the other's expression and manner were more vinegary. Yet Markham knew the two men had worked amicably in harness for many years and were well respected.

'Mary Priddy was just ten,' Maxwell told them. 'A shy, trusting little soul by all accounts. The mother was adamant she would never have wandered off by herself — had drummed into her all about Stranger Danger — so it would've been completely out of character.'

Fellowes took over the narrative. 'That's why we decided Mary must have been enticed away to the greenhouse by someone she trusted.'

'You had someone in mind?' Markham asked quietly.

The DI's handsome sculpted countenance, its air of calm distinction, somehow merely heightened by the passing years, was not without its impact on the retired detectives who remained silent for some minutes before Maxwell spoke up.

'A playground supervisor called John Sinnott—'

'*Sinnott!*' Noakes burst out. 'He's one of them volunteers we've been interviewing. Dead quiet, typical gentle giant.'

'What made you think he was involved?' Burton pressed them.

'He'd been in a relationship with Mary's mum, but they split shortly before the "accident",' Fellowes explained.

'Who ended it?' Noakes demanded.

'She did,' Fellowes replied.

'An acrimonious breakup?' Markham wanted to know.

'Both of them said not.' Maxwell's expression was impassive.

Burton's mind turned to alibi. 'Where was Sinnott when Mary went missing?'

Maxwell scratched his chin meditatively, looking more like a schoolmaster than ever. 'Apparently his shift didn't start for another hour and he took a wander round the park, the other side of the lake, over by the pinetum . . . the problem being that he didn't cross paths with anyone on his travels.'

'What was your impression of him?' Markham asked.

'The strong silent type . . . good with kids . . . trained as a youth worker later on.' Fellowes sighed. 'He was a model employee and popular with his colleagues. Never been in trouble or anything like that. Very reserved, but that's not a crime.'

Noakes cleared his throat. 'How did the little lass actually die? Was it from the fall or . . . had she been *interfered with* or owt like that?'

'She was found pretty quickly, about two hours into the search,' Maxwell told them sombrely. 'The greenhouse pit was around five feet deep with rubble and rocks at the bottom. Going by the bruising on her arms and back, the pathologist

— it was Dr Farooq in those days — thought it was possible she'd been gripped tight and pushed; cause of death was a broken neck, though skull fracture and haemorrhage would probably have done for her anyway. No signs of sexual interference.'

'She would have been found sooner,' Fellowes amplified, 'but the builders weren't due in that day, so initially no one thought to check out the greenhouse.' With an exasperated click of his tongue, 'They were bloody slack about security back then, considering it housed the Hollingrove Stones.'

'It was still early days in terms of academic research and that kind of thing,' Maxwell pointed out. 'The council took a while to appreciate what they had.'

'Yeah, as in potential gold mine,' Noakes cut in sourly.

'So, essentially anyone could've snuck in,' Burton said gloomily.

Maxwell's tone matched hers. 'Well, the place was pretty much a building site, and back then they didn't keep records of visitors to the stones. Nobody remembered seeing anything.'

'Who was on duty with the kids in the play area when Mary went walkabout?' she asked.

Maxwell made a disgusted sound. 'Two total birdbrains — nice enough girls but they were more interested swapping hair and makeup tips than watching the kids. It's different now that everyone's obsessed with health and safety and safeguarding, but things were much more lax in the eighties.'

Fellowes took them back to the disappearance. 'It was breezy but dry, first Saturday in March,' he said. 'Just a few kids in the play area while mums and dads went for a coffee. A couple of grownups wandered past but,' his tone was rueful, 'they were more interested in guzzling ice creams and throwing sticks for their dogs than looking at the climbing frames and swings and slides. Of course, once the alarm was raised it was a different story.'

'Who was first to notice that Mary was missing?' Burton asked.

'Her mum. She'd gone for a cuppa with her friend at quarter past ten and panicked when she got back just after eleven and couldn't see the kid.' Maxwell's mouth turned down at the corners. 'None of the other youngsters remembered seeing her leave, while Dumb and Dumber were just running around like headless chickens . . . It was total chaos.'

'Sounds like she were a lonely little girl, seeing as no one paid her any mind,' Noakes said almost angrily, and Markham knew that he was once again thinking of his own daughter.

'She was stick thin with flyaway brown hair, braces and big, ugly NHS specs,' Fellowes told them gruffly. 'But at least the glasses didn't break and her mum was able to get them back . . . *afterwards*.' He paused, as though struggling with some inner anguish, then resumed. 'Sinnott was our number one suspect because of his connection with the mother, but we couldn't shake him and there was no forensic evidence. Plus, there was some history student up at the house — cataloguing books or something like that — who corroborated his story about being sat on a bench over by the pinetum.'

Burton was puzzled. 'How could she see that far?'

'Telescope on the second-floor landing,' Maxwell answered. 'Antique piece — brass tripod and fittings — but it wasn't locked away or anything like that, so the work experience lot had a go from time to time.'

'Not an alibi, though,' Burton frowned. 'Not unless she kept an eye on him the whole morning.'

'She was sure it was eleven o'clock when she took a look and spotted him . . . said she remembered a grandfather clock chiming the hour.'

'He could still have done it,' Noakes mused.

'Assuming he was the one who abducted and murdered Mary, we're talking about a very limited window of opportunity if he was back at the pinetum for eleven,' Fellowes pointed out. 'It's over the other side of the park, so he would've had to get the kid over to the greenhouse, kill her and then make tracks in roughly half an hour.'

'Doable, though,' Noakes persisted.

'True,' Fellowes conceded, 'but the timings were a problem.'

Maxwell rubbed his eyes, suddenly looking very tired. 'In the end, we had to back off,' he said. 'Didn't have enough to make it stick.'

'What did your gut tell you?' Markham asked.

Maxwell returned the DI's gaze steadily. 'The bruises on her arms could've been down to horsing round like kids do . . . or whoever took her could've got rough, perhaps building up to a sexual assault. Or maybe the whole thing started out innocently enough but then somehow things got out of hand. Perhaps she said something cheeky or threatened to tell and they just lost it.'

'Either way, we didn't think it was an accident,' Fellowes concluded stoutly.

At that moment, the meeting was interrupted by Kate Burton's mobile.

'Excuse me,' she murmured, disappearing into the open plan office.

The DI was back seconds later, her face very pale.

'There's been another one,' she said.

## CHAPTER 6: SIGNS AND WONDERS

The mood in Markham's office on the morning of Thursday 21 March was decidedly tense as the team plus Noakes gathered for their emergency briefing.

Noakes kicked off proceedings. 'What the chuff were she up to mooching about that grove thingy by herself?'

'It's called a *pinetum*,' Burton corrected him patiently. 'Firs, maples, redwoods, cypresses and cedars . . . along with some very ancient oaks.'

Her colleague appeared seriously disgruntled on hearing this explanation, no doubt thinking that she sounded like a walking guidebook. Presumably, however, like Markham he had noticed the purple shadows under her eyes and therefore refrained from any sarcastic rejoinder.

'It was the same pinetum where John Sinnott was spotted all those years ago on the day that little Mary Priddy disappeared', Markham noted grimly.

'Maybe she fancied some time alone by herself in the great outdoors,' Doyle suggested. He had a flash of inspiration. 'Besides, she might've wanted to remember her mate, seeing as the park's the place where he died.'

'I reckon either she went there to meet someone,' Carruthers said, 'or else they were following her and knew where she'd be.'

'*But why'd she take the risk?*' Noakes demanded. 'There'd already been two murders, so why take the chance?'

'That's just it, though,' Carruthers said slowly. 'She didn't reckon *she* was in any danger . . . had a false sense of security . . . figured she could take care of herself.'

If so, it was a gamble for which Loretta Davenport had paid with her life.

'I don' like that "pi-ne-tum",' Noakes persisted stubbornly, enunciating each syllable after the fashion of a recalcitrant little Englander encountering foreign nasties. 'You c'n keep your oaks an' hazels an' all the rest of it, that wood's *way* too dark an' creepy — you think it's silent, but then when you stop to listen, there's all that rustling an' whistling an' pattering like there's folk hiding an' spying on you, only you can't see 'em.'

'Just a breeze blowing the leaves around,' Burton said prosaically, 'and wildlife in the undergrowth. The council's big on rewilding and conservation.'

'Then there's the tree holes an' knots an' hollows, like they're pulling faces at you,' Noakes continued, on a roll now. 'I c'n imagine them Stone Age types getting up to all sorts, dancing around in animal headpieces an' what have you,' he added balefully.

Doyle sniggered. '*Come off it, Sarge!* We're not talking the *Island of Dr Moreau*. There's benches and flowers and bits of art down there too.'

'Yeah, but Davenport went off the main path, right into the shadiest bit.'

'Maybe that's where she felt most comfortable, Sarge,' Burton theorised. 'Or if she was meeting someone, maybe she didn't want anyone overhearing, wanted to be private.'

'Same as Cathy Price,' Noakes put in. 'That poor kid most likely sloped off for a quick skive—'

'And paid for it with her life.' Markham concluded sombrely.

'There were nowt private about the way she were posed,' Noakes continued with a shudder. 'It looked like she were making love to that totem pole thing they strapped her to.'

'It's meant to be a shaman's staff,' Burton explained punctiliously. 'A piece of installation art that kind of honoured the park's Druid heritage, people coming there in ancient times for secret ceremonies—'

'Like human sacrifice,' Noakes interrupted.

'Well, priests going into trances, prophesying and making offerings,' she finished lamely.

'It looked a lot like that rag tree from the museum,' Carruthers volunteered unexpectedly. 'You know, the one in the engraving you asked about, ma'am. Devenish said the Druids hung up fabric and bits of clothing to mark a wood out as being haunted, possessed by spirits.'

'Yes, that's true,' she said slowly. 'They've got almost identical carvings of Janus heads and birds of prey.' She turned to Markham. 'That could point to the killer having a very specific hang-up, some sort of superstition which made it essential to finish Loretta off there, because the Druid connection was important to them.'

'D'you think there could've been something, well, something *sexual* going on, guv,' Doyle asked diffidently, 'with her skirt being hitched up and that beak or whatever it was sticking out between her legs?'

'The killer might have had a sexual motivation,' Markham acknowledged. 'Or they could simply have wanted to degrade Ms Davenport — demonstrate contempt for her.'

'Or want us to *think* it was some kind of sex attack,' Carruthers suggested.

'Dimples said she wasn't interfered with,' Markham replied, 'and forensics indicated there was nothing consistent with sexual activity. Which isn't to say there couldn't have been a sexual motive.' Analysis of the Cathy Price crime scene had reached a similar conclusion.

The DI pictured Loretta Davenport's deposition site again in his mind. She had been stabbed several times in the back and then lashed to the elm staff with a length of outdoor rope, her face pressed up against a carved raven head at the top so that only one eye was visible, filmed over and vacant in death. There had indeed, as Noakes observed, been something obscenely provocative about the corpse's embrace of the totem pole, especially the jackdaw's beak protruding from the rucked-up skirt. An archipelago of clotted rust-coloured stains covering her expensive linen jacket told them how she had died before Dimples confirmed it. Rigor not being fully established, he estimated she had been killed around four or five o'clock on Wednesday afternoon. This time it wasn't the face of strangulation that confronted them — the hideous swelling, cyanosis and tongue protruding between the teeth — but a deliberate, ritualistic choreography which carried echoes of the Pardoe crime scene. As for forensics, few clues were likely to come their way given the outdoor setting. In Markham's experience, scientific markers tended only to be useful once they had an identifiable suspect, a prospect that seemed further away than ever.

Now he said, 'The pinetum's secluded, with what I understand is a somewhat sinister reputation, so visitors mostly stick to the rhododendron walk and main paths. Visitor numbers were down on account of Mr Pardoe's murder, so it was a pretty sure bet that no one would interrupt Ms Davenport and her killer.'

'The stabbing would only have taken seconds,' Carruthers mused. 'Staking her out like that was the tricky part.'

'It needn't have taken all that long,' Doyle pointed out. 'And they could've taken pictures to remind themselves . . . a memento, for reliving the experience later . . . like Hindley and Brady.'

A profound silence followed this unsettling observation.

'Ms Davenport was tall but very slim,' Markham remarked finally. 'Dimples said it wouldn't have been impossible for a female assailant to manoeuvre her into position, especially given the adrenalin rush that most likely made them feel invincible.'

The DI's eyes were gritty with fatigue and he had the beginnings of a headache. 'I've got to brief the DCI,' he told them. 'And then there's Ms Davenport's next of kin . . . her

113

sister lives in France but is flying in later today.' He turned to his fellow DI. 'I need you with me for Sidney, please, Kate.' Even her talent for emollience would be at full stretch now there had been a third homicide. 'In the meantime, I want the rest of you chasing down witnesses and alibis.'

Burton cleared her throat. 'Seeing as the park's closed to the public for the time being, they're transferring the Spring Equinox celebration to Medway Mere, sir,' she said.

Startled, the DI asked, 'When's that meant to take place?'

'Tomorrow evening.' Observing him grimace, she added, 'The organisers don't want to cancel seeing as it's quite a big deal for local Druids.'

'No doubt the DCI will have an opinion about that,' Markham said heavily, thinking that any prospect of community tensions would most likely send Sidney & Co into their usual tailspin. Hopefully he could talk Olivia into attending the event with the team.

'Mr Pardoe's funeral is set for Thursday the 28th,' Burton continued. Under her boss's quizzical gaze, she added, 'The council's pulled strings to get it done and dusted before they appoint a new CEO.'

After the others had trooped off to their various tasks, Burton said, 'I know what Sarge means about the pinetum, guv. There *is* something spooky about it . . . something cold and oppressive, even on a fine day.' With a slight shiver she added, 'Apparently Miss Henwood was upset a few years ago when some archaeology researchers uncovered a horse cemetery nearby — skulls, ribs and various joints. The remains were Bronze Age, dating from the time when settlements were springing up, but she got it into her head that it must have been a site for Druid animal sacrifices.'

'I thought she was meant to be keen on that sort of thing.'

'Folklore yes, but not so much cruelty to animals. And she could be squeamish. According to Malcolm Devenish, she didn't much care to hear about pagan riders who went round with severed heads hanging from their horses' necks. And there was other stuff . . .'

'Such as?'

'The research team found little pipe-clay animal figurines that most likely belonged to infant burials . . . quite possibly infanticides . . . Miss Henwood didn't like that at all, particularly after what happened with Mary Priddy. Devenish said the whole topic of child deaths was pretty much off limits around her and she avoided the pinetum. She had a rose-tinted idea of paganism — hanging up garlands to Pan in the woods rather than devils wearing goat's horns or any black sabbath stuff.'

'"Age hath the privilege", as the saying goes, so I guess she was entitled to cherry-pick,' Markham observed.

'D'you think she ever wondered if her nephew was somehow mixed up in what happened to Mary Priddy and that's why she was so sensitive about dead kids?'

'I suppose it's possible, Kate, but I'm inclined to think, with her Merrie England mindset, she most probably idealised paganism and ancient rituals — Brother Sun, Sister Moon and all that jazz — but wasn't quite so keen to unpick the gorier strands.'

Burton nodded, acknowledging the logic.

'What line are we going to take with the DCI?' she asked.

'I believe Ms Davenport was acquainted with him,' he told her, before going on to explain the victim's inclusion in Sidney's Hall of Fame.

His colleague bit her lip.

'That's a tad delicate,' she said.

'Indeed. Though I believe we can rule out any connection of the carnal variety.'

She blushed at this, amusing him by her startled air such as a fawn might show.

Markham cast his mind back to the period of the Sidneys' estrangement. 'The Valkyrie may have played the field during their separation,' he said sardonically, using their nickname for the DCI's wife, 'but, by all accounts, Sidney just moped about with a face like a wet weekend.'

'I suppose he didn't connect Loretta with Tony Pardoe when you briefed him initially, sir.'

Her voice held a question.

'Presumably not. Though he'll sure as hell have joined the dots by now,' was the grim response. 'He'll be wanting a press conference too, something which steers well clear of any suggestion that there's a crazed Druid-worshipper on the loose.'

'Or a child-killer who's upgraded to adult victims,' she finished with a wry smile. 'Not to mention a sex attacker with a taste for adolescent girls.' The last being precisely the kind of sensationalist headline that was the *Gazette's* stock-in-trade.

'Quite.' Markham well knew that the idea of anything tending to a blot on the Henwood escutcheon would be complete anathema to his superior.

'We can tell the DCI we're checking out Druid activists, focusing on the, er, "lunatic fringe",' she suggested shyly. 'Ask if we can have some uniforms along for the Medway Mere thing — give him the idea that we're sussing out troublemakers and misfits, putting out feelers into the community so we can flush out local fruitcakes.'

He smiled at her. 'That sounds straight out of Noakesy's playbook.'

'Oh, don't worry, sir, I'll steer clear of pejorative language,' she replied gravely. 'But at least that way, the DCI won't worry about us circling too close to the more respectable elements.'

'Sounds like a plan.'

Markham got up and wandered over to his office window. Outside, the leylandii which bordered the station carpark swayed gently in a mild breeze, while further along the high street towards the town centre weeping willows, blackthorn and cherry plum were rich with the promise of spring, justifying Bromgrove's pretensions to be a 'City of Trees'. The overall effect, unfortunately, was to make his office appear staler, stuffier and shabbier than ever.

'What exactly *is* this equinox celebration, Kate?' he asked, turning back to his colleague, aware that he was postponing the evil hour with Sidney but lethargically reluctant to move. 'The only Druid festival I know about is Beltane but that's not till May, right?'

'Yes, that's the fire festival which commemorates how the Druids drove their cattle between two great fires as a symbolic protection against disease,' she told him with the conscientious air of an A level sociology student. 'The Spring Equinox celebrates the time when light begins to prevail against the darkness.'

'As opposed to the progress of our investigation,' he said drily.

Burton looked somewhat discomfited. 'It's all about fertility and new life,' she said earnestly. 'There's a tie-in with the resurrection, of course, the risen Christ rising from the tomb to spread the light.'

'Cue Noakesy's lament that it's turned into the feast of the Easter Bunny.'

He was pleased when she laughed at this, the solemn little face momentarily losing its pinched and anxious expression.

'So, what kind of activities can we expect to encounter?' he enquired.

'Most probably just some chanting . . . hailing the sunset . . . tree blessing . . . libations to the deities,' she said vaguely, 'that kind of thing.'

'Libations and chanting, eh?' he replied. 'All sounds very pacific. Just so long as no one decides to up the ante with a spot of arson or blood-letting.'

'Some sections of the community have been, well, *antagonistic* to local pagan groups in the past, sir,' she said apprehensively. 'It's a fair bet that tongues are wagging now, with three victims being linked to the park . . . though thankfully no leaks as yet about how they posed.'

'Talking of leaks, any further thoughts about Carruthers?'

'I haven't really had a chance to check in with him yet, guv, but there's no signs that he's passing stuff to the *Gazette*.'

'Let's hope it stays that way.'

Better get the DCI over with, he thought wearily. There was no point airing any theories about a killer in the grip of atavistic impulses connected with Druid culture. Sidney was sure to pour cold water over any such speculation in that awful crabbed way of his. Far better to stick with Kate's gameplan and divert his superior's attention to Bromgrove's "lunatic fringe".

'C'mon,' he told his colleague. 'Once more unto the breach.'

Her answering smile reassured him that she had his back. Which was just as well, with the likes of Bretherton and Ebury-Clarke ready to knife him as soon as the opportunity arose. He simply could not imagine CID without her . . .

Get a grip, Markham, he told himself firmly. There were now three victims demanding justice, and it was his job to see that they got it. His personal troubles would just have to wait.

\* \* \*

Early evening on Friday 22 March found Markham and Olivia at The Sweepstakes enjoying a "Chippy Tea", Olivia having declared that she required fuel before accompanying him on the expedition to Medway Mere.

'I guess we really ought to do something about our appalling takeaway habit, Gil,' she said idly, attacking her battered cod and mushy peas with gusto. 'There are times when I feel it's getting out of control. I get these massive guilt pangs every time I read something by Michael Mosley or Hugh Fearnley-Whittingstall about how we should ideally be eating eighty different types of plants a day to attain peak condition . . . as opposed to endless grease-fests.'

He grinned, enjoying her hyperbole.

'Junk food is an essential antidote to the strain of our high-pressured jobs,' he intoned.

'That's what I tell myself,' she laughed. 'And besides, whenever I pick up one of Ruth Rendell's detective stories, it seems that DCI Wexford and Mike Burden are forever feeding their faces in some pub or Indian restaurant, or sending out for curries and pizza, all in the line of duty, of course.'

'*Hmm*. I remember Wexford ends up being put on a strict diet to counteract the artery-furring effects of too many fry-ups . . . kicks up even more of a fuss about "rabbit food" than our Noakesy.'

She shot him a fond glance. 'You're a long way from furred arteries. And besides, Wexford's a demon for red wine and claret, whereas you're downright abstemious . . . except when it comes to Chateauneuf-du-Pape.'

'Oh, that may well change if I can't get Sidney to back off,' he gloomed.

'How is Judas Iscariot?' she asked with a wicked gleam.

'Let's just say he's deeply unsympathetic to the idea of supernatural shenanigans connected with the park. I try not to let anything about "dark magic" cross my lips.'

She frowned. 'Surely he can't ignore the fact there's something strange going on, seeing the way two of the bodies were left; the stones and the woods and all that.'

'Yes, but you know Sidney . . . he prefers the idea of its being down to some mad drug addict or local crazy to any notion that there could be a connection with the Henwoods or the park's management — or prominent businesspeople come to that,' he added, thinking of Jason Quirk.

'Is there any chance you could be looking at two separate murders? I mean, if Tony Pardoe and Loretta had quite busy personal lives — romantic complications and things — they could easily have triggered one of their exes.' Ruefully, she gestured towards a pile of books jumbled pell-mell in the battered rucksack she took to work. 'One of Hardy's characters — I can't remember which one — says: "Sometimes more bitterness is sown in five minutes than can be got rid of in a whole life." So, what if they each had some encounter or confrontation with someone they were involved with and then things flared up, spun out of control?'

'That could be true of Loretta. Less so with Tony Pardoe because, despite the dashing public profile, it doesn't look as if he had all that much time for women in terms of making an emotional investment. Of course, there was the on-off thing with Maureen Slattery, but it seems like that was pretty low-voltage on both sides.'

'What about men?'

Markham recalled Noakes's comments about the chances of Pardoe 'batting for the other side'.

'It's a possibility,' he said slowly. 'I still feel in my gut that the same person murdered both of them.' Of course, he had known better than to talk of his 'gut feeling' when closeted with Sidney. 'It's something about the park, Liv, that eerie setting . . .'

She sensed his discouragement.

'What about alibis for Loretta?' she enquired, changing tack. 'Have you been able to rule anyone out?'

He almost groaned. 'Malcolm Devenish, Tom Burke and Suzanne Mackie were wandering in and out of *The Reader Shop*; John Sinnott and other volunteers drifted about—'

'John Sinnott . . . the bloke people thought might've killed that little girl?'

'That's looking unlikely now, Liv — a witness placed him at the other side of the park at roughly the same time she was murdered.'

'Very fortunate for him,' Olivia rejoined in a deeply sceptical tone. 'What sort of witness?' she pressed him, intrigued. 'Any chance they could have been in cahoots with Sinnott?'

'She was a work experience student, only on nodding terms with Sinnott, just knew him to say hello to. Went abroad to do postgrad research afterwards, so that was pretty much that. CID didn't have any other witnesses.'

'Okay,' she said thoughtfully, forking up chips with undiminished enthusiasm. 'How about the rest of your suspects — what were *they* up to when Loretta was killed?'

'Apparently Jason Quirk and Marion Kirkwood — that's Pardoe's business competitor and the disgruntled PA — were having a late working lunch back at his place in Cinder Lane.'

'*Eeugh*, enough already . . . in other words, they fancied an afternoon quickie.'

'You've spent *way* too much time around Noakesy,' he said resignedly. 'Anyway, we can't disprove it, and the office manager confirms they weren't back till around seven that evening.' He raked a hand distractedly through the thick black hair that (a perennial grievance of Sidney's) curled over his collar. 'As for the mansion house café manager, she had her head down doing a stocktake, seeing as the park was closed to visitors and it was a chance for her to catch up.'

'Who else does that leave, Gil?'

'Bernadette Donovan, Miss Henwood's cousin . . . she was visiting an elderly neighbour. Then there's Maureen Slattery—'

'Oh yes, the teacher . . . I remember meeting her at some interschool shindig. She seemed relatively normal.' Unlike the rest of them, her tone implied.

'They do Enrichment on Wednesday afternoons — sport and extracurricular stuff — so she was back home early by around half three.'

'Collapsed in a heap, no doubt,' Olivia said with feeling. 'Especially if she had to run one of those goddamn after-school clubs.'

'She got off lightly by the sound of it . . . a creative writing workshop or something like that. Apparently, she escaped as soon as she could and poured herself a goldfish bowl sized gin and tonic before hunkering down with some box set or other.'

Olivia looked wistful. 'I wouldn't mind that.'

He raised an eyebrow. 'You astonish me, sweetheart,' he said with heavy irony. 'When exciting Druidical goings-on at Medway Mere await us.'

She made a noise that sounded very much like *Humph*.

'You're not expecting trouble are you, Gil?'

'I shouldn't think so. I believe it's mainly about hon-ouring the Earth Goddess and enacting various obscure rit-uals.' He couldn't imagine any sort of open warfare given the nature of the event, though he suspected Noakes was hoping for some argy-bargy between the pagan and anti-pagan cliques by way of enlivening proceedings.

'Well, hopefully we can wangle some time to ourselves tomorrow before we have to schlep over to Noakesy's for whatever Muriel's got planned.' She looked distinctly glum at the prospect. 'Roll on the tablescaping!'

'I'm going to Doggie Dickerson's in the morning with Noakesy.' His partner rolled her eyes at this mention of the dingy boxing gym in Marsh Lane. 'But the afternoon's free—'

'I suppose there's no way we can get out of Muriel's shindig.'

'C'mon, Liv, you're always the one who says, "anything for George".'

'Yeah, but this is above and beyond . . . gives a whole new meaning to the phrase "Easter Duty".'

He chuckled at that. 'Finish your chips and stop grumbling. Who knows what you'll learn tonight.' Despite the grousing, he knew she was curious about Druidical goings-on at the Mere.

'Enough to stun Muriel tomorrow with my dazzling inside knowledge of esoteric pagan cults,' she said sarcastically.

'Exactly!' he answered, though privately he didn't count on Muriel's dinner party producing much in the way of entertainment.

Tentatively, she asked, 'Any news about that poor kid who turned up dead? The *Gazette* made no bones about saying there might be a serial killer on the loose.

'Sidney wasn't at all happy about that,' he answered. 'The official line is that we're keeping an open mind, but it seems to me Cathy Price had the singular misfortune to encounter Tony Pardoe's killer.'

'Could she have been blackmailing them?'

He shrugged. 'It's one possibility, though by all accounts she wasn't the type to connive with a murderer.'

A grim silence ensued as they contemplated this scenario.

'Right,' she said eventually with an attempt at heartiness, 'better get togged up for tonight's fun and games.' Despite herself, Olivia could not help a tingle of anticipation. After all, it wasn't every day she got to observe pagan rituals.

* * *

In the event, Noakes considered the whole thing pretty much a damp squib.

'I've had more fun at a bus stop,' he muttered tetchily as the team plus Olivia huddled together on a woodland slope opposite a broad stretch of water that gleamed mysteriously in the failing light, reflecting the massed bluebells that carpeted its banks. Forming an effective boundary to the fifteen-acre Medway Allotments, it fell under the auspices of the council's Community Support Scheme, regularly hosting outdoor festivals of one kind or another.

'It's a picturesque setting,' Olivia commented, looking round appreciatively at the luminously opalescent landscape and the reservoir which put her in mind of some grey-green sea creature.

'We should've worn wellies,' Carruthers said ruefully, contemplating the muddy ground squelching round his immaculate brogues. Doyle likewise didn't look enthused as he batted away a low-hanging branch, almost losing his balance as the group waited in a thicket of overgrown foliage, doing their best to look inconspicuous.

Burton alone had come prepared, wearing an outsize donkey jacket and Paddington boots. Watching the DI almost jump out of her skin as a huge wood pigeon shot suddenly from a pile of bracken, Olivia suppressed a grin. Kate looked decidedly cold and forlorn, her nose turning pink in the misty evening drizzle.

'You need to watch yourself round here,' Burton told them. 'There are concealed dips all over the place, so it's quite treacherous.'

Possibly the last-minute transfer of the event to the Mere, together with the downturn in weather, was responsible for the low turnout, though Markham spotted the park's volunteers and personnel standing together next to a food van which was doing a brisk trade in hot dogs and paninis. Noakes's mouth turned down at the corners as he observed three uniforms joining the queue for food.

'Bleeding gannets,' he said disparagingly, only for Doyle to retort, *'Dear kettle, love pot.'*

*Heard it all before, duck's back stuff,* the older man's hunched posture and mulish expression replied without the need for words.

'Look at old Devenish and Burke,' Carruthers murmured. 'I mean, *what do they look like* in those weird tabards.'

Noakes squinted bad-temperedly at the ceremonial as though disappointed the participants weren't wearing antlers or some other fantastical headdress. As far as rituals went, it all appeared fairly lowkey, with someone leading a singsong chant and others lighting torches from a brazier. The contingent from the park seemed impressed if a little subdued, which was hardly surprising now they knew there had been a third murder on their patch.

'Hey, isn't that Bernadette Donovan?' said Doyle. 'Wouldn't have thought this was her kind of thing.'

'Pardoe's fancy woman's here too,' Carruthers noted, spying Maureen Slattery on the fringes of the crowd.

'She's with some teachers from her school,' Olivia pointed out. 'No law against it,' she added defensively, experiencing an odd spasm of professional solidarity.

'Brophy's here too,' Doyle said idly as he clocked the journalist. 'Good luck with this load of cobblers, fella,' he grinned, amused to wonder how the *Gazette's* finest would spin such a boring event.

Burton was watching the proceedings closely. 'Seems to be boys only,' she commented disapprovingly. Then, *'Oh no!'*

'What is it, Kate?' Markham said quickly.

'That's Mary Priddy's mother,' she replied out of the corner of her mouth. 'The grey-haired woman in the anorak over there . . . next to those boys from the Hoxton Estate.'

Suddenly they were all alert, aware that the Hoxton generally spelled trouble.

The next minute, a bottle suddenly whizzed through the air, landing next to a startled Tom Burke.

'*Fucking paedos!*' someone yelled. '*Effing devil worshippers!*' came from another.

'*You fucking child-killer, Sinnott! Rot in Hell!*'

Markham's face set in a granite hard expression as another bottle whistled past their ears.

'Get Liv out of here,' he instructed Noakes. Then to his colleagues, 'Break this up. *Now.*'

The Druids' circle had scattered and people were blundering blindly through the darkening trees. Overhead, squawking heralded a line of geese moving across the skyline, like symbols from some ancient augury, Markham thought uneasily as their hoarse cry rose further and further before fading into the distance.

His team and the uniforms brought things under control pretty quickly, watched avidly by Michael Brophy and gawping bystanders.

Along with Loretta Davenport's murder, this melee and the Priddy connection should keep the *Gazette* busy for days, he thought savagely.

It was a complication he could well do without.

On his return to the station, he received a call from Hollingrove Park's estate manager. Bill Whelan seemed casual and untroubled but 'felt you ought to know in case this might be significant,' before scanning over a picture of some doodle that had apparently turned up in one of the display cabinets at the museum. Markham didn't really see how it could be, but the sinister graffiti nonetheless gave him an unpleasant jolt in the pit of his stomach.

'Probably left by some joker when staff weren't looking,' Whelan said airily. 'Most likely a schoolkid.'

The DI somehow wasn't convinced, feeling that there was something ominous about the cross-hatched skulls with gaping eye and nose sockets — not something that your average visitor, far less a *child*, would secrete surreptitiously like that. But Whelan and Malcolm Devenish apparently saw nothing to worry about. The curator thought it might have been misplaced from elsewhere in the mansion house, perhaps from Miss Henwood's private collection so the little mystery would have to be shelved for the time being.

Nonetheless, Markham carried that image of sightless malignity all the way home, his scalp scrawling at the memory. Somehow it didn't bode well.

## CHAPTER 7: CONFLAGRATION

Olivia was resigned to Markham visiting Doggie Dickerson ('that awful old villain') on Saturday morning. He collected Noakes and headed for Bromgrove Police Boxing Gym in Marsh Lane.

Doggie, a 'legend in his own lunch hour' as Noakes put it, was absolute anathema to DCI Sidney and most of CID's top brass, on account both of his disreputable appearance and unsavoury reputation. He was a firm favourite, however, with both Markham and Noakes, the latter liking nothing better than to swap anecdotes about HM Armed Forces. The DI was long since inured to hearing salacious stories about various officers — invariably given an obscene adjectival pre-fix — and fierce debate about the merits of different NCOs, his friends reserving their especial scorn for 'blokes who got commissioned to supervise other blokes counting tins of spam' (aka the Army Catering Corps).

Olivia rolled her eyes when Markham tried to explain the mix of patriotism and comradeship that cemented such ties. 'Hired killers, that's really what soldiers are, Gil . . . ruthless hired killers.' Yet she never objected to Noakes's tales about ''orrible' drill adjutants and square-bashing and psychopathic 'sarn't majors', privately relishing his parade-ground gags and touched by his intense fealty to something bigger than himself.

Whereas Noakes had little time for Keats and Shelley, he took quite a shine to Rudyard Kipling (it helped that this poet's eighteen-year-old son got himself killed at Loos) and startled Doggie on one memorable occasion by reciting, 'For it's Tommy this, an' Tommy that, an' "Chuck him out, the brute!" But it's "Saviour of 'is country" when the guns begin to shoot.' It took a while for the gym's proprietor to recover from this outburst of poetic eloquence, but he soon rallied, coming up with bawdy limericks and scurrilous doggerel that would have turned Kate Burton's stomach to hear. In terms of "bragging rights", the score was about even.

'How d'you reckon Doyle and Carruthers would have got on in the army, George?' Olivia asked Noakes one day.

'A selection board would've had fun with them two,' the other replied, baring his teeth in what he fondly thought was a smile, 'especially Carruthers.' The grin became a grimace. 'I c'n jus' imagine the Wosbee trick cyclists deciding the lad were a fairy an' wanting to know how he got on with his mother.'

On Olivia raising her eyebrows, he guffawed, 'You c'n bet they'd get a bloody weird answer.'

In the circumstances, it was perhaps just as well the two young sergeants steered well clear of the gym, despite the fact that its raw, grimy authenticity suited a surprising number of station personnel, with detectives and local 'scumbags' slugging it out together in the ring before cheerfully reverting to their accustomed roles once back out on the streets.

Doggie's premises were undeniably on the dilapidated side (it was always touch and go whether the 'Premium' and 'Standard' locker rooms would make it through health and safety inspections), which led to DI Chris Carstairs, another regular, declaring that his credentials were on a par with those of Basil Fawlty. Markham and Noakes, however, were loyal to the gym and its proprietor, finding a characterful ambience that was notably missing from Bromgrove's blander health outlets.

Doggie himself ('You're better off not knowing, Liv', Markham said when his partner enquired curiously how the gym's owner had come by the moniker) had gone through various incarnations in the time that Markham and Noakes had known him. He'd started out looking like an extra in some Napoleonic Wars TV drama, the military frockcoat, horsehair wig and eye patch contributing to a decidedly sinister aura. There then followed his new age phase when, under the influence of one Marlene (of bingo hall fame), he became obsessed with astrology and adopted strange wizard-like attire as though auditioning for a part in *Harry Potter* or *Lord of the Rings*. With the arrival of sensible Evelyn to whom he was now affianced, he got his yellowing snaggle teeth fixed and replaced the eye patch with a glass prosthesis (quite the accessory for those wanting to channel their inner Vinnie Jones).

Neither the fiancée nor her trendy daughter Clare had managed to do anything about Doggie's nicotine habit and the aroma of Johnnie Walker which enveloped him, but at least these days he was more likely to be found in some kind of leisurewear which almost passed muster as a tracksuit, provided one didn't look too closely and ignored the down-at-heel slippers or flip flops he preferred to trainers. The straggling grey hair had been superseded by a dodgy mohawk, now mercifully replaced by something that was *almost* conventional — not exactly a short back and sides but what Doggie fondly imagined was the perfect Peaky Blinders haircut with Teddy Boy overtones.

'I got tired of Hells Angels coming up to me an' saying, "Come an' have a go if you think you're hard enough,"' was his laconic reply to enquiries about the defunct coiffure, though it seemed to Markham that the current northern gangster look was hardly likely to deter local bovver boys.

For all Doggie's sleaziness and local notoriety, he had his own code of honour that ensured he never let slip anything he learned from Markham and Noakes (a trait he had in common with Muriel Noakes, though she would doubtless have been outraged by the comparison). While Markham had the honour of being his 'fav'rite 'spector' — not least for the DI's qualities as a respectful listener — Noakes and Doggie were practically blood brothers by virtue of their former soldiering and, more importantly, a resolutely un-PC world view which came down heavily on anything remotely "woke" and contributed to a fierce patriotism that would have struck the likes of Kate Burton as xenophobic in the extreme.

Doggie was intrigued to hear about doings at the park and listened to Noakes's account of the lurid exhibits in Hollingrove's mansion house museum with a fascination that initially made Markham fear this might herald a relapse into the kaftan and zodiac phase. It seemed, however, that their friend was more ambivalent these days.

'People thought the Nazis would be big on paganism on account of they were right-wing nutcases,' Doggie said solemnly. 'But it was really only Himmler ever got into it.'

Markham's lips twitched at this while aloud he merely enquired, 'And weren't they . . . I mean, keen on it?'

'Not a bit of it,' came the reply. 'They were afraid of folk doing stuff in secret in case it led to 'em talking about politics . . . y'know, getting in a huddle an' having a good old bitch about Nazism being bad news. An' everyone knew Himmler wasn't right in the head . . . had a thing for Norse gods an' all that.'

'I never knew that,' Noakes said, impressed by Doggie's general knowledge. Not to be outdone, he said nonchalantly, 'The bloke who founded Wicca over here — the white witch lot — well, *he* started a coven in some naturist resort, how about that! Bit of a perv, jus' like that William Blake,' he added shooting a glance at Markham to show he hadn't forgotten the degeneracy of the Romantic Age, his perennial gripe whenever Olivia subjected him to poetry recitals.

Despite his willingness to embrace "high culture" for Olivia's sake, the more Noakes learned about the private lives of the nation's most celebrated poets, the less inclined Markham was to overlook such proclivities as opium use and — in Blake's case — nudism.

Suppressing the urge to tell Noakes he sounded like a prissy old woman, Markham moved them on to the subject of Miss Henwood's illustrious forebear Richard II. It was obvious that Doggie wasn't as enthused by this subject as by ancient holy men reciting spells and spitting curses, but he attended politely to Markham's account of the troubled medieval monarch.

'No wonder the king ended up feeling really small an' worthless with all them nobles bossing him around an' making him think everyone had it in for him.'

'*Infamy, infamy, they've all got it in for me,*' chortled Noakes, a great fan of the *Carry On* films, if not necessarily Kenneth Williams.

'You will have your little joke, Mr Noakes,' Doggie laughed politely. Then, 'Awkward for Miss Henwood if Richard was a bit, well, AC/DC,' he surmised.

'It sounds like she took it all in her stride, Dogs,' Markham said. 'The stardust of royalty most likely helped her overlook the, er, more *controversial* aspects,' he added wryly.

'You c'n understand folk going a bit doolally and dabbling in weird stuff — kind of detached from reality — if they're going through a bad patch an' don't know whether they're Martha or Arthur.' Doggie shook his head sagely as though summoning up some enigmatic hinterland of experience. '*I know all about tough times, see . . . been there, done that, got the t-shirt.*'

Markham wondered if these mysterious travails included sexual fluidity, recalling the other's Gandalf era and trying hard to dispel images of kabbalistic gender bending.

To his amusement, Noakes jumped away from the subject like a scalded cat. 'Ricky II jus' liked bigging hisself up,' he pronounced with pursed lips. 'Case of small man syndrome.'

'Only he was a six-footer, remember,' Markham pointed out with faint malice.

'He might've been tall an' strong to look at, but *inside* it were different,' Noakes insisted.

Hearing this, Markham recalled some words Olivia had recently quoted at him.

'Behind the big mask and the speaking-trumpet, there must always be our poor little eyes peeping as usual and our timorous lips more or less under anxious control.'

'I think both of you are right about Richard turning to the occult as a kind of crutch,' he said slowly. Even as he uttered the words, he felt as though they possessed some deeper meaning than he was somehow unable to lay hold of . . .

He became aware that Doggie had returned to the ancients and was waxing philosophical.

'Folk nowadays get dead worked up about their troubles, but if you think of Stonehenge an' all them places standing there for centuries an' centuries, it makes you realise the bad times are piddling really cos nothing lasts for long. Yeah,' with a comic lapse into the vernacular, 'someone should've told King Richard not to get his knickers in a twist.'

Moving on from historical conjecture, the trio chatted inconsequentially before Doggie prepared to tear himself away.

'Well, I'd better let you get on, gents.'

'Who've you got in today, Dogs?' Markham asked.

The proprietor brightened. 'A few of the usuals have dropped by. As it happens Boppo's in the ring warming up . . . ever so keen to have a crack at someone, Mr Markham.'

Boppo being the moniker accorded to the leader of Bromgrove's most infamous cosh gang, Markham knew he could count on a vigorous workout.

He grinned. 'You tell him to have a go if he thinks he's hard enough.'

As Doggie lurched away on his errand (no doubt via a detour to his office and the bottle of whisky stashed in the top drawer of his rickety filing cabinet), the DI began to get changed. He guessed Noakes was praying that he would pulverise Boppo (who had dubbed his friend 'lardy arse') and thus deliver a salutary lesson as to Bromgrove CID's superiority in the ring. Revenge might be a dish best served cold,

Markham thought with a wry smile, but as far as Noakes was concerned, this particular reckoning was well overdue.

\* \* \*

On their return to the station, Kate Burton met them looking apologetic.

'What's up, Kate?' the DI asked.

'Some kind of rumpus outside John Sinnott's house on Bromgrove Rise, sir.'

He shot her a look of anxious enquiry. '*Oh?*'

'Uniforms got over there quickly and defused things before it got ugly, sir,' she told him. 'Seemed like it was just a few protestors looking to make trouble.'

Markham could feel a vein pulsing in his forehead. *This was all he bloody needed.*

'What put them on to Sinnott?' Noakes demanded.

'We're not sure at this stage—'

'But Sidney's doing his nut, right?'

'That's about the size of it,' she replied.

'We'd better get ourselves up there,' Markham said woodenly. 'Might be better if Kate and I tackle this one, Noakesy.'

If Sidney was 'doing his nut', his wingman's presence would only add fuel to the fire.

The DCI was indeed incandescent, demanding to know what had put Bromgrove's newshounds on to Sinnott.

Burton, as Markham observed afterwards admiringly, 'lied like a rug'.

'We're *totally* on it, sir,' she assured Sidney with unblinking sincerity. 'Local muckraking and neighbourhood gossip.'

Sidney's mouth was hard and narrow. 'Just so long as you have this *situation* under control, Inspector,' he glowered at Markham. 'Not distracted by any Iron Age *projects* and such like?'

The DCI somehow made him sound like a low-rent version of Alice Roberts or one of those other TV anthropologists who seemed to be all the rage these days.

Markham's tic was getting worse, but he fastened a rictus smile onto his face. 'I'll be getting to the bottom of it first thing Monday morning, sir.' It had better not involve Carruthers, he thought grimly.

There was a press conference scheduled for Monday afternoon, Sidney reminded him with a basilisk glare.

Markham recalled Noakes's withering denunciation of the DCI's oratorical abilities. 'Applauded in an' then clapped out,' was how his friend characterised Sidney's performance on such occasions.

'You can be assured we'll have every angle covered, sir,' Markham assured his boss with bland insincerity.

*Good luck with that*, Burton's expression seemed to say.

'You get off now, Kate,' he told her after they had been ushered out of The Presence. 'Whatever Monday brings, we'll cope somehow.'

He had the feeling his colleague wouldn't have minded hanging round, but ushered her out of CID with unusual decision. Whatever the state of play with Nathan Finlayson, she needed time off to take a breath.

*Next week could wait.*

\* \* \*

Saturday evening saw Markham and Olivia at what she wickedly described as the 'punishment posting' chez Noakes. There being no chance that Muriel would fall down a manhole and have to cancel, she indulged herself in a whinge beforehand.

'I can't *stand* the way she looks at me, Gil . . . casts me as the screaming neurotic who somehow snared you through unspeakable sexual wiles,' she complained.

'"Anything for George,"' he reminded her calmly, hoping that she would grit her teeth and get through the evening somehow.

Muriel's Easter "tablescape" almost undid Markham's own attempt to simulate respectful gravity. There was so much Maidenhair and other assorted ferns that it appeared more Jurassic Park than tasteful spring décor. Their hostess was wearing a dreadful sprigged milkmaid number which presumably aimed to create an effect of demure simplicity but in conjunction with the hard lacquered bouffant, and heavy pantomime makeup, made her look like Jane Austen on a bad day. *Nightmare at Pemberley*, he thought, trying desperately not to catch Olivia's eye. Judging by the expression on his partner's face, it was clear this was her idea of a waking nightmare.

Markham was pleased to note, however, that she was touched by Noakes's pride in his wife's 'flair' and managed to endure with equanimity a long monologue about how Muriel had drawn inspiration from reading about the 'dear late Queen's little tricks for making people feel at home'. The Windsors' genius for hospitality didn't do much for poor Princess Diana, she muttered sotto voce as Muriel chuntered on.

Luckily their hostess appeared oblivious to any mutiny in the ranks.

'It's all about *making an effort*, isn't it,' the other gushed, laying a crimson talon proprietorially on Markham's arm. '*Not letting one's standards slip.*' There was a certain something in her eyes as she contemplated Olivia's unbound red hair, floaty skirt and loose shirt which suggested she considered there was room for improvement in that department.

Mischievously, despite being aware she was under the scrutiny of the beadiest eyes in the western hemisphere, Olivia contributed an anecdote of her own — a story about Lady Soames who, when obliged to host various assorted royals with a predilection for bed-hopping, memorably declared, 'Pray let the claret be good.'

It was obvious from Muriel's stony reaction that she didn't care for such risqué titbits, but Markham was swift to distract her with amusing patter about the Duchess of Edinburgh (gleaned from Sidney whose crush on this particular royal had its uses).

Nailing a bright, strained smile on her face, Olivia made inroads into the red wine that accompanied their boeuf bourguignon (at least Muriel never did "tweezer food"), with due appreciation for its anaesthetising properties. Markham was relieved to hear that Natalie would be joining them after the meal, well aware that the spectacle of mother and daughter fawning over him was something that invariably set her teeth on edge.

To his amusement, he learned that Natalie had decided on an outdoor Celtic-style handfasting ceremony for her nuptials.

'Of course, they could have opted for something more lavish,' Muriel confided.

*Of course.*

'But in the end they settled on something simple and meaningful; so refreshingly *unpretentious* and *natural* when for most young couples it's all about showing off and making a splash.'

She was putting a brave face on it, thought Markham, but no doubt Muriel would have loved to wipe the eye of Natalie's prospective mother-in-law (a hard-faced, brassy woman who hadn't exactly welcomed Natalie into the bosom of the family) with the most ostentatious display that could be devised — even at the risk of bankrupting poor Noakes.

He endeavoured to be utterly charming about it all, listening patiently to lots of rubbish about a crown of flowers (yuk) and boho-chic garlands (double yuk).

'It sounds delightful,' he said easily. 'A rented dress . . . barbecue in the garden . . . all very unshowy and relaxed.'

Muriel looked pleased at this, quite forgetting to frown at Noakes's joke about how he was afraid a 'posh do' meant having to pawn their furniture so they could afford it.

Again, Olivia couldn't resist putting a spoke in the wheel.

'Kenneth Grahame, who wrote *Wind in the Willows*, was quite browned off when his wife refused to wear a ring or traditional dress,' she said innocently. 'Went all back to nature on him; rolled around in the dew and stuck a coronet of flowers on her head to establish her pagan credentials, then turned up at the church in this wrinkled, sodden rag of an outfit with a face like a thundercloud. You can see why that marriage never really stood a chance.'

As two red spots appeared on their hostess's cheeks, Markham shot his partner a warning glance. 'Of course, Natalie's wedding will be an altogether more *civilised* affair,' he said smoothly. 'There's really something quite engagingly modern about such informality, very confident and *individualistic*.'

Muriel's tinkling laughter in response signalled that a dangerous moment had been safely navigated. Thanks to Markham's skill in drawing her out, she was in high good humour by the time it came to pudding (Bakewell tart á la Mary Berry).

The talk turned to gardening, and Olivia dutifully admired Muriel's spring begonias and petunias.

'My favourite time of year,' the other sighed sentimentally, with a languishing glance at Markham.

'I prefer autumn,' Olivia countered. '*Season of mists and mellow fruitfulness.*'

'Oh God, not that Keats again,' Noakes, who was pretty mellow himself by this stage, groaned. 'I can't stand all his mystical gibberish about that female nutter.'

On Olivia looking somewhat mystified, he enlightened her, 'You know, "Bird say if thou art cuckoo" or summat.'

She grinned. 'I think you mean Wordsworth,' she told him.

'Same difference,' he muttered, having a decidedly low opinion of the man who fell in love with the lakes.

'You have to remember this was the "Age of the Romantics",' she pointed out.

'Yeah, usually about twenty-five,' he retorted. 'After that they all grew out of it, 'cept for Keats an' Shelley. I mean, all that twaddle about flowers . . . *Go, lovely Rose* . . . *Get lost, Lily* . . . An' that Keats got kicked out of medical school, prob'ly high on bleeding belladonna or morphine an' all that stuff he took.' With a renewed sense of grievance, he added, 'I'll never forget that pigging awful recital you dragged us to down at Hopeless.'

'*An Evening with Yeats*,' Olivia laughed. 'I seem to remember it wasn't really your cup of tea.'

'Too right. All that godawful stuff about linnets an' glades an' the countryside, an' old Doc Abernathy droning on 'bout his rhythm and iambic whatsits. Mind you, I'll say one thing for Yeats, he ain't half so bad as Kelly an' Sheets.'

'Don't forget Robert Browning,' she said, starting to enjoy herself.

'Oh aye, the gravy fella. Think I prefer *sensible* types — the ones who write poems for cup finals an' coronations an' the King's birthday, instead of whittering on about flowers an' nature an' all that malarkey.'

'Wordsworth *was* pretty practical,' Olivia insisted. 'Even let his sister Dorothy darn his socks, which is probably how she became immortal as the "Lady of the Lakes".'

As it appeared that Noakes was likewise enjoying their repartee (and glad of a break from the begonias), she added, 'Speaking of flowers, one of our NQTs had this problem with a kid who had the most horrendous B.O., so she wrote a note for his mum asking if he was sufficiently careful about "personal freshness". Mum wrote back a note which said that Mikey was a normal healthy lad and not "a bleeding geranium".'

Noakes roared at this.

'The coup de grace was her pointing out that he came to school "to be learnt not *smelt.*"'

'Talking of B.O.,' Noakes said once his mirth had subsided, 'I've always wondered about that washing the feet thing they do in church coming up to Easter—'

'In memory of the Last Supper when Jesus washed the apostles' feet,' Muriel cut in repressively.

'Yeah, thass right . . . Well, jus' imagine if one of 'em had stinky feet!'

Olivia burst out laughing. 'Jesus probably had more to worry about than sweaty feet, George.'

Muriel's expression, which had darkened during the anecdote about B.O., positively froze at this sacrilegious dialogue (not at all suitable for her dining table).

Noticing his hostess's dark looks (clearly a cordon bleu sanitaire was about to descend) and suspecting that Noakes was poised to embark on a tale referencing how he was a martyr to his feet or something about athlete's foot and odour-eaters, Markham swiftly turned the conversation.

They were on to the coffee and petit fours (the usual Richard Clayderman and Perry Como had been superseded by Max Bygraves, which wasn't much of an improvement) when Natalie joined them. Usually prickly and antagonistic around Olivia, in contrast to the full-beam adoration she bestowed upon Markham, the daughter of the house was disposed to be smug, seeing as she was finally getting Rick Jordan down the aisle — or the flowerbeds, he thought, observing with amusement how Olivia smiled gamely at the talk of al fresco marquee and buffet till it looked as though her face must crack with the effort.

Eventually, however, their conversation moved to Hollingrove Park. Natalie seeming genuinely interested in the Druidic overtones, pronouncing them (with a simper in Markham's direction) all 'very romantic'. She wouldn't be quite so keen if she had any idea how the latest victim was left, Olivia thought nastily, mindful however of Markham's injunction to let nothing slip about the obscene manner in which Loretta Davenport had been displayed. As for the investigation, Natalie opined maybe their killer was the sort of weedy inadequate who got off on thinking they had magic powers.

'Related to King Arthur or Merlin perhaps,' Olivia suggested sweetly, but Natalie failed to register the sarcasm.

'Yeah, someone who can't cope with real life or change, so it's kind of like *escapism*,' Natalie declared with a confidence which suggested that, as the proud possessor of a BA in History, she felt herself to be quite the intellectual equal of Ms Smarty-Pants Mullen.

During the post-prandial chit-chat conducted largely by Muriel and Markham, along with the occasional contribution by Noakes and Natalie, Olivia found her thoughts drifting . . .

Markham's gentleness towards their arch, maddeningly pretentious hostess was a characteristic which attracted and annoyed her in equal measure — all part of the compassion for "the halt and the lame" that underpinned his professional life. It was just a pity she hadn't experienced the same tenderness when *she* was coming apart at the seams.

But that was the problem with Gil. It seemed to her the troubled childhood (complete with alcoholic father and abusive stepfather, not to mention his lost sibling) and that disastrous relationship with his mother had somehow hollowed him out and left him with little emotional capital to expend on anyone else. As she saw it, his past had somehow resulted in a stunting of the inner man along with a weirdly idealised vision of womanhood. God help Little Miss Muffet (as she contemptuously designated Kate Burton) if she decided to take him on.

Watching as he listened attentively to Muriel wittering on about her latest charitable project, she reflected that Gil's generalised compassion for suffering humanity was another impediment to real intimacy. She could not help feeling it acted as a protective shield, keeping others at bay, and enabling him to focus with ruthless detachment on his job. The truth was, he didn't really want *anyone* getting too close — except perhaps George Noakes. It was a state of affairs that made her feel excluded . . . *redundant*.

Listening with one ear as her partner effortlessly charmed Muriel and Natalie, Olivia tried to pin down what exactly it was that gave her the feeling he found her somehow *wanting*. She suspected it had something to do with the way he struggled to integrate the two sides of himself, on the one hand wanting straightforward "normality" and a settled domestic existence while on the other possessing an airy idealism that was impatient with mundane constraints and couldn't settle down to ordinary existence.

It appeared that he was somehow in quest of an ideal female, imagining that he could somehow give his whole life for her but in fact never really *seeing* her. Obviously, Kate Burton thought the sun shone out of her boss, but Olivia wondered almost dispassionately how she would handle his obsession with placing women on pedestals.

Perhaps, she thought sadly, herself and Gil were chasing what they couldn't have of each other, locked in a pattern with no sign of resolution. The physical chemistry between them was as strong as ever but somehow their souls kept missing each other, and without that essential connection the relationship felt doomed. Of course, her fling with Mat Sullivan hadn't helped matters, she brooded, wondering if her partner had ever really forgiven her for what happened between herself and Hope's Deputy Head when she and Markham were on a break from each other . . .

Olivia suddenly became aware that their hostess was regarding her with a jaundiced eye (*not making the effort*, Muriel's expression said) and roused herself to take an interest in Natalie's woo-woo new age chatter.

'I think I actually preferred Natalie in her nightclub phase,' she said afterwards as they walked home.

'Don't be such a snob,' he reproved her. 'It was quite sweet the way she wanted to know all about the museum and medieval stuff.'

His partner gave a reluctant chuckle. 'It was priceless when George came out with that gem about having discovered that Edward the Confessor's the patron saint of people who choose to walk alone. You should've seen the dirty looks Dracula's Child was giving me — like she couldn't *wait* for you to rejoin the ranks of desirable singletons.'

'*Enough, Liv.*' Despite the reproof, his tone was indulgent. 'It was odd, but I had the feeling that something she said back there was important, maybe even the key to cracking this investigation . . .'

'*Wow.*' Olivia was surprised and, if truth be told, secretly a little nettled. She wasn't at all sure she liked the idea of Natalie Noakes being Boswell to his Johnson. Endeavouring to be charitable, she went on, 'George was delighted when you said she'd be an asset to the volunteers at *The Reader Shop.*'

'My motives were mixed, Liv,' he admitted ruefully. 'Somehow, I can't get a handle on our suspects, so another pair of eyes and ears would be welcome. It could be dangerous, though, so perhaps it's just as well that she's busy with the wedding.'

His partner gave a little shiver and he drew her protectively closer.

'Don't worry, sweetheart, there's the press conference tomorrow. Who knows, but it might blow things wide open.'

Markham spoke confidently but was all too well aware how little they had to go on.

* * *

Once they got home, Olivia took herself off to the refuge of the bathroom for a scalding hot bath, declaring that only a luxurious wallow could compensate her for 'Ordeal-by-Muriel'.

Aware that she was unlikely to emerge any time soon, Markham retreated to his study, first pouring himself a glass of Chateauneuf-du-Pape since (unlike his partner) he had been relatively abstemious at the Noakeses. (It paid to keep one's eye on the ball when socialising with Muriel).

Standing at the picture window that looked out onto the gathering twilight, his thoughts were uneasy and restless. He sensed that Olivia was struggling with some inner resentment but was unsure how to handle his partner's eggshell sensitivity. Taking a long draught of wine, he pondered the state of their relationship.

Deep down, he knew his remoteness was the problem . . . had always been the problem. But, he reasoned, his was really the detachment of a survivor — an ability to sweep away emotions when they overwhelmed him and to start over or just keep going.

That's why they thought him a cold fish in CID. It was impossible for his colleagues to intuit that the crevices of ice inside him were scar tissue formed over many years, acting as a self-protection that meant he was forever destined in some deep interior part of himself to pull away and remain aloof. Certainly, his unfailing ability to immerse himself in an investigation had proved to be one of the saving graces of his personal life — as though through dedication to the job he could redeem his life's wrong turnings and somehow make amends to those he had let down.

Strains of Tchaikovsky floated down to the study, making him smile. Clearly Olivia was exorcising her demons with some ballet music. His partner's favourite composer never failed to help restore her good humour. Mind you, he thought uneasily, right now her mood seemed spikier than usual.

He knew she resented what she saw as his detachment or coldness despite insisting that she understood its origins. The problem was that his heart simply did not translate love into the more usual channels that occupy a life, which meant that romance was fitted in round his all-consuming passion for work, relegated to the intervals between investigations.

'Prince Myshkin,' she nicknamed him after Dostoyevsky's remote and troubled mystic, and though he had laughed, her words nevertheless stung him. 'A second-hand heart' was another taunt she had flung at him in one of the arguments that preceded their previous split. If what she meant was that he had the kind of heart that essentially wanted to be left alone and allowed to love in a simple, detached way, then he guessed she was right. He needed to be allowed to carry on solving cases without messy distractions. A case of 'Keep your distance, I promise to send roses,' Olivia had commented sardonically, and he couldn't deny it. Sex was undoubtedly there in the air around them — his heart still skipped a beat whenever he set eyes on her — but, these days, despite the physical electricity, there was something shadowed about it, something maimed and off-colour.

His thoughts turned to Kate Burton and the possibility that he might lose her to Tower Bridge CID. That he was so shaken at the prospect of losing her made him realise how much solace, sanity and discipline his career provided. It was common ground, too, with his fellow inspector, who shared the same energy, excitement and mutual respect. So it was only natural that Olivia should be jealous — though of course she wasn't exactly blameless, he thought, taking another gulp of wine, having put him through an emotional wringer when she took up with Mat Sullivan.

Was the increasing closeness between himself and Burton a revenge of sorts for having been dumped by Olivia? If so, it didn't cast him in a very attractive light, he admitted to himself wryly. At least these days, however, he was trying harder to involve her in his professional life, finding solace in sharing his doubts and fears.

Sighing, he moved away from the window to his desk, still revolving pictures of the two women in his mind. A noise from outside made him jump, but it was just a pigeon coming to roost in the neighbouring cemetery. Swallowing the last of his wine, he suddenly felt cold and forlorn.

He wouldn't mind a bath himself, he concluded, though somehow he didn't imagine Olivia would welcome him joining her in that soapy lake she favoured! Nor did he imagine that lovemaking was on the cards tonight.

Perhaps it was just as well, he shrugged. Time to get his head down and catch up on some sleep.

Out there somewhere was a killer with a growing appetite for murder.

## CHAPTER 8: BOMBSHELL

The team meeting on Monday morning turned out to be an uncomfortably subdued affair. Markham made no secret of his intense frustration at this latest turn of events, the *Gazette* predictably having made sensational capital from the Medway Mere fiasco and disturbance outside John Sinnott's house.

'All bets are off with Brophy,' Noakes told them in doom-laden tones, between stuffing his face with refreshments from *Costa* provided by Burton ('getting her priorities right', as he called it). 'You can't expect him to ignore a cracking story like that.'

'True,' Markham agreed then added heavily, 'It's par-ticularly unfortunate that Mary Priddy's family have been dragged into it. Maxwell and Fellowes are going to meet her mother and do some turbo-charged grovelling, but Sidney's got steam coming out of his ears.' Not least as it appeared stories about police insensitivity and ineptitude were likely to be headline news for days (if not weeks) to come.

Doyle was puzzled. 'Was it *Brophy* who tipped the pro-testors off then, sir?' he asked. 'I mean, I thought you said he was willing to keep schtum till we had someone in the frame.'

'When we talked in his office, he seemed amenable to holding off,' the DI said bleakly. 'I spoke to him on the phone before going in to see Sidney and he swore blind he had nothing to do with what happened at the Mere and Bromgrove Rise.' Markham didn't add that he believed the journalist on this score but simply moved on to discussion about tactics for the afternoon press conference.

He wasn't particularly surprised when Carruthers lingered in his office after Doyle and Noakes had left.

Quietly, Burton gestured the DS to a seat. Markham said nothing but merely waited, anticipating the confession that must follow.

He was taken aback by Carruthers's first words. There was no beating about the bush.

'It was me who gave Brophy the heads-up that we were reopening Priddy, I admit it . . . but I never breathed a word about John Sinnott or had anything to do with those thugs and their anti-paedophile demos.'

Carruthers's white-faced sincerity was convincing. Markham believed the assertion that he hadn't put the word out about John Sinnott, since there were others who would have known about the police interest in him after Mary Priddy's body was found. His DS was looking unwell, Markham thought, not least as the hair that was normally immaculately gelled into place now appeared as though he could not stop running his hands through it. His complexion looked rough and unhealthy, too, with a flowering of acne. The BBC accent had unconsciously slipped and a northern twang was detectable behind the usually carefully enunciated vowels.

'Look sir, ma'am, I may've slipped the odd story the *Gazette*'s way,' Carruthers pleaded with them. 'I hold my hands up to that. But no way did I put anyone on to Sinnott . . . *no way.*'

'Did the *Gazette* pay you for leads?' Burton's voice was surprisingly gentle despite her fierce dislike of anything that smacked of corruption.

Markham knew she really rated Carruthers, both for his intelligence and loyalty (not easy considering he was Bretherton's nephew). Strangely, despite the fact that they were contemporaries, there was something verging on the *maternal* in his colleague's attitude to both Doyle and Carruthers, almost as though she found in them the family she showed no signs of building with Nathan Finlayson.

'Once or twice in the past, yeah.' Carruthers took a deep shuddering breath. 'I don't even know why I did it.'

But Markham knew. One-upmanship — a need for Carruthers to prove to himself that he was still "in the game"; a need which derived from some kind of personal insecurity about his prospects. The DS hadn't experienced the smoothest of honeymoon periods on joining the 'Gang' (and doubtless attracted resentment from his peers into the bargain) plus, Markham now recalled, there were those rumours that he had split from his girlfriend and was living on the never-never. As someone who valued his own privacy, with the result that the persona he projected was chilly and aloof (earning him the station nickname 'Lord Snooty'), the DI was loath to pry into his colleagues' personal affairs. Carefully, he said, 'I'm assuming that after this, it won't happen again.'

The flare of hope in Carruthers's eyes was almost painful to behold.

'You mean you're not going to report me, sir?'

'No, I'm not,' was the decisive reply. 'You're a good detective with considerable potential. I've no wish to see a promising career derailed.'

'You won't regret it, guv,' the DS positively stuttered, removing his glasses and wiping them vigorously as though they had suddenly steamed up with the force of his emotion.

Afterwards, all Burton said mildly was, 'Let's hope no one from the *Gazette* decides to dob Carruthers in. If that happens, we're *all* screwed.'

Markham's face wore an implacable expression that was all too familiar. 'I rather think it won't come to that, Kate. And if it does, let's just say Noakesy has enough dirt on Gavin Conors and the rest of them for it to come in handy as a bargaining chip.' Not to mention his own ammunition, was the unspoken message.

'If neither Brophy nor Carruthers tipped those lowlifes off, then who the hell did?' she wondered, looking troubled. 'Someone must've wanted to create trouble for Sinnott, make sure the spotlight's on him.'

*The killer?* Her unspoken question hung in the air between them.

'It should make for an interesting press conference,' Markham replied, his mouth twisting.

She groaned softly. 'What line are we going to take, sir?'

'The line of least resistance,' he told her flatly. 'We go with what you fed Sidney.' Mechanically, he listed the various bullet points as if reciting from an autocue: 'Recent muckraking by local troublemakers deplorable; Hollingrove's previous history — including Priddy — obviously relevant, but there are *several* lines of enquiry; Press should refrain from ill-informed speculation which could potentially prejudice the investigation as well as hurting innocent people, blah blah.'

'What line should we take on Cathy Price?'

'We say there's nothing to show any link with the other two murders and talk up its being a vicious and unprovoked attack without any obvious motive — essentially move them away from the idea of a serial killer.'

'What if they ask about John Sinnott?' Burton pressed him. 'Conors or one of them is bound to say something about the bloke being public enemy number one.'

The DI smiled thinly. 'We remind them of the law relating to defamation, throw in something about perverting the course of justice and intimidation while we're at it,' he added blandly.

Burton looked more confident on hearing this. Markham suspected that she could hardly wait to consult her trusty copy of *Archbold Criminal Pleading, Evidence and Practice* with a view to composing something suitably legalistic.

'Maybe I'll blindside them with stuff about Druid hocus pocus,' she said, a grin finally breaking through her hitherto solemn expression. 'Newspapers always go a bundle on anything to do with the occult and black magic.' She frowned. 'Not that Malcolm Devenish and his volunteers from the park are going to like me sending it up.'

Markham smiled at her encouragingly, glad to park their current woes for a short time, as always, finding her company curiously soothing. Seeing her rise to go, he waved his colleague back into her chair, wishing to extend the moment.

'What do *you* make of it all then, Kate?'

'Well, somehow it doesn't seem right to make fun and turn the Druids into something out of *Horrible Histories*,' she said slowly. 'By all accounts, they were impressive folk. It was only when the Romans got the wind up about rebellions and things that they started those stories about them being barbarians—'

'And then later on, the early Christians decided to go one better — misrepresented them as creepy magicians by way of eliminating the competition,' he observed wryly.

'Yeah, bit of an unfair press all round, guv,' she said shyly. 'I don't like playing up to all that Wicker Man prejudice.'

'You could always focus on the, er, *bardic* side of it . . . the Celtic Revival . . . Celtomania,' he suggested with a mischievous glint.

She threw up her hands in mock horror. 'Oh God, you mean the Eisteddfod angle.'

Noakes would just *love* that.

'Or you could talk about that mad vicar Devenish mentioned—'

'Stukeley?'

'Yeah, him . . . And there's Stonehenge to fall back on, that always makes good copy.'

She sighed. 'When I was a kid, I thought the Druids built Stonehenge, kind of half-believed the storybook stuff. Stukeley did too — thought the world was only six thousand years old — didn't have a clue about timelines or the "deep human past", so had to make it all fit somehow—'

'Squeezing in Abraham and Moses and Ancient Egypt while he was at it,' Markham chuckled, recalling their tour of the mansion house exhibits. 'And then would you believe it, all those tiresome field archaeologists and scientists came along, spoiled everything by insisting that he was talking rubbish, because the Druids were only around from the fourth century BC and Stonehenge was way older than that.'

'Well, Tom Burke said we've got to think of the Druids' roots being much deeper than anyone realised, so it's more than likely they *were* connected with the building of Stonehenge.'

The air of flushed triumph with which she gave this verdict amused Markham, who could easily picture the senior volunteer's delight at her interest.

'What the heck, I say go wild, Kate! Chuck in Stukeley, Stonehenge and anything else you can think of . . . just so long as it steers Gavin Conors and the rest of them away from the Priddy case and John Sinnott.'

She pulled a face. 'I won't mention anything about human sacrifice, though, boss.'

'Hell no. "Altars running with blood", or whatever it is Tacitus said about ritual slaughter, is strictly *off* the agenda.' Side-tracking the reporters with some neolithic history might be a useful stratagem, but it needed to be judiciously filtered, otherwise Sidney would be after *his* blood!

Burton's solemn brown eyes seemed full of soft light, exuding sympathy with his predicament.

'Ask Noakesy for some ideas,' Markham told her. 'He's bound to go all *Time Team* on you but might come up with something startling that'll strike the press vultures dumb.'

She laughed at that, looking much less careworn than before. He was intrigued by the metamorphosis.

'How's it going with Sarge's private eye business, guv?' she asked him.

'Well enough that when I told him about this case, he didn't need asking twice.' Markham suspected that even if his friend's agency had been in the doldrums, nothing would have stopped him coming on board the Hollingrove Park investigation. 'No doubt he'll invite you along to view his cubbyhole in Medway now it's halfway decent.'

'He must miss Rosemount though,' she mused. 'I mean, that whole country house set-up . . . very posh, like something out of the National Trust,' she added wistfully. Burton had been quite overawed by the splendour of those manicured surroundings, he remembered.

'I believe it *was* something of a wrench to leave all his war heroes,' Markham observed drily, recalling the portraits of Nelson, Captain Cook, General Gordon and other luminaries which adorned Rosemount's premises. 'The décor in his new place has less of a "patriotic" accent. He was keen to put up a picture of his latest crush — General Custer — but Olivia talked him out of that idea on the grounds that it might spook potential clients.'

She laughed again, a full-throated peal that totally transformed her.

'*General Custer . . . Oh my days!*'

Markham grinned back. 'Oh yes, all moustachioed, long-haired and wild-eyed. I honestly don't think Medway's quite ready for anything like that.'

'I'm surprised the long hair didn't put Sarge off,' she marvelled.

'Well, neither that nor the fact of Custer being nicknamed "Fanny" seems to have troubled Noakesy — military credentials trump all the rest.'

'Oh dear. Tom Burke told me the Druids were exempt from military service. Sarge won't like that.'

The gleam was back in Markham's eyes. 'I think you'll find, Kate, that if it means getting one over on Gavin Conors and the rest, Noakesy will be only too happy for you to talk about the Druids till the cows come home.'

And so it proved, the assorted 'reptiles' proving surprisingly susceptible to heavy-handed hints about devil worship and sorcery, with Burton skilfully diverting attention away from the Priddy case and almost — but not quite — implying that they were on the trail of deranged Satanists.

'I'm a bit worried I overdid it back there, sir,' she said afterwards as the team convened back in Markham's office.

'You sounded jus' like that Dan Snow or one of them other boffins, luv,' Noakes said heartily. 'Conors were *lapping it up*,' he chortled. 'Nothing like a bit of Stonehenge mania to get 'em all excited. He forgot all about Cathy Price with all that stuff about mistletoe an' cycles of the moon an' whatnot.'

'Sidney was practically *purring*,' Carruthers put in eagerly, looking far more cheerful now he had made a clean breast to Markham. 'Anything that gets them thinking this is all about some random maniac with a thing for sacrifices and witchcraft is good news from the DCI's point of view.'

'Only we're not *really* looking for some mad devil-worshipper are we, guv?' Doyle asked warily.

'No, Sergeant,' came the firm reply. 'I believe these murders are linked to the Mary Priddy case and our killer is someone we've already interviewed.'

He was unable to shake off his strange conviction that the mansion house museum could shed light on the deaths of Tony Pardoe and Loretta Davenport, if only he could interpret its message . . .

'Forensics are done with the park,' Burton interrupted his thoughts, 'so *The Reader Shop*'s going ahead with its Easter Tea Party tomorrow afternoon.'

Doyle's expression was dubious. 'Won't that look a bit, well, *callous* seeing as there's three people dead.'

She shrugged. 'The council want it to go ahead as planned . . . Look at the positives,' she urged. 'It'll give us a chance to review our suspects in a relaxed setting where the killer might be off their guard and let something slip.'

At least there was no question of dragging everyone back to that creepy convent, Noakes thought with an inward sigh of relief. Not exactly the cheeriest venue for a bunfight.

'I've scheduled a psychological profiling session for tomorrow morning,' Burton continued, 'which should cue us up for the tea party. Then we've got Mr Pardoe's funeral on Thursday at St Edward the Confessor, followed by his wake at The Storybarn.'

'*The Storybarn?*' Noakes repeated blankly. 'What the chuff's that when it's at home?'

'The old stable block round the back of the mansion house,' Burton replied patiently. 'It's been converted into a kind of reading retreat for families.'

Noakes pulled a face, clearly visualising soft play areas and CBeebies.

'Don't worry, Sarge,' she reassured him. 'There's two or three meeting rooms and the café staff are catering it. Apparently, Mr Pardoe had great plans for the place — holiday clubs, birthday parties, mums 'n tots groups — so that's why the council chose it for the wake.'

'Handy advertising opportunity too,' Carruthers muttered caustically, the cynicism a sure sign that he was well on the road to recovery after the recent hiatus over press leaks.

'Be that as it may,' Burton said severely, 'it's another chance to monitor our suspects.'

'What's happening with Priddy?' Doyle wanted to know. 'Is that all secret squirrel now the press are onto it?'

'I've arranged for us to catch up with Maxwell and Fellowes on Wednesday afternoon,' she replied crisply. 'Hopefully by then they may have come up with more from the family.'

'Excellent, Kate. In the meantime, let's revisit everything we've got to date,' Markham instructed. 'Witness statements, alibis, *everything*, no matter how inconsequential or insignificant.'

'Yeah, "deep dive".' Noakes smirked as he parroted Sidney.

Burton ignored the sarcasm. 'I'll come by later and update you, boss,' she informed Markham as the team dispersed to their various tasks.

*Deep dive.*

The words reverberated mockingly in the DI's ears.

The killer was lurking out there in the depths of Hollingrove Park, but he felt as far away from solving the case as ever.

\* \* \*

Before Burton returned to give Markham the promised update, he took a call from Nathan Finlayson regarding the profiling session scheduled for the following day. At the end of the call, he was startled when the psychologist said with a slight edge to his voice, 'By the by, I hope you can talk Kate out of this latest mad scheme of hers, I really do.'

'What mad scheme?'

Was it his imagination or was there a subtle note of satisfaction in Finlayson's voice as he replied, 'She hasn't said anything to you then?'

'About what?'

'That she's thinking of leaving the police to join a convent.'

'*Become a nun?*'

Markham struggled with a chaos of thoughts, suddenly recalling Burton's easy familiarity with Sr Renata at Maryvale House and the revelation that she was a regular visitor to the convent, together with his sense that something was afoot. He hadn't really taken it in when Noakes mentioned that her increasing religiosity was a problem for Finlayson, but now things were falling into place.

The DI felt that loyalty to Burton required a calm and neutral manner. Afterwards, he barely knew what he had said, but it seemed to satisfy Finlayson. In the circumstances, it was a relief to learn that the psychologist would not be conducting the next day's session personally, delegating this responsibility to Dr Eleanor Shaughnessy whom Markham had consulted on previous investigations and held in high esteem.

There was little time to gather himself before Burton appeared, ready — with her usual quiet competence — to summarise the state of play.

Still reeling from Finlayson's call, Markham took in almost nothing of what she said, his thoughts skidding and repositioning themselves in skeins of baffled conjecture.

'Are you okay, boss?'

She was peering at him in concern.

He decided to have it out with her. Finlayson was bound to disclose that he had brought up the subject of her religious conversion (if that's what it was) and the situation would become awkward if she suspected people were gossiping behind her back. Besides which, if this was some deeper personal crisis, he wanted to offer help. If he was being honest with himself, he also wanted to stop her making some sort of irrevocable decision that meant he would lose her.

'I understand you may be thinking of pastures new, Kate,' he dashed at it headlong, striving to keep any hint of disapproval from his tone.

'*Pastures new?*'

God, he was making a real hash of this.

'As in joining the Carmelites.'

Aware how lacklustre and toneless this sounded, he added quickly, 'A wonderful vocation.' As a lapsed Catholic, he wasn't at all sure he considered it anything of the kind, and besides didn't she already *have* a vocation — with the police.

His fellow DI coloured up violently but, being Burton, she was a past mistress at taking herself in hand. The flush receded and she managed to speak in tones that, if not perfectly steady, reflected her usual habit of self-control.

'I suppose Nathan let it out,' she said without rancour. 'It's true that I'm at some kind of crossroads, but nothing's been decided.'

This sounded less cut and dried — less extreme — than Finlayson had allowed him to imagine, and he experienced profound relief that she wasn't panting for admission to the convent's ranks.

He felt a brief flare of anger at the psychologist for ambushing him like that and panicking him into concluding that his colleague was on the brink of making some utterly irrevocable decision about her future. But in simple fairness, he realised he shouldn't begrudge Burton's fiancé the satisfaction of putting the cat amongst the pigeons, especially if Finlayson happened to suspect the depth of their feelings for each other.

Markham's warm gaze searched hers. 'What's brought all this on?'

'Everything changed after dad died,' she said simply. 'I thought if he's not *here*, boss, then I've got to go look for him and the nuns can help with that. I mean, life beyond the physical has to be where the real action's at. Why should I spend life thinking about murder and violent crime when I've got a *soul?*'

It sounded to Markham as though she was looking for a new kind of home — one far removed from CID. He recalled Eleanor Shaughnessy saying that after losing a parent, the mind often had to reinvent itself in order to deal with a different universe. His own salvation had been *Work and More Work* (often to the detriment of his relationship with Olivia), but Kate Burton needed something different.

'I've visited Maryvale a few times,' she continued, encouraged by his sympathetic demeanour. 'With the peace and quiet and beauty of their life, you feel like you're on the threshold of another world.' A world free of mutilated corpses and psychos, he thought grimly. 'Most people are convinced that nuns live like the dead, sir, but it seems to me they're more alive than the rest of us. And the silence makes everything stand out so my mind can unspool and I can hear myself *think*.'

It was rare for Burton to talk at such length about herself, and he sensed that it came as an exquisite relief. 'There's this idea about nuns,' she said earnestly, 'that they hate the world or something.'

'It would be understandable if they *did*,' he smiled, 'considering how messy and sordid it can be.' An image flashed into his mind of Loretta Davenport's features frozen in death — that staring, empty mask, a rigid carving like the rest on the totem pole to which she had been bound. With an effort, he dismissed the memory. 'I imagine it's more a case of your nuns aiming for detachment so they can get in touch with something deeper.'

Her eyes were moist. 'You *understand*, guv . . . not like Nathan.' She bit her lip. 'That's not really fair. I guess it's not very flattering to learn your fiancée is thinking about withdrawing from the world. He says that I need to let him know whether we have a future together, that he feels like he's sitting on a fence and just can't sit there any longer.'

'Poor old Shippers,' Noakes said later when they met up for a drink in *The Grapes*, Burton having given her permission for Markham to tell his wingman how matters stood. 'No wonder the lad's depressed. Sounds like she wants to be some holy sweet pea, one of them simpering plaster saints in the cathedral, all candlelight an' holy water an' meeting up with Daddy. Mebbe what she *really* needs, guv, is a few days in some detox centre, like that spa wotsit in Old Carton, somewhere she can go an' chill out.'

Seeing that Noakes didn't have a high opinion of such places, this represented quite a concession. It was also a shrewd acknowledgement that Burton needed space to be mended and put back together again — a chance to unplug herself from the claustrophobic human landscape. Markham recalled the time his friend had spoken about Burton needing a break from policing and, not for the first time, marvelled at the intuitiveness that lurked beneath Noakes's uncouth exterior.

After a brief hesitation, he confided, 'Kate said she doesn't feel marriage is really for her. It should be a total commitment and if she's not ready to make that commitment, then the fairest thing for herself and Nathan is to call off the engagement.'

With a sensitivity and delicacy for which few would have given him credit, Noakes said nothing about the issue of Burton's feelings for *Markham*. He simply shook his massive head dolefully. 'Dunno how I'd feel about seeing her through them weirdy bars or grille or whatever they call it. An' then she needs to think about what it's like not having enough grub an' spending all that time down on your knees.'

Markham could not help but smile. 'Convents aren't as austere as they used to be, Noakesy, but it's certainly a hard life.'

'What if the lass is jus' mixed up right now an' changes her mind later?'

The DI recalled Burton's eager voice. 'I'm afraid of going in and then realising I've made a huge mistake — haven't walked to God but just taken a wrong turn . . . He's not there waiting for me after all and it's some massive delusion.'

He took a hefty swig of his red wine before answering Noakes's question. 'I told Kate there'll always be a place for her here, no matter what.'

'I reckoned that's what you'd say,' his friend replied comfortably. 'If you ask me, Burton's got some idea that whatever journey her dad's on — to heaven or the other place — her going into this convent will make things easier for him. Once she gets that out of her system and realises CID's where she's meant to be an' thass what her dad wanted for her, she'll be fine.'

There was something very consoling to Markham in this theory.

'If the boss woman's got any sense, she'll see what's what an' sort Burton out,' his friend concluded.

It amused the DI that, despite Noakes's sturdy Methodist aversion to nuns and convents, he had every faith in the 'boss woman' (aka the Prioress) making things right. 'I'll have to leave it to Kate's Svengali then,' he said lightly. 'You do that, guv,' the other nodded sagely. 'Tell Burton to go an' stay with 'em at Maryvale over Easter . . . they'll mark her card right enough.' He knocked back the last of his beer. ''Sides, there's the mad hatter's tea party thingy tomorrow. She'll be too busy looking for nutters to worry about God.'

Noakes's common-sense perspective somehow took the edge off Markham's anxiety. Time out at Maryvale could even be packaged as some sort of sabbatical for his fellow DI to research a Heritage Crime Unit pilot. What mattered was that Kate Burton remained in the force . . . and in his life.

Lingering over his drink after Noakes had departed, he tried to make sense of his feelings for the two women in his life.

Olivia *seemed* to have made peace with the idea of Kate's importance to him, though, on the other hand, it was not so long ago that she had poured scorn on what she termed his colleague's 'pathetic infatuation', declaring, 'It's downright abnormal for a woman of her age to dote on her boss like a teenager with a schoolgirl crush on some rock star. If you give her the heave-ho, she'll get over it. What she really needs is someone to blast her out of adolescence.'

He knew there was some truth in Olivia's words. Knew that he was as flawed as any other human being and Kate Burton needed to see him in the light of unvarnished reality: the workaholic habits that acted to the detriment of personal relationships; the detachment that kept people at arm's length even when he cared about them; the solitary nature that made true intimacy difficult if not impossible; the arrogance that he knew to be the flip-side of his humility; the meticulous, chilly professionalism that he wore like armour; the bruising aloofness and austerity that he deployed to shut out truths he found too difficult to bear. Like Kipling's cat, he walked by himself, Olivia maintained, but was as lethal as any lion on the prowl. 'You need to discard those blinkers of yours, Gil,' she had urged, her words scoring deep gashes across his consciousness. It was all such a tangle, however, that he struggled to see the way forward . . .

Real love isn't selfish and possessive, he told himself, thinking of Burton. He should be wanting the best for her rather than luring her onto emotional rocks and wrecking her future. It was an indisputable fact, however, that she somehow patted down and smoothed out all his jagged edges so that he was able to face whatever the job threw at him. Indeed, he sometimes felt that she was literally the only person capable of defusing the extreme stress he battled from day to day. Although he told himself he wanted her to move on and be happy, he knew that the non-possessive love on which he liked to plume himself was a sham and, in reality, the thought of Kate finding happiness in any other quarter (even with a convent of nuns!) made him jealous as hell. He might honestly have wanted to attain an ideal of selfless purity, but reality buried deep at the bottom of his mind lay quite elsewhere.

During the Tower investigation, one DCI Len Knevitt had shown a distinct interest in Burton, but as yet nothing seemed to have come of it. He almost wished that Knevitt would declare himself. At least that would force a decision one way or the other.

He acknowledged ruefully that Burton's engagement to Nathan Finlayson had been a useful arrangement, seeing as it meant the "other" man took care of mundane husbandly duties and the tiresome demands of daily life. Were he and Burton ever to take the plunge and hook up, honesty compelled him to admit to himself that the sheer humdrumness of real life might throw a spanner in the works, to say nothing of the fact that he still seemed to need Olivia — like she was some sort of witch who had him under a spell.

He became aware that the beer garden had emptied and the evening meal rush would soon be in full swing. Having no desire this evening for conviviality or companionship, he decided to make tracks.

Sidney & Co were fast losing patience with the snail-like process of this investigation.

*Give me a breakthrough*, he implored the deity in whom he still believed despite everything. *Before anyone else dies.*

## CHAPTER 9: RIPPLES

In advance of the Easter Tea Party at Hollingrove Park on Tuesday afternoon, there was the psychological profiling session to get through.

Noakes and Markham met in his office half an hour before the others for a private chat.

'Can't believe they've got the heating on in this place,' the older man muttered wrathfully, savagely twisting the valves on the radiator under Markham's window this way and that in a vain attempt to regulate the tropical Center Parcs temperature. 'Like freaking Siberia in winter and then they put it on full blast in time for Easter.'

The DI grinned as he listened to his friend's choleric monologue.

'Here you go, switch this on,' he instructed, disinterring a portable desk fan from the metal storage cabinet behind his desk.

More muttering followed, but the fan helped and Noakes eventually stopped grumbling about the state of the premises (admittedly well due for an overhaul).

Markham smiled as he contemplated his friend whose chunky body, florid complexion and bushy salt and pepper hair gave him the air of an eighteenth-century huntsman out of an old-fashioned sporting print despite his stab at an ensemble suitable for the afternoon picnic: viz mustard cavalry twill trousers teamed with a red fisherman's jumper and the inevitable George boots. The overall effect was positively Pickwickian, but Markham imagined this wasn't so incongruous when one thought of Hollingrove's mansion house, a veritable relic from the past with all that heavy mahogany furniture — the enormous sofas, high-backed chairs and musty velvet hassocks. Yes, in that setting Noakes might almost pass for a country squire.

Aware of Markham's appraisal, the other bridled self-consciously. 'Looks like it's gonna be a nice day, so I opted for smart casual.'

The DI's idea of "smart casual" was a million miles removed from his wingman's, but he merely said self-deprecatingly, 'And here am I encased in pinstripe. Should have taken a leaf out of your book, Noakesy.'

Well pleased at the implied compliment, Noakes eyed his too-tight trousers complacently.

The weather was certainly ideal for an outdoor party, Markham reflected, savouring the balmy, soft breeze that came through the window, heavy with the scent of newly fledged trees and cherry blossom from further down the main thoroughfare that led into the town centre. Yes, it was a glowing morning alright, which made the thought of their upcoming review in CID's stuffy seminar room distinctly unappealing. He sighed as he recalled the lines of daffodils bordering the gravelled paths of Hollingrove Park and the masses of golden celandine spangling its woods . . .

Noakes's voice recalled him to the present.

'Jus' as well Blondie's doing the session today an' not poor old Shippers. That'd be well awkward seeing how things stand with him an' Maria von Trapp.'

'*Maria von Trapp?*'

'Y'know, the nun from *The Sound of Music.*'

'Very droll. For God's sake don't let the others hear you call Kate that,' Markham admonished. 'And it's *Doctor Shaughnessy*, not Blondie.'

Noakes merely grinned. 'It'll be good for Burton to go ten rounds with the doc,' he concluded. 'She'll be so busy trying to show she's up on all the latest psychological boffin talk, that it's bound to keep her mind off convents an' holy joes an' all that. Besides,' he added, 'she's desperate to crack this case . . . get you more gold stars so you don' have to worry about knobheads like Ebury-Clarke an' Bretherton.'

'Oh, like the poor, those two will be always with us,' Markham riposted, a note of buried mockery in his voice.

Noakes chortled to signal his appreciation of the biblical allusion. 'Don' worry, guv,' he reassured the DI, 'I won't drop any clangers round Burton. I mean, I won't wind her up or owt. She'll be embarrassed enough about me knowing all about this mad convent scheme without making things worse.'

Noakes fondly imagined his reputation as an irascible curmudgeon meant colleagues thought of him as a tough nut, whereas it was well known that in many respects he had a loud bark and no bite at all. Beneath the uncouth exterior beat a soft heart, though he fell into paroxysms of embarrassment at ever being detected openly in an act of kindness. That was why Burton hadn't baulked at the notion of Markham sharing her secret with his number two: she knew he only ever wanted her good and wouldn't make sport of her personal circumstances around others.

In the event, Noakes was as good as his word, his demeanour almost preternaturally solemn and respectful around Burton, to the extent that Markham was worried he would overdo it. Luckily, she was sufficiently absorbed by Dr Shaughnessy's insights to put her colleague's unusual behaviour to the back of her mind.

Eleanor Shaughnessy always gave good value, making a compelling case for histrionic/narcissistic personality disorder as the key to their killer, not only on account of the murders' 'performative' aspects but due to the fact that both Tony Pardoe and Loretta Davenport were flamboyantly dominant characters capable of triggering feelings of acute inferiority in an emotionally vulnerable, even schizoid, subject.

'What about how Davenport was found?' Carruthers wanted to know. 'How does sex fit in?'

'Inappropriate sexual behaviour or exhibitionism falls within the symptomology, likewise persecutory delusions and grandiosity.'

As Dr Shaughnessy discussed the impact of shifting psychological environments on an unstable personality, Markham felt a flash of recognition and something nibble at the edges of his consciousness, as if she was describing someone he knew . . . someone he had recently met. The problem being that he couldn't match her template to any of their suspects.

'D'you reckon the same person who murdered Pardoe and Davenport killed Mary Priddy?' Doyle enquired.

'I believe so, yes,' the statuesque blonde academic (or Norse goddess as Markham always thought of her on account of the long flaxen hair and piercing blue eyes) replied, her gentle voice with its hint of an Irish accent full of calm assurance. She went on to explain her conviction that ancient Hollingrove Park held powerful significance for the killer, such that it was the inevitable locus for eruptions of violence. After a lucid exposition of geographical coefficients in profiling this particular offender, she added, 'I don't see the motive as sexual . . . more that this was all about some perceived threat to the ego which meant the little girl *had* to die.'

'Like a crime of passion then?' Doyle sounded puzzled but the psychologist nodded. 'Displaced animosity or hostility towards the child's mother perhaps,' she suggested.

'That fits John Sinnott cos the kid's mother had dumped him,' the DS said eagerly. 'Could be he was looking to punish her.'

'The timings are a problem,' Carruthers reminded him.

'What makes you think it couldn't have been some sex game gone wrong?' Noakes challenged the psychologist.

'The fact that the greenhouse was a bit of a building site at the time,' she replied. 'Your typical paedophile prefers to *linger* over an assault, wanting to be comfortable while doing it.'

Carruthers exchanged telling looks with Doyle as Shaughnessy and Burton began a spirited debate centring on various research papers pertaining to the neurobiology of paedophilia.

Markham found the psychologist's arguments absorbing, however, once again he couldn't seem to reconcile the notion of a fractured ego with anyone from their suspect pool. He wasn't aware that Maxwell and Fellowes had uncovered a link between any of the volunteers or park staff and Mary Priddy's mother (apart from John Sinnott), but perhaps that meeting scheduled for the morrow would shine a light on the Priddy family background . . .

'Earth to Inspector Markham, come in please.'

The psychologist was aware that he had drifted off but not at all offended, her voice teasing.

'Any pointers for us as to our killer's gender?' he asked, somewhat embarrassed to have been caught wool-gathering.

'There are both male and female signifiers,' she told him regretfully. 'I haven't been able to isolate anything definitive one way or the other.'

'Any chance of joint enterprise?' This was Burton.

Noakes's shaggy eyebrows shot up. *Two killers!*

'Again, I can't rule that out. The occult dimension could point to some sort of shared obsession. Adherence to a pagan cult would certainly bolster a narcissist's need to feel special and superior—'

'The possessor of secret knowledge, like the Druids,' Doyle chipped in.

Her smile of approval was so radiant that the young DS blinked in confusion, dazzled.

'Exactly like that, Sergeant.'

Noakes didn't care to see CID's Young Turks carry off the laurels.

'If it's a bloke, what're we looking for, luv,' he demanded bluntly. 'I mean, the Hollingrove lot . . . well, they're all dead ordinary an' boring, nothing to show they've got a thing about witches' nipples or owt like that.'

Doyle snickered at this, abruptly swallowing his amusement in the face of Burton's flinty disapproval.

'I believe you're looking for the proverbial "*Street Angel House Devil*",' the psychologist told them. 'Someone whose mask is so firmly in place that nobody could possibly suspect the existence of an alter ego.'

'A fat lot of use that is,' Carruthers complained as the meeting broke up.

Burton, however, begged to differ.

'We should dig deeper into people's personal histories, guv,' she told Markham. 'See if any psychological markers jump out.' She frowned. 'I know we can't go round demanding clinical records — patient confidentiality and the rest of it — but maybe there's career "blips" . . . blank spots . . . something that went wrong.'

The expression on Carruthers's face suggested he was biting back a sardonic 'Good luck with that'.

'Excellent idea, Kate,' Markham told her, something in his eyes squelching the acid riposte forming on his sergeant's lips. 'We're missing something here, so it's got to be worth a shot.'

He was amused to see that, despite a certain competitiveness where Eleanor Shaughnessy was concerned (not least because some female instinct alerted her that Markham found the blonde psychologist attractive), Burton was champing at the bit to apply everything they had learned from the profiler. That was the thing about his fellow DI, he reflected. Professionalism and commitment to duty (along with loyalty to himself) conquered all. She was clear and translucent as spring water, with a complete lack of artifice that made other women (even, if truth be told, Olivia) seem meretricious and petty.

Noakes meanwhile was engaged with Dr Shaughnessy in an energetic discussion about whether she didn't think "snowflakery" had gone too far and what did she reckon to reintroducing national service. Standing in what Noakes would doubtless designate an "at ease" position, the psychologist's demeanour was attentive and respectful.

His friend was highly gratified by the outcome of their conversation. 'She liked that one about the RSM telling the officer cadet sprogs when they called him "sir" an' he called 'em "sir", the difference were *they meant it*.'

Markham flashed Eleanor Shaughnessy a glance which somehow comprehended the entire history of his relationship with Noakes, the number two who confronted the whole world in battledress.

Like Burton, he knew that she understood.

He had found the profiling session useful, even though the psychologist had been unable to shed any light on Cathy Price's murder. 'There's a sense of choreography with what happened to Tony Pardoe and Loretta Davenport,' she said, 'whereas Cathy's murder seems clumsy and rushed. If it's the same killer, then they lost control over events . . . were somehow taken by surprise, which might account for the ferocity of the punishment they dealt out to that poor girl.'

* * *

What Noakes persisted in calling the mad hatter's tea party was actually a decorous affair (admission by ticket only) held in the picnic area adjacent to the mansion house café.

The edibles were varied and imaginative, though Noakes snorted disdainfully at the Easter Bunny Salad and pig cheeks with apple gel, zeroing in on the cheese scones and red velvet cake. 'Don' mind if I do, luv,' he hailed a teenaged waitress, cheerfully accepting a Get Set for Spring Cocktail as Doyle and Carruthers watched enviously. Being a "civilian contractor" meant that the older man had no compunction about availing himself fully of the hospitality on offer, while his police colleagues were obliged to decline the alcoholic beverages.

'We should call this "Operation All You Can Eat",' Carruthers muttered as he watched Noakes's attack on the buffet table, reaching crossly for a Kiddies Mocktail.

'Stop whingeing,' Burton snapped under her breath. 'You're here to *work*, remember.'

For all that he had seemed to be auditioning for a spot on *Man v Food*, Noakes missed very little. When the team retreated indoors to the shade of the café for a conflab, he reported, 'That Bernadette Donovan looks very cosy with the Chuckle Brothers.'

'*Eh?*' Doyle was puzzled by this latest nickname.

'Devenish an' Burke . . . Keep up at the back,' the other guffawed.

'Don't let anyone catch you calling them that, Sarge,' Burton pleaded, looking askance.

'Keep your wig on, luv,' he chided. 'It's nice an' discreet in here . . . no risk of anyone overhearing us.'

She smiled weakly. 'Bernadette's of an age with the other two, so I guess it's hardly surprising if they're friendly.'

'Well, turns out them, along with the café manager woman, an' Pardoe's girlfriend got caught up in some kind of hoo-ha with the locals accusing 'em of witchcraft an' all sorts.'

'*Woah*, hang on a minute.' Carruthers was anxious to reel it back. '*Witchcraft!* Are we talking about that snippy Catrina Walsh and Maureen Slattery?'

'Yeah, thass right.'

'D'you mean to say them and the oldies were mixed up in some kind of *cult?*' Carruthers persisted.

'I'm jus' getting to that,' Noakes reproved.

'Sorry, Sarge.' Carruthers waited to be enlightened.

'Turns out they asked the parish priest from St Edward the Confessor to do some sort of blessing ceremony.' Noakes screwed up his eyes. 'This was after Miss Henwood got all upset over that ancient knacker's yard them archaeologists discovered out in the grounds — horse bones an' what have you. Anyroad, folk roundabout got the wrong end of the stick an' accused 'em of being Satanists an' devil worshippers an' all sorts. Right upsetting.'

'But if it was a *priest* doing the exorcism thingy or whatever it was,' Doyle's vocabulary wasn't up to this, 'then surely that made it *respectable*.'

Noakes shrugged eloquently. 'Some folk didn't like it.' Or maybe had a specific grudge against the participants, Markham thought.

'Malcolm Devenish . . . Tom Burke . . . Bernadette Donovan . . . Catrina . . . Maureen . . . They seem pretty odd bedfellows,' Carruthers ventured.

'Zackly what I thought,' Noakes rejoined unperturbed. 'But them new age thingies,' with an air of holding his nose, 'seem to attract all sorts.'

'There's kind of an overlap between occult groups and mainstream religion,' Burton said uneasily. 'Plus, the whole "white witchcraft" scene manages to include right wingers and the exact opposite.'

'Bloody weird if you ask me.' Doyle clearly couldn't get his head round the concept of a movement which embraced, at one extreme, Hollingrove Park's senior volunteers together with Violet Henwood's prim and proper cousin and, at the other end of the spectrum, the spiky café manager along with Tony Pardoe's ex.

'Did Loretta Davenport's name come up?' Markham enquired without much hope.

Noakes scratched his chin. 'That Catrina one said Davenport were snarky about mystic stuff — plus she were besties with the police, so they kept her out of it.'

*Besties with the police. As in Sidney?* Layer upon layer, thought Markham wearily.

'Y'know that fat bird who used to work for Pardoe? Well, she's knocking around here somewhere,' Noakes continued.

'Marion Kirkwood,' Burton said, aware there was no point pulling him up for un-PC terminology.

'Yeah, her an' that Jason bloke she's knocking off were slobbering over Tweet Tweet.'

'Councillor Songhurst,' Burton amended, stony-faced.

'Don' worry, luv, I stayed well clear,' Noakes reassured her cheerfully. With a wolfish leer he added, 'Wouldn't want to spoil the love-in or owt like that. But after they'd finished sweet-talking him, Kirkwood made a beeline for Pardoe's girlfriend — the one who teaches over at Medway High — seemed like she were having a go at her.'

Burton wanted to be clear about this. 'You mean Maureen Slattery?' she asked. 'Are you sure?'

''Course I'm sure,' Noakes said huffily. 'Jus' cos I'm a private dick don' mean I'm past it.'

'Sorry, Sarge.' She thought of the soft-spoken teacher. 'It's difficult to imagine Maureen being in a catfight.'

'Oh, she were dead ladylike . . . did the death stare, like Kirkwood were summat she'd scraped off her shoe. Then ole Jason barged over all red in the face like a turkey-cock an' kind of dragged Kirkwood away before she made a scene.'

It sounded as though Jason Quirk had defused a potentially nasty situation, Markham thought, wondering why exactly Marion Kirkwood had targeted Tony Pardoe's ex and what was the history between them. Female rivalry? The jealousy of an older woman who had been passed over for someone younger and better looking? Some imbroglio involving Pardoe and Jason Quirk?

'Stilettos at Dawn,' Carruthers yawned as Doyle sniggered, before abruptly subsiding at Burton's glacial expression. Sensing the drop in temperature, Carruthers hastily changed the subject. 'Brave of John Sinnott to rock up,' he said.

'Well, he's one of them volunteers,' Noakes pointed out. 'An' he ain't been convicted of anything.' *Yet.*

'Folk were giving him a wide berth back there,' Doyle observed. 'Like they might catch something if they get too close.'

'Suzanne Mackie was sort of shepherding him around and filling up his plate.' Carruthers rolled his eyes. 'She was a bit too obvious about it, though — lots of false gaiety and whooping with laughter whenever Devenish and Burke cracked their idea of a joke.'

'It *was* a bit forced,' Burton acknowledged, 'but they were trying to protect him, wanted to be kind.'

'Tweet Tweet an' Councillor Allbright managed not to see him,' Noakes chuckled. 'Eyes staring straight ahead, even when Mackie practically pushed the poor sod in front of 'em.'

'God yes, that was awkward,' Doyle agreed. 'Sinnott looked like he wanted the ground to swallow him up. I expected him to make a quick exit after that.'

Carruthers grinned. 'No chance of that. Not with Mackie clinging on to him for dear life and Devenish pretending nothing was wrong.'

Markham contemplated the scene beyond the French windows.

What lay beneath all those bright, impenetrable smiles? Which of the visitors out there was concealing murderous thoughts behind a social mask?

'Seems like Sinnott's finally had a bellyful,' Carruthers murmured as the tall figure strode towards the picnic site exit, to the visible consternation of his fellow volunteers, their mouths comically agape at this outcome.

'Devenish looks like a guppy fish,' Noakes commented heartlessly. 'Poor old Burke's catching flies an' all.'

Catrina Walsh seemed to have matters in hand, though, weaving through the throng and directing waitresses with considerable aplomb. She looked very fetching, Markham thought, with her hair in a softly flattering loose style and wearing a simple print dress that suited her angular frame. Judging by Carruthers's appreciative gaze, the café manager's efforts hadn't been wasted.

'We'd better get out there and give it another ten minutes or so,' Markham told them, even though he knew in his heart they were unlikely to gather up any further crumbs of gossip or intrigue.

'Yeah, I fancy some of that chocolate mousse,' Noakes said firmly.

The DI had a sneaking suspicion that his friend wouldn't be above passing out a few cards to advertise Medway Investigations. If so, he would make sure to look the other way.

* * *

Markham and Olivia quarrelled that night.

She had reacted scornfully, almost callously, to his revelation that Kate Burton had thoughts of becoming a nun, or at any rate retiring to a convent.

'At least maybe now she'll stop making cow eyes at you,' was her dismissive verdict. 'I mean *for God's sake*, all that goggle-eyed devotion!'

'You shouldn't talk like that, Liv,' he reproved her. 'It's got nothing to do with me . . . Kate feels she's reached a crossroads of some sort and—'

'*Give me a break*,' was the frigid response. 'She's been hung up on you for years. George knows it . . . most likely everyone knows it. I wouldn't be surprised if this wasn't a ploy to keep you interested, like some pathetic fantasy straight out of El Cid: she heads off to a convent and then the hero discovers he can't live without her.' Olivia mimed sticking two fingers down her throat. 'Totally pukeworthy.'

Her words struck him like the crack of a whip.

'It isn't anything like that and you know it.'

'*Do I?*'

A pain had somehow lodged in his heart and was travelling upwards, almost depriving him of speech.

'*Oh for fuck's sake, Gil, you've got unfinished business with her and I'm fed up of the whole psychodrama.*'

Angry words bubbled to his lips but somehow he choked them back.

'I think the "psychodrama" is in your imagination,' he said quietly.

He was aware even as he said it that this sounded patronising, but her contemptuous dismissal of Kate Burton stung. Also, selfishly, he wanted to close this discussion down — put the whole thing on ice till he felt able to deal with it.

'No, it bloody well isn't all in my imagination,' she insisted. 'To quote the late lamented Princess Diana, "there's three of us in this relationship" and I need you to make a choice.'

His heart took a dip.

'There's no choice to be made, Liv.' He swallowed hard. 'Look, I thought we decided after,' he groped for the words, 'after our time out, that we were going to make things work . . . give our relationship a chance. What's changed since then?'

'That's just it, Gil . . . *Nothing's really changed.* Somehow I feel we're just treading water.'

She had never looked more vibrant and beautiful, the grey-green gaze flashing as though an electric current had passed through it. 'Look Gil,' she continued remorselessly as it seemed to him, 'School breaks up for Easter on Thursday the 28th.'

The same day as Tony Pardoe's funeral, he recollected dully.

'I plan to head up to my parents then and give you some space.'

Things had to be bad if she proposed to escape to her chilly, remote family.

'I don't need space,' he said dully.

'Sure you do.' It seemed to him her manner was oddly constrained and he wondered bitterly whether she had confided in Mathew Sullivan, Deputy Head at Hope Academy.

Why the hell did everything have to be so damn complicated, he raged internally.

Outwardly, however, he had himself well under control.

'Whatever you like then,' he told her with ironclad courtesy.

The rejoinder was cold, but in the circumstances there was little choice but to fall back on his usual coping mechanism. He wanted to rail at her. How could she do this to him in the middle of a complex investigation, one with potentially grave consequences for his job if he screwed up? The station vultures were always circling. She *knew* that . . . *knew* what was at stake for him.

Deep down, though, he was aware that some part of him had seen this coming and reluctantly acknowledged the justice of her charge that the romantic triangle with Kate Burton had put a strain on their relationship. He had settled for the status quo without appreciating the effects of this on Olivia.

'I'm leaving the field clear for Ms Startled Fawn,' she continued. 'It's crunch time, Gil. Me or blank blank Kate Burton.'

And with that, parting salvo, she stalked off.

There was no time to ponder his partner's ultimatum. He was on a treadmill with regard to the current investigation. His dismay was acute but he couldn't press pause and take time out to make things right.

With what felt like a Herculean effort, he went through to his study, trying to refocus. Maxwell and Fellowes were next up. And after that, Tony Pardoe's funeral.

The breakthrough had to come soon, he told himself.

*Before another tragedy.*

## CHAPTER 10: SERPENT IN THE GARDEN

It was an unpleasant shock on Wednesday morning to wake up and find Olivia's side of the bed cold and empty, but with a sense of dull resignation, Markham supposed that he had better get used to it. Somehow this breakup felt worse than last time, as though Olivia really *was* calling time on their relationship. He felt flat and numb, but knew he couldn't afford to succumb to self-pity at this stage of the investigation.

Once back at his desk in CID, his mood wasn't improved by discovering that he had missed a voicemail from Natalie Noakes the previous evening while rowing with Olivia. Her cryptic request to come and see him 'with information she thought might be useful to the investigation' didn't exactly fill him with hope of a breakthrough, but at least it offered some respite from briefing notes, spreadsheets and endless tense conversations.

DCI Sidney was swift to comment on his subordinate's ravaged appearance, observing with something almost like compassion that he 'looked under the weather . . . hopefully not coming down with anything,' before spoiling things by asking with feigned solicitude 'how his lady friend was doing these days.'

The DCI and Olivia hated each other's guts, and the DI knew this was Sidney's way of getting his own back after Markham finally brought up the subject of his boss's acquaintance with Loretta Davenport. He had done so as tactfully as possible, but Sidney nonetheless chose to take umbrage. '*You surely aren't suggesting anything untoward in my relations with Ms Davenport,*' he honked in tones of deep affront, leaving his subordinate to extract an alibi the hard way with all the bowing and scraping required to smooth down the DCI's seigneurial outrage.

Markham's face was set and hard by the time he returned to his office. At least he was able to stop worrying about Sidney's involvement with the third victim, he told himself, the DCI having been in a 'top-level' meeting with Bretherton and Ebury-Clarke about CID budgets at the time she was murdered.

He was pleased when Maxwell and Fellowes arrived to distract him from depressing thoughts about Sidney and the rupture with Olivia, whose absence the previous night he had minded more than he thought possible.

In the event, they didn't have anything new for him about the Priddy family. Helen Priddy and her estranged husband had solid alibis for the time of their daughter's death and were never in the frame, the same applying to their extended family and neighbours.

Nevertheless, Markham found it useful to listen once more to the retirees' memories of that spring weekend, trying to visualise the park's green boskiness and that shadowy figure waiting in the wings, poised to blot out the daylight for one little girl. He was interested, too, when they expressed their increasing reservations about John Sinnott's guilt.

'It's not just the timings,' Fellowes said, his earnestly cherubic face intent on Markham's. 'The guy's temperament just doesn't *fit*. My cousin knows him from *Hollingrove Bowling Club* and says he's the easy-going type — pretty shy around all the lady members and there's never been a whiff of scandal about him.'

Maxwell followed up with an exasperated, 'Sinnott was our number one suspect on account of his personal history with the mother, but we couldn't make it stick back then.' *And we can't now*, his expression said more clearly than words.

'We've tracked down as many witnesses as possible, those who are still around at any rate,' Fellowes said. 'We're having another look at the family and neighbours, just in case we missed anything,' Maxwell added before the pair took their leave, 'but so far no joy.'

Not long afterwards, the rest of the team assembled in Markham's office. He had just brought them up to speed, when a call from the desk sergeant announced the arrival of Natalie Noakes.

Markham was fond of Noakes's daughter, their acquaintance dating back to the days when he fished her out of various dodgy fleshpots patronised by the local *jeunesse dorée* (or what passed for such in Bromgrove). While undeniably vain and obsessed with social status (taking after her mother in this), she didn't lack courage, as he had discovered during previous investigations. And there was something positively *gallant* about the way she had got her life back on track after an undistinguished early start, obtaining her History degree against all the odds and finally getting her man, despite the best efforts of the "mother-in-law from Hell". Yes, there was something about Natalie's sheer bullishness that went straight to Markham's heart, sensing as he did the vulnerability and insecurity that lay beneath her spray tan brassiness (now considerably toned down from her nightclub days). Like Noakes, she had a keen interest in true crime documentaries and Markham was often surprised by her astute observations.

The DI welcomed his visitor warmly, touched by her obvious gratification that Noakes was front and centre in this investigation. He was amused by her governessy attire — pie-crust-collar blouse, pleated beige skirt and (wonder of wonders) a padded velvet Alice band. Clearly she had decided that backcombed "big hair" and generous embonpoint wouldn't strike a sufficiently serious note. Judging from the way she kept smoothing her skirt and patting her hair, she was feeling nervous and self-conscious about this visit to CID. Notwithstanding which, a look of terror passed across Doyle's face at her arrival, the youngster unlikely ever to forget Natalie's overtures to him in her man-eating days. Taking pity on him, Markham deputed him and Carruthers to sort out refreshments ('the good biscuits mind', instructed Noakes) and then dispatched them with Kate Burton to digest the latest developments (such as they were). Aware of Natalie's self-consciousness, he figured she could do without too large an audience for whatever insights she wished to impart.

The arrival of tea and the presence of Noakes seemed to give her confidence, as did Markham's deferential courtesy and keen attentiveness.

'What you said about the killer having an inferiority complex was most interesting,' he told her. 'Our psychological profiler tends to agree with your theory that such a mindset could well have fuelled a fascination with the occult.'

Clearly pleased, she confided tentatively, 'I heard something about one of the Hollingrove Park crowd, though I'm not sure if it really amounts to anything.'

'Why don't you let us be the judge of that, luv.' Noakes was expansive.

'Well, it came about like this.' She fidgeted nervously with the pleats of her skirt. 'Catrina Walsh — you know, the café manager — is doing the catering for me and Rick. She does jobs for private clients now and again. Very *professional* without people paying out a fortune.'

Markham heard the defensiveness in her voice. He reflected that most likely the formidable mother-in-law elect's advice weighed heavily in the cost-benefit equation and that, given her dislike of this alliance with the Noakeses, there was no great enthusiasm for a lavish show.

'How clever of you to decide on Ms Walsh,' the DI said smoothly. 'Given her connection with the park, she sounds like the ideal person to cater your handfasting ceremony.'

Natalie brightened immediately.

'That's right,' she said happily. 'With us having it in the garden of Old Carton Retreat Centre and Cat knowing the owners, it made sense to use her.'

'So Ms Walsh mentioned something about one of the people at Hollingrove?' Markham prompted gently.

'She said it was just a bit of gossip from way back,' the other continued hesitantly. 'Didn't make it sound like it was any big deal . . .'

Natalie was afraid of sounding foolish, Markham thought compassionately — afraid that bringing this titbit of information to them might make her look stupid. He suspected she was also worried she might be getting someone into serious trouble without having any solid grounds for her suspicion.

'Naturally, being a detective's daughter you took the view that maybe we ought to know,' he said in his suavest tone.

She took heart from this.

'Well, Cat said Suzanne Mackie was mad keen on John Sinnott back in the day.' In prehistoric times, she could have added. 'Only he wasn't interested, cos he had something going with Helen Priddy.' Doubt crept into her voice once again. 'When Dad said someone could've killed that little girl to get back at Mrs Priddy—'

'You wondered if that gave Mrs Mackie a motive,' Markham finished.

'Yeah.' The note of doubt was even more pronounced now. 'The thing is, sometimes Cat exaggerates and makes stuff up, kind of for effect . . . she's a bit of a show-off that way. She couldn't even say where she got the story.'

'Nat thought the girl might've been having her on,' Noakes explained. 'Making trouble like, to stir things up.' It sounded as though he could well imagine Catrina Walsh being prone to a spot of mischief-making.

'Have you ever had much to do with Mrs Mackie yourself, Natalie?' Markham enquired.

'Not really,' she admitted, 'though I've seen her down at *The Reader Shop* when I helped out there for a bit.'

During her hippie phase, Markham thought, suppressing a grin.

'Did you ever pick up on any signs of her being romantically interested in Mr Sinnott?' he asked, thinking this would be the kind of behaviour she was likely to notice.

'They just seemed like good friends. I mean, all the volunteers are well thick with each other . . . *cliquey*, if you know what I mean.' There was an undertone of pique, as though she resented not having been able to penetrate this tight-knit group.

'So you didn't notice Mrs Mackie nursing some kind of grand unrequited passion for Mr Sinnott?' the DI pressed.

'*Nah*. She's just one of those women who acts silly and cackles a lot around blokes.'

"Stones" and "glasshouses" came to mind on hearing Natalie Noakes, of all people, disdain feminine wiles and artifice!

'To be fair,' Natalie continued with a flash of memory, 'there's something a bit odd about old "Suzi", something not quite right.'

'How do you mean?' Markham was flatteringly interested.

'She can be dead intense, takes things the wrong way unless you're careful. And I remember seeing her lose her rag one day in The Storybarn. It was one of those school reading events. I went along with my friend Paula and her two little ones. Some kid was throwing a tantrum . . . kicking off big style. I remember seeing Mackie give her a shove.' Natalie's eyes gleamed maliciously. 'Made me think the old bat's Bo Peep number was a bit of an act.'

'Any other signs of aggression?' Markham probed. 'Of *violence?*'

Natalie shook her head reluctantly, honesty forcing her to admit, 'I can't imagine her actually *killing* anyone . . . And to be fair, some of the kids that day were a right pain in the ar— backside . . . Paula said they needed a good slap. Hardly surprising if Mackie got fed up.'

It didn't sound promising, the DI thought glumly.

'What did you mean by saying that Mrs Mackie struck you as intense?' he asked.

'Dunno . . . She just seemed kind of wide-eyed and star-struck whenever the museum bloke or one of his helpers went off on one about Stone Age stuff, like she bought into all of it. Got snappish with people in the shop if it looked like they didn't take it seriously, Stonehenge and Richard the wotsit,' she said vaguely, breezily jumbling up times and dates. 'I remember there was some teacher who came in to help one weekend and she bit her head off about something.'

Maureen Slattery, Markham thought automatically.

'Mind you,' Natalie continued with a judicious air, 'Cat said the woman who lived with Miss Henwood and the old fogeys who helped out in *The Reader Shop* were every bit as bad as Mackie. A massive revamp was coming down the tracks apparently, but the whole lot of 'em had fingers in their ears shouting *La la la . . . this ain't happening.*'

'Did anyone else mention that Mrs Mackie and John Sinnott had history . . . or suggest there was anything unbalanced about Mrs Mackie's behaviour, anything out of the ordinary?'

'Nah.' Natalie sounded regretful. 'I kind of got the feeling she's a bit possessive about everything to do with the park. But the gerries who run the show are *all* like that, so she's no different from the rest of them really. The museum bloke acts like he owns the place, and you wouldn't believe the airs Bernie the Bolt gives herself.'

'*Bernie the Bolt?* Sorry, Natalie, I'm not quite with you . . .' Markham said faintly.

'Bernadette wossname,' with a hint of impatience. 'Y'know, that old biddy who lived in the mansion house with Miss Henwood . . . the cousin or companion or whatever she called herself.'

Markham's lips twitched. '*Ah*, I believe you mean Bernadette Donovan.'

Sheepishly Noakes explained, 'I used to watch *The Golden Shot* as a kid . . . Bernie the Bolt were the fella who loaded them crossbows. Guess Nat musta heard me calling her that.'

'Sounds like it wasn't all sweetness and light behind the scenes at Hollingrove Park,' Markham mused.

'*Too right.*' There was suppressed venom in Natalie's voice. 'The boss man's PA was a right stuck-up cow, really threw her weight around before he decided he'd had enough and gave her the push.' Wistfully, she added, 'You need someone tactful with solid client-facing skills for a job like that,' an assertion which made Markham wonder if she had ever fancied her chances as Marion Kirkwood's successor.

Later, the DI and Noakes mulled the latest intel.

'Mackie's a bit flaky alright, but no more than the rest of 'em,' his wingman reasoned. 'Plus she went an' got married in the end, so it's not like she spent the rest of forever mooning after Sinnott.'

It was obvious that Noakes didn't see the widow as a killer, despite his wish that Natalie's input should be treated with due reverence.

'We'll have a chance to scrutinise Suzanne Mackie and the rest of them more closely at Tony Pardoe's funeral tomorrow, Noakesy,' the DI said, adding carefully, 'It was extremely useful hearing Natalie's take on things.'

Honour was satisfied, Noakes's mastiff's countenance radiating approval.

'You still reckon Priddy an' the other murders are linked, boss?' he asked.

Markham nodded, recalling those words of Eleanor Shaughnessy the previous day about how she believed Hollingrove Park possessed an irresistible attraction for the killer which made it the 'inevitable locus for eruptions of violence'. While the research data the psychologist cited in support was doubtless open to debate (Doyle and Carruthers hadn't appeared enthused by 'geographical circle theory', though Burton was predictably entranced), the DI felt instinctively that she was correct and that Mary Priddy's murderer was drawn to attack Pardoe and Davenport in the vicinity of their previous kill.

'Seems like how it don' matter who Sinnott were courting back then,' his friend pointed out using the old-fashioned phraseology of his youth. 'Unless we c'n make a link with Pardoe an' Davenport, we're stuffed.'

Never was a truer word spoken, Markham reflected. Some kind of tenuous "hunch" based on what Natalie had given them led nowhere. Furthermore, nothing had surfaced to show that the rabbity, over made-up Suzanne Mackie ever fell out with either Tony Pardoe or Loretta Davenport. Quite the opposite, in fact, seeing how Carruthers had reported that it was obvious she thought the sun shone out of the CEO's backside and Markham himself had observed nothing but cordiality towards Davenport. The woman presented as somewhat vacuous and fussily overeager to please, almost obsequious; but that was hardly a crime, certainly not enough to elevate her to the status of prime suspect. No doubt she shared the older volunteers' generalised resentment at the notion of being "put out to grass", expected to retire gracefully and make way for new blood. But as a motive for murder it fell a long way short, not least as Bernadette Donovan had said they were bound to 'come round in the end' courtesy of united efforts by Pardoe and Davenport to pour oil on troubled waters. If it came to it, Markham could more easily imagine spiky Catrina Walsh as a killer, or Bernadette Donovan herself given the woman's probable resentment of Pardoe. On the other hand, what Natalie had told them established some kind of connection between Suzanne Mackie, John Sinnott and Helen Priddy, a connection lacking in the case of the other two . . .

There was a weary slump to Markham's shoulders and a grimly taut look about his mouth that caused Noakes to eye him shrewdly.

The DI was only too well aware that he looked pinched and wan — what the other was wont to term 'like death warmed up' — and hardly projecting the kind of confidence required to bolster his team's morale.

'Mebbe Burton'll come up with summat from them background checks,' Noakes said encouragingly. 'Red flags from work; mebbe a failed relationship or two; p'raps a spell in the nuthouse . . .'

Markham gave a short hard bark of laughter.

'I imagine it's too much to hope that any of them had a psychotic break which landed them in the Newman,' he said, referring to the special hospital situated behind Bromgrove General on the outskirts of Medway.

Noakes pursed his lips. 'Burton's like a bloodhound,' he said. 'If there's owt dodgy going on with any of 'em, she's bound to winkle it out.'

The ghost of a smile hovered about Markham's lips at this. Bloodhound was an apt description of Kate Burton once she had the bit between her teeth.

The DI gave himself an internal shake, realising that he needed to get a grip. Judging by Noakes's concerned expression, it was obvious his wingman thought his despondency arose from 'Trouble At Mill' — that Burton's convent scheme had badly unsettled him with the result that he'd had a row with Olivia about it.

Knowing Noakes as he did, he imagined the whole weird triangle thing was a source of utmost bafflement to his friend, who would doubtless maintain that no one in their right mind would look twice at Kate Burton if they had Olivia Mullen waiting back at home. Noakes was fond of Burton — ready these days to concede that she was a "good egg" and had loosened up considerably in the last few years — but, in thrall as he was to Olivia's ethereal personal charms and sparky wit, there was little likelihood of him subscribing to the idea that Burton could represent any sort of romantic competition. Fortunately, it was tacitly understood between himself and the guvnor that it didn't *do* to yammer about emotional stuff — only sissies did that — so Markham reflected with relief that they could park the problem for now.

'C'mon, let's check in with Kate and see what she's got for us,' he said, abandoning the tangle of his thoughts. 'It's Mr Pardoe's funeral and wake tomorrow, so we could do with a strategy.'

There would then be the chance to observe Suzanne Mackie more closely, the DI told himself.

A chance to decide if *she* was the serpent uncoiling in Hollingrove Park, or if someone else carried the poison, a tiny invisible sac of it just waiting to be discovered . . . if only they looked hard enough.

## CHAPTER 11: BREAKTHROUGH

The tall, narrow church of St Edward the Confessor (patron saint of those who walked alone, as Noakes helpfully reminded the DI) was a greystone, neo-gothic, sooty monstrosity on the outskirts of Old Carton. Squeezed between a community centre and an office supplies warehouse, its architecture was not such as to raise the spirits, Markham thought as he and Noakes stood on the pavement outside at 10.15 on Thursday 28 March. The Requiem Mass (for the Henwoods were Roman Catholics) was due to start at 11, but as was their wont on such occasions, the two men had arrived early to 'get a feel for the place'. Noakes was privately proud of Markham's enthusiasm for 'mouldy old churches', feeling that this characteristic endowed his boss with unusual distinction.

The day was overcast, with a cold drizzle falling and sullen, pewter-coloured clouds scudding overhead, in keeping with the sombreness of the occasion. As ordained by the council, the cremation service was to be a strictly private affair with mourners directed to The Storybarn in Hollingrove Park for a 'cold collation'.

'Cold collation . . . whassthat when it's at home?' Noakes asked suspiciously.

'Relax, Noakesy. It's just posh-speak for a buffet.'

The other's expression cleared at this assurance that "Operation All You Can Eat" was still on. Markham knew better than to enjoin self-restraint on his friend or issue any injunctions against 'being a gannet', since Noakes positively gloried in the fact that his new (usefully opaque) status as an independent contractor rendered him immune from Sidney's wrath. No doubt, he told himself wryly, he would come in for a vicarious share of the DCI's displeasure should his boss be treated to the spectacle of Noakes shovelling up assorted savouries. At least the private investigator's attire was unexceptional (apart from the duffle coat, but you couldn't have everything).

The interior of the church came as a pleasant surprise to Markham after the late-Victorian horrors outside, boasting five bay nave arcades of pointed moulded arches in gleaming white stone supported by white marble columns on either side of pine pews. The atmosphere was airy and light-filled, the effect being enhanced by the soaring white stone sanctuary with large rose window in its gable. Its double row of carpeted crimson steps and gilt tabernacle stood out vividly against this backdrop.

'Too much white,' Noakes muttered. "S'like a bleeding aqueduct with all them arches.'

Even he had to admit, however, that the elaborately carved white painted reredos behind the altar had a certain charm, with four medieval saints each under its own gabled canopy, two on either side of the soaring ebony crucifix and corresponding icons in a row of smaller carved niches beneath. The glorious turquoise, green and red facets of the traceried rose window, its circle of clover-shaped panels showing the twelve apostles surrounding an inner wheel of prophets, irradiated the sanctuary with a luminescence that recalled some biblical city of sapphire and rainbow.

'You'll make yourself dizzy staring up like that,' Noakes said gruffly.

'"Had I a tongue in eloquence as rich. As is the colouring in fancy's loom, t'were all too poor to utter the least part of that enchantment,"' Markham quoted softly.

Noakes's face fell, with the look it assumed when he feared it was time to batten down the hatches seeing as the guvnor was spouting poetry.

'One of them Romantic poets?' he asked warily.

The DI grinned. 'No, Dante. And don't worry, I'm not going to "go off on one".' Suddenly his expression turned bleak. 'Just some lines I remember Liv reciting one time.' The despondent tone of his voice as he mentioned his partner confirmed he was nursing some raw, unhealed wound that ached and throbbed.

Noakes cleared his throat and waved a pudgy hand towards the side aisles whose walls were lined by numerous alcoves containing plaster saints illuminated by votive candles. 'Don' think much of them,' he groused. 'Why do holy folk always have to look as if they're paralysed or having a stroke?'

It did the trick and Markham chuckled, always amused by his friend's sturdy Protestantism which he suspected was bolstered by *Maria Monk* style fantasies about Catholic iniquity.

'You can't have everything, Noakesy, and at least the Counter-Reformation architecture's pretty uplifting.'

'Oh aye.' His portly wingman pivoted, squinting at the paired clear glass lancet windows in the nave. 'They should do summat about the bird droppings,' he said firmly. 'Spoils the look.'

The two men did a leisurely circuit of the church, Noakes venturing that he reckoned King Richard II would have loved all the gilt and trappings — the galleon-shaped hanging lamps, memorial tablets and tiny shrines to Our Lady shoehorned into spare corners.

'*Hey*, there's John the Baptist,' he exclaimed, spying a framed painting near the back of the church. 'According to old Devenish's spiel, Ricky were *well* into him — had one of his teeth as a relic.'

Trust his friend to have latched on to the more grisly aspects of the story, Markham thought with grim amusement.

'Hmm . . . the plaque says it's a reproduction by one of those obscure, impossible to pronounce Dutch artists — I'll give it a go, though: Geertgen tot Sint Jans, lay brother of the Order of St John. Died in his twenties. Reproduction of his panel *John in the Wilderness* . . . the haloed lamb represents the Lamb of God, his special symbol.'

'It ain't zackly a wilderness, though,' Noakes pointed out prosaically. 'Looks almost like Hollingrove Park with the trees an' sunshine an' stream . . . little birds an' rabbits an' all,' he said peering closer as he took in the scenery.

It was true, thought Markham. The delightful pastoral backdrop held nothing of the desert, resembling more some delicious green sward out of a fairytale, with rich grassy glades and picturesque copse in the background. Even the lamb looked more like the saint's pet, to be scooped up in his cloak, rather than a solemn reminder of Christ's sacrifice. Maybe the painting looked forward to Paradise and the eternal reward awaiting believers . . .

'John's got chuffing *enormous* feet,' Noakes interrupted his thoughts. 'Right old clodhoppers.'

'They're crossed at the ankles — maybe a nod to the crucifixion,' Markham hazarded.

'Poor bloke looks proper depressed,' Noakes continued. 'Sitting there in that ratty monk's getup with his head on his hand like he don' believe in hisself anymore. Weird that, seeing he's meant to be warming 'em all up for Jesus, the main event like.'

He meant it to sound as though the Baptist was some sort of divine support act, Markham reflected, trying not to laugh.

'Somehow he ain't impressive an' heroic,' Noakes groped for a comparison, 'not a bit like when Michael York played him in that film.' He thought hard for a minute. 'More as if he's having a mid-life crisis. Looks kind of small an' puny, sort of *swamped* by all that countryside. Yeah,' Noakes delivered his verdict with finality, 'jus' some saddo, bit inadequate an' ordinary . . . not glamorous or uplifted or owt like that.'

He thought back to the figure in the diptych at the museum. 'He should be big and strong with long hair and beard . . . all ready to stick it to sinners.'

Now Markham *did* laugh. 'He was meant to be a wild-man wandering round in camelhair and living off locusts, not some athletic male model!'

Noakes was mildly indignant at this but pleased to see the cloud had lifted from Markham's countenance.

'Wonder what we're in for,' he muttered as the under-taker's people arrived with oak trestle, flowers and orders of service, the two men sliding into a pew at the rear of the church. 'Hope it's not any of that soppy kumbaya rubbish.'

The DI couldn't help but be diverted, reflecting that given his friend's character, it wasn't surprising he favoured the Boanerges style of preacher who could deliver 'marrowy' sermons on hell fire and eternity, or sorting the wheat from the chaff. Certainly, he was not enamoured of the Reverend Simon Duthie's charismatic tendencies and had been heard by outraged parishioners to mutter 'Take your partners for the last gospel' when the priest mounted his pulpit.

Duthie's choice of modern hymns and recessionals also didn't go down well, sparking one of Noakes's most infamous interjections. '*Voici le résultat des votes du Church of England: Morning Has Broken, Nul Points!*' he had rumbled in his execrable cod French.

'Give the poor man a break,' was Markham's plea. 'It's not his fault he belongs to the evangelical wing of the church.'

'You won't say that when he decides to bring in limbo dancing or sticks a helter-skelter in the porch,' the other countered darkly.

The Reverend Duthie was by no means Noakes's only clerical enemy, since Markham suspected it would be a long time before his friend was forgiven for various faux-pas with visiting Irish ministers. 'Did you hear about the Kerryman who took his car in for its first service an' crashed it into the pulpit?' was one quip that had conspicuously failed to break the ice last St Patrick's Day.

Just remembering these comical eccentricities momentarily lifted the profound gloom that had descended on him with Olivia's departure. Having George Noakes at his side was a guarantee against despair.

He was reasonably sure, whatever Noakes's fears, that *this* occasion promised to adhere to the tribal rites of the Catholic Church, his opinion confirmed by a dignified sacristan who came out to prepare the altar.

Noakes watched proceedings with avid curiosity, no doubt engaged in an inner monologue about papist eccentricities. Markham, however, found his thoughts returning to his friend's commentary on John the Baptist.

*Mid-life crisis . . . puny . . . inadequate . . . ordinary . . . not glamorous . . . mid-life crisis.*

Why did he feel the words possessed some significance that might, if he only concentrated hard enough, unravel the mystery of these murders.

But the congregation was arriving and he had to let it drop.

\* \* \*

The funeral passed for him in the amorphous blur invariably induced by swathes of black mourning.

His suspects were all there.

Malcolm Devenish and Tom Burke with an almost clerical air in their dark suits.

Bernadette Donovan composed and elegant, her head becomingly draped (to Noakes's obvious fascination) in a black lace mantilla. As the sole family representative, she took her place with great dignity in the front left-hand pew.

Catrina Walsh in very high heels and a too-short, too-tight, black two-piece, hair flowing about her shoulders as though in a TRESemmé ad.

Maureen Slattery in a simple black jersey dress with jacket, her hair coiled into a neat chignon.

Suzanne Mackie sporting a fussy befrilled outfit of the kind Muriel Noakes would have favoured, teetering on high heels and wearing a monster fedora skewered by some kind of feather.

John Sinnott was loyally escorting her, a firm hand beneath her elbow. In the circumstances, it took some guts to come, Markham thought, hoping the *Gazette* photographer he had spotted slinking in alongside Michael Brophy (quite raffish in a belted gaberdine raincoat) wouldn't manage to snap the poor fellow, whose height and good looks marked him out in the little troupe of volunteers.

It was a surprise to see Jason Quirk and Marion Kirkwood, muffled respectively in charcoal overcoat and black cashmere pashmina. Judging by the hostile looks the latter shot Maureen Slattery, whatever ill-feeling had surfaced at the Easter Tea Party still lingered.

The congregation was on the small side, but there were pockets of smartly attired business people and a smattering of conservatively dressed elderly parishioners to swell the ranks.

Markham felt despondent as the Requiem Mass wore on. What had he really expected to see, he asked himself. Watching the body language of Suzanne Mackie and John Sinnott, one would only think them old friends . . .

Something of the church's earlier radiant aura was dispelled when the electric lights came on, but as the skies darkened ominously outside, the extra illumination was welcome.

The celebrant Fr Aidan Kennedy, bluff and balding, made a decent fist of things in the circumstances. As the sermon got underway, it was clear he aimed to be inclusive. Welcoming those of other denominations, he intoned, 'Different religious traditions share the characteristics of the patriarchs: Abraham stands for Faith, Jacob represents Sacrifice and Isaac literally means Laughter.'

'I'd settle for the first two of 'em,' Noakes muttered darkly, this being his dour assessment of such determinedly upbeat joviality. 'Bet they come from yards around to hear this.'

'Shut up, Noakesy, he's doing his best,' Markham admonished out of the side of his mouth.

'He should jus' plug everyone into the Holy Ghost an' then get out of the way,' came the surprising retort, which struck Markham as an interesting commentary on the preacher's art.

Noakes always enjoyed it if non-churchgoers didn't know whether to stand up or sit down, bobbing up and down or crouching and kneeling at the wrong moments. 'Church is pretty much a spectator sport for Sarge,' as Carruthers put it waspishly. On this occasion, however, Noakes was destined to be disappointed, since it appeared everyone either knew the form or was swift to copy the initiated.

Kate Burton, needless to say, appeared absorbed by the readings and homily, listening attentively as the celebrant discussed the gospel parable about 'having life and having it more abundantly'. Was that what she looked forward to in her convent, Markham wondered. The message was somewhat confusedly mixed in with meandering metaphors of vines, branches and pruning which had Doyle and Carruthers groaning softly under their breath. Their anguish at this, however, was as nothing compared to their embarrassment during the hymns when Noakes responded enthusiastically to the injunction that worshippers should "raise ye a joyful voice unto the Lord", doing so in a fashion that saw Sidney and various other high-ranking attendees swivel round to stare. At the recessional *Come every pious heart*, the two young sergeants had their revenge on their portly colleague. *Come every pie-ous heart*, they enunciated pointedly to Burton's scandalised dismay.

As the team gathered in the church forecourt (Sidney & Co having swept out behind the coffin with assorted councillors and business folk), Markham observed his sergeants' visible relief to be back out in the fresh air, then reflected wryly that congregants rarely left the house of God without some anxious longing for escape.

There had been no eulogy and (more surprisingly) no tribute from the Hollingrove Park or council contingents.

Nor was there any mention of Loretta Davenport or Cathy Price other than a veiled reference to 'our departed brothers and sisters in Christ'. Yet, in spite of all, Fr Kennedy had done his best to infuse the occasion with a degree of spiritual fervour, touching the DI with his final prayer from a poem of George Herbert which described death as 'going from earth to paradise as from one room to another'. He thought with a pang how much Olivia would have liked that before turning with forced heartiness to his colleagues. 'Better head for The Storybarn,' he instructed them after they had watched the hearse on its way.

'*Hey*, isn't that the nun from the convent place?' Doyle exclaimed suddenly.

Burton followed his gaze. 'It's Sr Renata,' she said. 'How nice of her to come and represent Maryvale. You go ahead, boss,' she urged. 'My car's here . . . I'll catch you up once I've had a quick word.'

It struck Markham that the nun looked bothered about something, but perhaps it was simply dismay at the prospect of being caught in a summer shower, great flat drops falling out of the clouds as thunder rumbled overhead.

Without further ado, the team headed for their cars.

\* \* \*

The Storybarn 'collation' — held in the grandly named Banqueting Suite — was in fact as substantial a spread as Noakes's heart could desire, with a wide range of sandwich choices, salads, savoury options (including, joy of joys, pork pies aplenty) and sweets (brownies, lemon drizzle, scones and fruit cake). Tea and coffee were in generous supply along with soft drinks but no alcohol, which at least spared the two sergeants a repeat of what Carruthers wittily called 'Mocktail-gate'.

Everybody behaved disappointingly well, however, though no doubt the presence of the police including the head honchos (a sea of epaulettes) and the two recent murders had something to do with the subdued and wary atmosphere. The fact of its being a 'dry' funeral, moreover, appeared to inhibit people's tongues, even Suzanne Mackie failing to exhibit her usual volubility, though her glassy-eyed expression made Markham wonder if she had fortified herself before the obsequies.

'No chance of getting any gossip,' Doyle muttered. 'At least not unless we can get the café woman or that teacher on their own.'

There were some suspects, the DI reflected wryly, that his young sergeants would always find it a pleasure to interview. Certainly, Catrina Walsh and Maureen Slattery looked young and blooming beside the older mourners.

Several of the business contingent and councillors headed off early after murmuring polite condolences to Bernadette Donovan, followed in short order by Sidney, Bretherton and Ebury-Clarke who were visibly, as Noakes put it sourly, gagging for a few stiff ones. The scorching glance Sidney shot Markham's wingman upon leaving suggested that his inroads on the edibles had been duly noted.

Kate Burton made her reappearance, something about the way she looked immediately alerting Markham that his fellow DI might be about to announce a breakthrough.

Noakes, too, noticed her air of suppressed excitement.

'Summat's happened, right?' he prompted her softly. 'Summat to do with that little nun?'

'Better wait till we get back to the station, Sarge,' she replied levelly, though her cheeks were pink with elation.

At that moment, there was a terrific crash of lightning which suffused the interior of the banqueting suite with an eerie glow that, to Markham's overwrought perception, transformed the mourners' faces into sickly-green gargoyles like creatures from Hades. Outside, the boughs of great oaks and beeches were sobbing and creaking violently as though mysteriously aware that the final drama of the investigation was about to break.

Quietly and unobtrusively, the gang made their way out.

*This was it*, Markham told himself, the blood singing in his ears and the throb of his heart so strong it seemed that everyone must hear it.

Tony Pardoe's body was by now turned to dust, while Loretta Davenport lay stiff and silent in a hospital morgue. But he meant to throw open their graves and recover the past so they, and perhaps the ghosts of little Mary Priddy and Cathy Price, could all four finally be free.

# CHAPTER 12: AID FROM ABOVE

Arriving back at the station in a thunderstorm, it was a thoroughly bedraggled little crew who tramped through CID and into Markham's office.

Despite their discomfort and steaming suits, the gang was alight with anticipation to hear Kate Burton's news.

'I arranged for a car to pick Sr Renata up from St Edward the Confessor and bring her straight here,' the DI told Markham.

'In case she did a runner,' Noakes chortled.

Such was Burton's eagerness, that she barely noticed the irreverence.

'If she had something to tell us, why not come to the station before now?' Carruthers demanded with his customary impatience.

'Apparently she only found out about it yesterday.'

'Found out about *what?*' Doyle, too, was on tenterhooks.

'She couldn't speak freely outside the church,' Burton replied. 'There were too many people listening. But she said one of the other sisters had seen something that could be significant.'

'*One of the nuns!*' Doyle sounded deflated, as though he didn't count on anything useful reaching them from that particular quarter.

Carruthers had a similar reaction. Probably one of the old dears fancied herself as a crime-solving nun, like Sister Boniface from that TV series. And, God help them, now they'd have to listen politely to some far-fetched yarn.

When Sr Renata was ushered into Markham's office, however, Carruthers became more hopeful as the nun, having declined the offer of refreshments, briskly commenced her narrative.

'Members of the community who need nursing care are accommodated on the third floor of Maryvale House. Ideally, we want to keep them inside the enclosure — that's to say our part of the building,' she explained, seeing that Doyle and Carruthers were baffled by 'enclosure'.

Noakes had caught on quickly. 'She means the extension,' he told them. 'The nuns' private bit out the back.' Then, 'Why don't you have your own hospital section . . . infirmary thingy? Seems only fair after all that time spent down on your knees praying for folk an' . . . scrubbing floors an' peeling vegetables.' He had obviously cottoned on to the concept of "manual work", Markham thought, trying not to catch Burton's eye.

'Our current infirmary is in the process of being remodelled,' Sr Renata said, taking Noakes's inquisition in her stride. 'So it's only a temporary arrangement. There's a lift in the main house and, as things stand, it's less disruptive than our trying to provide care in the middle of building works.'

Carruthers was divided between his anxiety to be respectful and a growing impatience.

'So where does this fit in with Loretta Davenport?' he asked.

'I'm coming to that.' Clearly the nun was not going to be rushed.

Despite the tension in the room, Markham could not help but be amused by the long appraising look she levelled at Carruthers, who cast his eyes down meekly like a refractory schoolboy.

'Sr Mary Annunciata's recovering from a bout of pleurisy. One of the carers from social services who came in to look after her let slip about Loretta Davenport, how she'd been found murdered in the park.' Sr Renata's lips tightened. 'Really she shouldn't have been gossiping like that, but perhaps it's providential—'

'*Providential?*' Like Carruthers, Doyle was desperate to move things along.

Sr Renata was imperturbable, weighing her words carefully. 'Maggie — that's the carer — showed Sr Mary the local paper which had a piece about the murders along with Ms Davenport's picture.'

The atmosphere in the room was now taut as a bowstring.

'Well, Sister said she remembered seeing the woman in the picture only the other day from her window.'

'*From her window . . .* how come?' Noakes was baffled.

'Her wheelchair was over by the window. There's a lovely view of the park from there, the south side where it backs on to the Hollingrove Triangle. Sister loves to sit and watch people walking their dogs, buying ice creams, that kind of thing. Anyway, she saw Ms Davenport . . . noticed her because she seemed to be having an animated discussion with another woman. At first she wasn't sure who the other person was, but then they turned round and she recognised them.' She paused deliberately, smoothing the folds of her habit.

*Talk about milking the drama*, Carruthers thought crossly, but, given the earlier reproof, he made no attempt to move things along.

The nun was so cool and precise that she would make an excellent witness, Markham decided.

Sr Renata resumed, 'Mrs Mackie helps out at St John the Baptist— '

Noakes cut in, 'But how would this Sr Mary know her? I mean, ain't the nuns' chapel screened off from the church so nobody can gawp at 'em? Ain't that why you have the fence thingy . . . the grille wotsit . . .'

Markham suspected that the innocent looking nun rather enjoyed watching Noakes tie himself in knots.

'The convent also has a room where the nuns can meet people from outside,' she replied demurely. 'There's the grille and a curtain which they can draw back to talk to visitors. Mrs Mackie came several times with other lay helpers, so Sr Mary had a good look at her on those occasions.' Her tone dry and amused, she added, 'Sister hasn't *always* been sick, Mr Noakes, though she's become much frailer of late. As I said, there's nothing wrong with her powers of observation — she's quite emphatic that it was Mrs Mackie she saw. It was just over a week ago, around 2 p.m. on Wednesday 21 March, and unusually there was no one else near the Triangle — no other walkers or passers-by — so the two women stood out and it looked from their expressions and body language that things were getting pretty heated.'

Again, she paused impressively.

'When I finally heard about this, I realised the police needed to know.'

'Why'd it take so long?' Noakes asked. 'I mean to say, with Hollingrove Park being in the news, you'd think this Maggie would've joined the dots.'

Another compression of the lips. 'Maggie assumed that Sr Mary probably mistook Ms Davenport for someone else. I suspect she was only listening to her with half an ear. Sr Mary only mentioned it to me yesterday evening. I think up till then it hadn't occurred to her that what she saw might be significant, seeing as Mrs Mackie's one of our parishioners. Also, she's a very . . . *trusting* . . . soul . . . slow to imagine ill of people.'

Unlike Sr Renata who was clearly a far tougher proposition, Markham thought, suppressing a smile: realistic and downright despite her calling, a veritable religious "bruiser".

'How good is Sr Mary's eyesight?' Doyle demanded. 'Easy to get it wrong from up at a window,' he added dubiously.

'She wears spectacles but her distance vision is very good. More to the point, though, Mrs Mackie's dress sense is quite distinctive,' the nun replied evenly. 'Apparently, she was wearing a floral knitted poncho embroidered with poppies . . . Sr Mary described it perfectly. In any event, I've seen Mrs Mackie in that same outfit.' Once again, her lips thinned. '*Most* unsuitable for cleaning church brass work.'

Markham waited, sensing there was more to come.

'Hearing what Sister saw made up my mind to come to you. You see, I'd had my doubts about Mrs Mackie.'

'How so, Sister?' he prompted her courteously.

'There's something not quite right with the woman. Our parish priest at St John the Baptist recently told me she's one of those church "groupies", by which he means tiresome women he finds it difficult to shake off. But more than that, apparently, there's been a history of her making trouble for female parishioners she thinks are too close to the clergy — she tries to see them off, if you like, by spreading malicious gossip or making poisonous remarks about inappropriate behaviour.'

Hearing this, Markham recalled what Natalie Noakes had said.

*There's something a bit odd about old "Suzi" . . . something not quite right . . . dead intense . . . takes things the wrong way unless you're careful . . . made me think the old bat's Bo Peep number was a bit of an act.*

Not for the first time, he marvelled at Natalie's gift for picking up on traits the casual observer was likely to miss. Perhaps she had missed her calling and Noakes should consider recruiting her as his Girl Friday! Judging by his friend's complacent expression, he, too, was remembering Natalie's summing up.

'Father Flynn's the most *charitable* man,' the nun continued, with an inflexion that suggested she considered this particular virtue to be vastly overrated. 'Positively *saintly* . . . hates to think badly of anyone. I believe that's why he couldn't make up his mind to say anything before now, probably hoping I might be able to have a word . . . get to the bottom of things.' Markham suspected she regarded this as a typical instance of male cowardice. 'He felt maybe Mrs Mackie needed *professional* help.'

'Prob'ly fancied your boss woman for the job,' Noakes ventured.

This elicited a wintry smile. 'Of course, our *Prioress* Mother Augustine gives *spiritual direction* to a wide range of people, but it seemed to me from what Father Flynn said that something more *clinical* was in order.'

'Yeah, I c'n see how a cosy little chat an' a cuppa wouldn't cut it,' Noakes agreed cordially as Burton audibly winced. (Sr Renata smiled kindly at her as though to say, *We all have our crosses to bear*).

Hastily, Markham asked, 'So Mrs Mackie is familiar to you. I take it you didn't know Loretta Davenport, weren't aware if she and Mrs Mackie had previously crossed paths?'

'That's correct. As far as Ms Davenport is concerned, I only know what was published in the *Gazette*.'

Markham thought hard. 'You said Sr Mary thought they were having an *animated* discussion. Did she mean animated as in angry? Or was this just an intense conversation?'

'Sister couldn't really be sure about that . . . she thought their faces looked cross but couldn't swear to it.'

'You've been most helpful, Sr Renata,' Markham said warmly. 'If possible, we'd like to speak to Sister Mary Annunciata when you feel she's up to an interview.'

'Just telephone Maryvale and I'll arrange it, Inspector.' Judging by the gleam in her eye, he imagined this would prove an agreeable diversion from the daily routine.

'It ain't enough,' Noakes pronounced after the visitor had departed. He turned to Burton. 'Don' want to rain on your parade, luv,' he said kindly, 'but even if Mackie's a bit of a screwball on account of that stalker-type stuff with the padre — warning off the competition an' all that — she ain't the sort to start offing folk in the park—'

'Even assuming she had the strength for it,' Carruthers concluded.

Burton wasn't going down without a fight.

'What if she'd set her sights on Tony Pardoe and he turned her down?'

*That* brought them up short.

'Go on,' Carruthers said slowly.

'If he rejected her, that could've triggered something. And then she went after Loretta because Loretta and Pardoe were best friends and she hated that—'

'Or Loretta could've been on to Mackie,' Doyle cut in excitedly.' Twigged that something was "off" and tackled her.'

'Loretta Davenport was the type who'd have come straight round to us if she thought Mackie had anything to do with Pardoe's death,' Carruthers demurred. 'No messing around.'

'She might not have suspected Mackie of murder at that point,' Burton replied. 'It could be that Mackie was making mischief — gossiping about her and Pardoe — and she simply asked her to stop.'

'Only Mackie decided this meant Davenport was getting suspicious so she'd be better off dead,' Doyle reasoned.

Noakes took over. 'Mebbe Loretta jus' figured there were summat wrong with Suzanne Mackie . . . had some vague, unformed suspicions floating round in her head that Mackie were a wrong 'un but didn't seriously believe she could've done murder or owt like that.' He turned to Carruthers. 'I mean, it's like you said, Mackie wouldn't be physically up to it.'

'Dimples said not to rule out a woman,' Markham pointed out.

'Yes, and the tox screen showed alcohol in Pardoe's system,' Burton said eagerly. 'So if she got him drunk—'

'But she still wouldn't have had the strength to lug him halfway across the greenhouse and stretch him out across that big stone,' Doyle said defeatedly. 'Same with Davenport. Even with an adrenalin rush, posing her like that'd need some muscle.'

'What if she had help?' Markham said quietly.

Three pairs of eyes stared at him. '*Help?*' Doyle repeated stupidly.

'Dr Shaughnessy said she couldn't rule out joint enterprise,' the DI reminded them calmly, 'particularly if there was some kind of shared obsession with the occult and similar narcissistic traits.'

'What about Priddy?' Noakes demanded, changing tack. 'Where does Mackie fit into *that*?'

'Bear with me,' Markham said. 'According to what Catrina Walsh told Natalie, there was a time when Suzanne Mackie was apparently "mad keen" on John Sinnott . . . only he wasn't interested because he was involved with Mary Priddy's mother Helen, a relationship which didn't work out. Isn't it possible that *she* could have killed the little girl through rage at the child's mother for thwarting her chances of a relationship with Sinnott?'

Doyle leaned forward. 'Hold on, boss . . . I thought Dr Shaughnessy said it was a case of displaced hostility and that fitted *Sinnott* as the killer cos Helen Priddy went and dumped him.'

'She talked about a fractured ego and displaced hostility but didn't say that meant it had to be Sinnott.' As ever, Burton's powers of recall could be relied upon.

'*Exactly,* Kate,' the DI said approvingly. 'So, you see, there's no reason it couldn't have been Suzanne Mackie punishing her rival, as well as making trouble for Sinnott, because in the circumstances suspicion was *bound* to fall on him.'

Markham allowed the silence that followed to stretch as his colleagues absorbed this.

'What were Mrs Mackie's alibis for the two murders, Kate?' Markham asked. 'Remind me.'

'Working on a newsletter the night Mr Pardoe was murdered, no witnesses,' she said crisply. 'In and out of *The Reader Shop* the afternoon Loretta died, but no one had eyes on her the whole time. It was just the older volunteers around and they were vague about timings.'

'And for Priddy?' Noakes butted in.

Burton frowned. 'Suzanne Mackie wasn't one of those questioned in the original investigation. As far as I remember from background checks, she was a student back in the eighties, Ancient History or something like that; hoped to do a Ph.D. but that never came to anything; did admin at the university; then later married an accountant who died several years back. All pretty unexciting and ordinary.'

'Look, forget Priddy for a moment . . . If we say Mackie killed Pardoe an' Davenport, then *who the chuff helped her?*' Noakes burst out, still struggling to get his head round the concept of joint enterprise.

Markham sighed. 'That I can't say.'

'So, where's it leave us then?' His wingman's corned beef complexion turned even redder with frustration.

'We need to bait a trap, Noakesy,' the DI said steadily.

'As in, get her to confess to one of 'em from Maryvale?' his wingman scoffed. 'Bleeding *Sister Act.*'

'Now *there's* a thought.'

Markham's tone was silky-smooth. Together with the sudden flare in his keen, unwavering gaze, it made Burton shiver. 'Sr Renata has her head well screwed on and appears to have seen through Suzanne Mackie,' he said.

'You ain't *serious*, guv?' Noakes asked incredulously.

'Never more so,' was the laconic reply. 'Assuming, of course, that she's up for it — and providing Sidney and Plus Thomas agree.'

'*Plus Thomas?*' Doyle goggled at Markham like he thought the guvnor was losing his wits.

'He means Bishop Thomas Kelly, the suffragan RC bishop for Old Carton,' Burton explained. 'He usually puts the sign of a cross before his signature hence "Plus" Thomas.'

'Very funny,' Noakes sniffed as though to say, *I make the jokes round here.*

Markham laced long, tapering fingers under his chin. 'Technically, I believe the bish also has responsibility for convents in his diocese, so best to get his approval.'

'Sidney'll never wear it,' Doyle breathed, almost overcome by the audacity of the scheme.

Markham caught Burton's eye.

'He will if we present Mackie as our prime suspect,' the DI retorted with a grim smile, 'all neatly packaged with a bow on top.'

His fellow DI whipped on her glasses and produced the trusty notebook out in a trice. 'What do you want us to do now, boss?'

'Speak to that priest Sr Renata mentioned—'

'Father Flynn.'

'That's the one. Find out as much as you can about the stalking and other unusual behaviour. Take a statement from Sr Mary Annunciata — once you've got permission from the Prioress — and have a chat with Catrina Walsh about Mackie's history with John Sinnott.'

'Isn't there a risk that Walsh might tip Mackie off?' Burton asked.

'Not if you give the impression no one's looking at Mackie as a suspect . . . you're just trying to build up a clearer picture of *Sinnott*: his character, relationships with women, that kind of thing. Come at it obliquely and see if you can get her to spill the beans about Mackie, as in, providing evidence of instability. Oh, and while you're at it, try and find out what was the score between Mackie and Tony Pardoe — was it a case of hero-worship, did he ever have trouble fending her off, stuff like that.' With a wry smile, he said, 'If Doyle and Carruthers mount a charm offensive and make it look like they enjoy chatting up an attractive witness, I'm sure Ms Walsh can be coaxed into indiscretion.'

The two young sergeants shuffled their feet self-consciously but were clearly not displeased at hearing this.

'Loretta and Mackie seemed perfectly friendly when we saw them with the volunteers at the café,' Burton mused, 'that time when we visited the museum.'

'Yet, according to Sr Mary, later that same day — Wednesday 21st — Loretta confronted Mackie at the Hollingworth Triangle,' Markham said, 'so there must have been some sort of undercurrent. With luck, Catrina may have picked up on that.'

'She's definitely our best hope for a bitchy backstory,' Burton agreed.

Markham could see his fellow DI had bought into the strategy. 'I think provided you're *casual* about it all, and she thinks you're just gathering more background, you may get something useful out of her.'

'We'll check out Mackie's time working at the university, see if there were any issues with other staff, any time off work, medical problems,' Burton continued.

'Good. Also, have a look at the Druid and Folklore Societies to see if she made any ripples there. Again, we need details that will allow us to present the DCI with a pattern of unbalanced behaviour.'

Noakes fell naturally into his role of Greek chorus.

'Sidney won't like it, what with Mackie being a respectable citizen.'

*Understatement of the year*, Markham thought grimly.

'We'll consult Dr Shaughnessy and see what she reckons to Mackie as our prime suspect,' he said. 'Hopefully, she can weave it all into a profile that will satisfy Sidney, in addition to helping us come up with a script for Sr Renata.'

'You *really* think Mackie'll cough to that little nun?' Noakes asked disbelievingly.

'Why shouldn't she, provided we can bring her to the tipping point?' Markham countered.

'You're not planning to stake out the convent are you, guv?' Doyle sounded equally mistrustful. 'I mean, bug the rooms or cells or whatever they call 'em?'

'Take it easy, Sergeant, this *isn't* a replay of *Nuns on the Run*.'

His ruefully indulgent, quizzical tone made Doyle colour up to the roots of his ginger thatch.

The DI took pity on him.

'Don't forget, Sr Renata's an *extern sister*.'

'Externs are like the guardians of the enclosure,' Burton took over. 'They liaise between the enclosed nuns and outside — do the shopping, welcome visitors, take messages, look after guests — so that the contemplative sisters can concentrate on prayer and worship.' Seeing that Doyle still looked bemused, she added, kindly, 'They wear the habit and are bound by similar rules, but their role is more, well, *practical*.'

'She sounded fairly practical alright,' Carruthers conceded. Quicker than Doyle to grasp the implications of "extern", he continued, 'You're not aiming to have her meet up with Mackie in the convent then, guv?'

'No.' Markham paused deliberately. 'I was thinking more of the *park*.'

Watching their faces closely, he pursued the argument. 'It's clear from what we've learned of Suzanne Mackie that the park has a powerful hold on her imagination. If she killed Mary Priddy there, then she's even more likely to have a superstitious attraction to the place.'

'You'd think that would be enough to make her stay away from it forever,' Doyle said with a shudder.

'She has strong pagan sympathies,' Markham pointed out, 'as well as being conventionally religious. The two aren't mutually exclusive, as we've seen with Miss Henwood . . . also Malcolm Devenish, Tom Burke and any number of others.' He allowed this to sink in before continuing. 'As Dr Shaughnessy pointed out, we're dealing with a histrionic narcissist whose mental pathology falls outside the scope of normal responses.'

Burton snapped her notebook shut. 'What time's the next briefing, guv?'

'Give me what you've got first thing tomorrow. Then I'll present Sidney with the whole caboodle, get him to give us the green light and — assuming the convent's onside — supply Sr Renata with a script to use when she contacts Mackie.'

'If Mackie *really* killed Pardoe and Davenport, does that mean we're looking at her for Cathy Price too?' Doyle asked. 'I mean, why'd she attack her like that?'

'It could've been blackmail or, if she's as unstable as Sr Renata makes out, then maybe something Cathy said flipped a switch, set off something inside Mackie and she just lost control,' Carruthers suggested.

'Or she got someone else to do it,' Doyle said, his mind still running on the idea of an accomplice.

After his colleagues had dispersed, Noakes disappearing on the eternal quest for refreshments, Markham found he could not shake off a persistent uneasiness.

Repeatedly during the investigation, he had been visited by a feeling that a clue to these murders was to be found at the mansion house museum, almost as if it was some kind of forensic Rosetta Stone. Time and again, there had been the sensation that its treasures, especially the Ricardian exhibits, were pointing him towards a prime suspect. He had experienced the same uncanny awareness a short while back as he and Noakes contemplated that painting of St John the Baptist in the wilderness. While he was now leaning towards the conclusion that Suzanne Mackie was profoundly unbalanced and a killer, it was as if part of the jigsaw was missing and the suspect profile somehow imperfect . . . *incomplete* . . .

He had been sitting lost in thought for some time when Noakes reappeared bearing a paper sack from *Greggs* along with black coffee for Markham.

'Where *do* you put it all, Noakesy?' the DI asked as the other tucked happily into a jumbo sausage roll and cappuccino. 'I'd have thought that buffet at The Storybarn would see you through.'

'This is brain food,' was the prompt reply. 'And 'sides, it's been ever so long since that wake.'

Registering the other's appraising glance, the DI felt blear-eyed, heavy-lidded and somehow ravaged, aware that Noakes was bound to put it down to difficulties with Olivia.

'I got you a bacon an' cheese roll,' Noakes muttered awkwardly, shoving a paper bag across the desk. 'Jus' to put you on an' soak up all that black coffee.' It was obvious he thought Markham wouldn't welcome any overt sympathy and was better left to wrestle his demons without interference.

Touched by his friend's solicitude, and with difficulty repressing a shudder, Markham did his best.

After the "brain food" was consumed (leaving his office smelling like a greasy spoon), the DI shared his misgivings that he was missing something.

'I reckon you're on the right track with Mackie, guv,' Noakes said finally. 'But she must've had help.' He scratched his grizzled face thoughtfully. 'The problem being, none of the others looks screwy enough for the job. Seems to me Jason Quirk's the only one with the brawn for it . . . but then, what's the connection between him an' the bunny boiler?'

Seeing Markham's despondent expression, he continued, 'Happen Mackie'll give up Mister X.'

'Only if we manage to press the right buttons.' The DI's tone suggested it was a big *if*.

'Are you gonna authorise surveillance for Mackie?' Noakes asked.

'You mean before the DCI okays it?'

'What Sidney don' know won't hurt him.' To Noakes it was that simple.

'I don't believe anyone's in immediate danger from her, but it's probably a wise precaution,' Markham said.

'Get Blondie to say we need eyes on Mackie twenty-four seven, that should cover you.'

'I'll leave it to *you* to liaise with *Dr Shaughnessy* about that,' the DI said tartly, belatedly aware from Noakes's wolfish leer that the assignment wouldn't exactly prove to be a penance.

After Noakes had bustled away, the DI wandered across to the window. It was still grey and cold, the sky full of rain. A perfect match for his mood.

He wouldn't allow himself to think about Olivia. *Couldn't.* Once all of this was over, he would make a clean breast of it to Noakes. As one who loved them both, his friend would give him a sympathetic hearing. But he wouldn't be soft and would most likely dispense a few home truths that Markham knew he needed to hear.

He felt his shoulders, already stiff with tension, tighten even more.

What if he was clutching at straws? What if he'd got it all wrong and that strange, fussy little woman had nothing to do with the murders? What if he was pinning too much on Sr Renata's suspicions and the words of an elderly nun? What if . . .

His spirits sank even further as he remembered there would be no Olivia waiting at home for him tonight, since this was the day when school broke up and she planned to head off on her "break".

Angrily, he yanked himself back from the precipice of despairing thoughts and wrenched his mind back to the job in hand.

He would take another look at all the witness statements and suspect profiles, both for the current investigation and Priddy. That way, he would be open to anything, any sub-liminal hint buried in those papers, that might point the way to Suzanne Mackie's accomplice.

Then he'd make tracks for home.

He'd be sure to spin out the evening glass of Chateauneuf-du-Pape lest it become three or four.

Tomorrow was *Do or Die*.

## CHAPTER 13: NEW HORIZONS

The Old English Garden in Hollingrove Park was an enchanting space, Markham thought the following day as he surveyed the site of their stakeout, Sr Renata having suggested she should meet their prime suspect in that location. All those splashing fountains in the Japanese Garden with its bamboo pipe water features meant she'd be needing the loo every five seconds, she explained in a matter-of-fact fashion which rather endeared her to the DI who increasingly felt she would have made an excellent policewoman.

He was almost glad that the final act of the drama — for such he increasingly felt it to be — would take place in this tranquil, utterly English space untouched by spectres of bloodthirsty Druids and echoes of ancient savagery. The mild spring weather favoured an outdoor meeting, so Sr Renata's suggestion of the rendezvous had aroused no suspicion.

Reached by a narrow cobbled footpath, the garden teemed with glorious colour, a row of old glasshouses along its eastern wall housing various rare specimens.

'Too many chuffing benches,' Noakes groused. '*To the memory of* . . . practically every Tom, Dick 'n Harry in Bromgrove . . . bleeding *morbid* if you ask me.'

Markham, however, fell under its spell immediately.

Likewise Kate Burton, delighting in the trellises covered with climbing plants, secluded paths and pond with water lilies. 'It feels so private and peaceful,' she breathed.

'If you c'n forget our obbo in that glasshouse,' Noakes pointed out sourly.

'God Sarge, where's your *soul*?' she laughed. 'It's *paradise*.'

'Better 'n Maryvale,' he conceded grudgingly. 'Imagine us trying to set up in one of them funny whatchamacallit *parlours*, like some kind of freaking *air lock* in case the nuns get *contaminated . . . infected* or summat.' Clearly Markham's wingman was offended by what he perceived as the bacteriological connotations of monastic enclosure.

'It's not like that, Sarge,' Burton protested earnestly. 'The idea isn't that people from outside are dangerous or dirty.'

'Oh aye.' This was uttered in stentorian tones as though to say, *Stop Digging*.

'It's all about making sure the nuns stay focused on their job.'

'Whass that then?'

'Praying for the world,' she answered simply, shooting an embarrassed look at Markham.

Noakes's expression suggested to the DI that his friend preferred not to labour any such obligation to Rome, but the other merely muttered an unenthusiastic '*T'riffic.*'

'The park's cordoned off, sir,' Burton said, 'and there's plain clothes officers posted out at the Hollingrove Triangle with orders to ring through any unusual activity.'

'Excellent, Kate.'

In the meantime, the glasshouses were a perfect observation post, rigged so that the micro transmitter Sr Renata wore was guaranteed to relay every word of her conversation with Suzanne Mackie.

The nun played her part to perfection. She could have given Sarah Bernhardt a run for her money, Carruthers said afterwards in tones of profound admiration.

Slowly, inexorably, step by step, following the script agreed with Dr Shaughnessy, Sr Renata cranked up the pressure on their prime suspect until she finally reached the crucial tipping point.

'My dear,' she said, as though deeply uncertain and perplexed, 'I simply don't know what to make of these reports from Father Flynn and our parishioners.' Then, in a dithery, confused and flustered manner, like one who saw only the best in everyone and was unworldly to a fault or not of this world at all — which Markham knew was as far removed as possible from her sensible and perspicacious personality — the nun sprang her trap.

'My dear,' she began again, 'it's come to my ears that you may have . . . *had hopes* of Mr Tony Pardoe . . . behaved indiscreetly . . . given rise to rumours . . . Of course, as you know, in the convent we try never to credit gossip but—'

'*You dried up old prune.*' The words were uttered in a sibilant hiss which Markham barely recognised as Suzanne Mackie's affected trill. He didn't need to see the speaker's face to know it would be mottled, covered with an angry flush, the lipstick-flecked rabbity teeth drawn back in a snarl and madness shining behind her eyes.

'*What makes you think you can look down on me?*'

The detectives in their hiding place were tense, poised to spring, but with a peremptory gesture Markham signalled to them to wait.

*We need a confession.*

Now there was barely any need for Sr Renata to improvise, the nun's voice shrill with alarm.

'I'm so sorry, my dear, I didn't mean to cause any offence. It's just that with these murders . . . You see, I hardly know what to think . . . *inconceivable that you could be mixed up in such wickedness*, but still I wondered—' Her voice held a tearful plea.

'Obviously I did them both.'

The admission was so flat, so devoid of affect, that Markham could scarcely credit it. But still he kept his hand straight up, palm turned towards the team.

*Not yet.*

214

Sr Renata knew what was required. In a stuttering voice, she quavered, 'You mean you *killed* them . . . Mr Pardoe and that poor woman?'

'Those two had it coming, both of them! And now I've got to dispose of *you*.' Her voice rasped with impatience, like someone contemplating a tedious domestic chore.

'*PLEASE NO, GET AWAY FROM ME!*'

And now, at Sr Renata's strangled shriek, Markham gave the signal.

Bodies ricocheted through the air as the detectives, together with uniforms posted around the perimeter of the garden, hurtled towards the two women.

As Suzanne Mackie was pinioned, she gave a barely audible cry.

But Markham heard.

And knew what it meant.

Minutes later, when the call through to Burton notifying an RTA at the Hollingrove Triangle came, he had the sense that this denouement was preordained and his investigation could have ended no other way.

\* \* \*

'The burly lorry driver's face was working with distress. 'I swear to God, that bloke came out from nowhere,' Markham heard him telling a couple of uniforms. 'One minute he was on the pavement and then the next he just stepped straight out in front of me.'

'Take it easy, sir,' the older one said. 'Nobody's saying you're to blame.'

If anything, this appeared to increase the unfortunate man's agitation.

'Tell them,' he appealed desperately to a little gaggle of onlookers. 'I had *no chance* of missing him. It's as if he *wanted* it . . . walked right out into the road with this dead creepy smile on his face, like some sort of *sleepwalker*.'

'That's right, I saw how it happened,' a pedestrian volunteered. 'The way he was stood there swaying backwards and forwards and muttering to himself, I thought maybe it was someone who wasn't right in the head or something. Your man here,' he gestured at the frantic driver, 'was coming up towards the Triangle, not speeding or anything like that. The guy on the pavement waited till the lorry was almost level — the last split second — and then practically jumped in front of it . . . It seemed like slow motion, but I'd lay money he *meant* to do it . . . just something about the way he looked.'

Markham moved forward with calm assurance.

'I'll take over here,' he told the uniforms in a tone that did not admit argument before directing them to divert traffic and throw up a cordon round the Triangle. Turning back to the lorry driver, he said quietly, 'You aren't responsible for what's happened here, sir. The victim's identity is known to us.'

Noakes's jaw sagged.

*Is it?*

'*Think*, Noakesy,' the DI murmured under his breath. 'She had her mobile switched on so he could listen in to the meeting with Sr Renata. She cried out his name as we moved in.'

'I remember now . . . *Tommy*,' Kate Burton muttered. 'Tommy . . . As in *Tom*.'

*Tom Burke.*

'She was calling out a warning, telling him to get clear,' Markham's fellow DI explained, ashen-faced as she watched the pool of viscous blood widening before her eyes.

Noakes looked dazed. 'I thought she'd wigged out, calling on some dead rellie for all I knew . . . thought she were jus' spouting gibberish.' His voice dropped an octave to a hoarse whisper. 'I never thought of *Burke* . . . never *him*.'

Afterwards, Markham personally supervised removal of the accomplice's mangled remains, suspecting it would be a very long time before he would be able to expunge the image of Tom Burke's head pulped to the consistency of a grapefruit, clotted brain tissue and shards of bone mashed into his sober tweed suit. Most pitiful of all was the straggling hairpiece ground into the dirt. As the shrouded stretcher left in a little procession heading from the Triangle to Bramfield Road and Tom Burke departed Hollingrove Park for the last time, Markham said a quiet prayer for the dead man.

*Peace at last for this tormented soul and justice for those innocents he helped destroy.*

* * *

It was shortly after Easter that Markham and Dr Eleanor Shaughnessy found themselves in the beer garden at *The Grapes*.

The hostelry's formidable landlady Denise — a pneumatic peroxide blonde whose towering lacquered beehive was one of the wonders of Bromgrove — was delighted by the handsome inspector's compliments on her little empire, ushering them to a secluded nook where roses twined round a newly erected pergola.

In no time at all, Markham was settled with a large glass of Chateauneuf-du-Pape while the psychologist savoured a crisp white Chardonnay.

At first, they talked easily about trivial matters, both by instinct postponing discussion of recent events. Gradually, however, their conversation turned to the Hollingrove Park investigation, Markham accepting her congratulations on the *Gazette*'s flattering coverage with an air of ironic detachment. He had never been interested in press attention or notoriety and far preferred to remain in the background, even if this meant assigning his superiors a far greater share of plaudits than those gentlemen warranted. Somehow, he had managed to keep his own picture and backstory out of the newspaper, which meant readers were treated to the unctuously unappealing trio of Sidney, Ebury-Clarke and Bretherton in full fig. Not exactly the Three Musketeers, he thought with an inward chuckle, reflecting that he had no appetite for playing d'Artagnan.

Idly, he asked himself if there was any possibility of a relationship developing with Eleanor Shaughnessy, who had no doubt heard on the grapevine that all was not well with Olivia.

Too soon, the voice of caution told him. As things stood, he was content that she seemed willing to give him space and simply follow where he led.

'Do you remember when you gave that session on histrionic narcissism?' he asked her.

She laughed.

'Indeed I do, though I wasn't sure at the time that all your team were necessarily on board with it.'

'Oh, believe me, they found it far more interesting than the usual HR seminars.'

The psychologist chuckled again. 'I can't imagine Mr Noakes having too much patience on those occasions.'

'Let's just say I was always mortally afraid he'd heckle the speaker or come out with something outrageous at Q&As but when it comes to criminal profiling, he and Kate Burton are fertile ground thanks to their insatiable appetite for *CBS True Crime*.' He drank some more of his wine before continuing. 'Anyway, during that session I couldn't help thinking that I'd met someone *exactly* like the personality you were describing . . . only I wasn't able to place them.'

'How intriguing.'

'It was somehow all tied up with my feeling that the answer to the investigation lay in that little museum at Hollingrove Park.'

Her eyes kindled with interest. 'Oh yes, the quaint one with all those exhibits on the Druids and Richard II.'

'I realise now that *Richard II* was the ultimate narcissistic personality — puny son of a great warrior who suffered all his life from comparisons with the Black Prince and was unable to have children so couldn't even found his own dynasty—'

'If he saw the childlessness as a slur on his virility, then that, allied to physical puniness, might well have set up a neurosis — become dangerously pathological.'

'*Precisely*.' Markham was delighted by her response. 'Added to which, he was sexually conflicted and obsessed with his self-image, had to see his kingship as making him semi-divine and superior to people around him, otherwise he simply couldn't cope. His interest in the occult was another side of the same coin — a way of investing himself with a special aura that made up for other deficiencies.'

'All of it leading to grandiosity, detachment from reality and even paranoia,' she said gravely.

'That's right,' Markham said eagerly. 'The museum curator, Malcolm Devenish, called Richard a narcissist and said his vindictive streak surfaced big time after he was forced to accept a takeover by some of his nobles. When this happened again towards the end of his reign, he developed all kinds of persecutory symptoms and essentially experienced a psychotic break.'

'Where do my pearls of wisdom from the seminar fit into all this?' she asked lightly.

'You talked about how an unstable personality might respond to shifting psychological environments and *that's* what happened with Richard . . . the tectonic plates shifted when his nobles started plotting against him. It's also what happened with Suzanne Mackie and Tom Burke.'

'*Tectonic plates* . . . Hmm, I like that image,' she murmured. 'But tell me how *those two* fit the profile.'

Markham took another long draught of wine. 'Here goes then . . . This is what we've pieced together from putting their lives under the microscope and talking to other people. On the surface, Tom Burke was a somewhat prim and fussy elderly widower on the fringes of Violet Henwood's circle, though it appears she never had much time for him. He was highly possessive about the Henwood family and anything to do with the estate, so much so that he gradually became obsessed with the idea that he and the other volunteers were somehow guardians of ancient culture. Along with Suzanne Mackie, he was a member of the local Druid Society, but that attracted more than its fair share of eccentrics and oddballs so their monomania wouldn't necessarily have marked them out.'

The psychologist leaned in, flatteringly absorbed.

'It's emerged that since being widowed, Burke was struggling with his feelings for men — seeing a therapist about it.'

Her eyes widened at that. 'Go on,' she breathed.

'He was deeply closeted in the sense that he'd never acted on his homosexual impulses, but there was some raging internal conflict, probably not helped by the fact that he was helping to curate exhibits about Richard II and his male "favourites"—'

'Do you think he may have been attracted to Tony Pardoe, may have betrayed his feelings and then been rejected?' she interrupted, fascinated by the scenario he depicted.

'We'll never know. By all accounts, it was *Suzanne Mackie* who had a predatory interest in Pardoe, but people thought that she was just — how to put it — mutton dressed as lamb, always desperate to be attractive to men, more to be pitied than anything else. Anyway, the café manager Catrina Walsh recalled an event at the mansion house where Pardoe made fun of the pair of them . . . apparently he was an excellent mimic and took them off to perfection. Ms Walsh said that behind their backs he nicknamed Mackie "Poison Ivy" — because of the way she twined herself round men — while Burke was "Beetroot Face" and "the old fussbudget". He also jeered at their fixation with Druids and the occult.'

'Did the third victim — the woman who turned up tied to a tree — join in ridiculing them?'

'Loretta Davenport was at the same event, but we don't know for certain what part she played. It's likely Mackie was extremely jealous of Loretta due to the woman being Pardoe's best friend and the epitome of social sophistication — everything she herself aimed at but always ended up missing by a country mile. Apparently, she'd tried to foster some sort of connection with Loretta as a way to inveigle herself into Pardoe's circle but got nowhere with it. . . . There were probably any number of slights or imagined slights that galled Burke and Mackie . . . I've learned that Burke was morbidly sensitive about the fact that he and his wife were unable to have children — yet another parallel with Richard II

— so if Pardoe or Davenport ever joked about that, it would really have flicked him on the raw. I remember noticing that Malcolm Devenish seemed worried about Burke's reactions when we were looking at exhibits and the subject of Richard's childlessness came up . . . it was strange how he seemed oddly watchful and solicitous as if this was somehow a sore point.'

She looked startled. 'D'you think Mr Devenish had any suspicion that his friend was dangerous?'

'I don't suppose we'll ever know as he certainly hasn't been prepared to talk about it. But it was interesting that he seemed very uncomfortable when I asked if there had ever been any break-ins or interference with the exhibits, brushed it off as a case of absent-mindedness.'

'But you think now he may have suspected Burke of somehow gaining access out of hours?'

'Well, there was an unsettling report that came in about something that turned up in one of the display cases but nobody knew where it had come from — a sheet of paper covered in drawings of skulls. Devenish never reported it to us, but word got out somehow and the estate manager, Bill Whelan, made a call to the station.'

'Burke again?'

'If Devenish knows, he isn't saying, though I think it may have been by way of a calling card, some kind of twisted outlet for the rage and paranoia Burke kept bottled up for most of the time.'

There was a pause while she took this in.

'He and Mackie probably also deeply resented the fact that Pardoe's plans for the future of Hollingrove Park most definitely did not include a role for *them*,' Markham resumed.

The psychologist sipped her Chardonnay thoughtfully. 'Was *that* what tipped them over the edge?'

'Again, we'll probably never know for sure, but both felt rejected and snubbed . . . had built up a head of steam about it. They hatched the plot between them and Mackie somehow lured Pardoe to a meeting at that greenhouse. He probably went along thinking it would be fun to lead her on, watch her make a fool of herself. He wasn't averse to having a drink in the process, so she managed to get him tipsy and then *hey presto* out came the wire garotte, taking him completely by surprise. Burke helped her pose the corpse — something that I imagine gave them both considerable satisfaction.' He took another gulp of wine. 'I'd go so far as to say it unlocked something in them — sexual release, disinhibition, revenge . . . The obsession with the Druids played its part too, since at a level, they were starring in their own atavistic psychodrama.'

Despite the warmth of the day, she shivered. 'Powerful stuff.'

'I had the strangest sensation on a visit to the museum that there was evil there, literally stroking my neck, but couldn't pinpoint the source.'

'Only now you know it was Burke.'

'Yes, he and Mackie were ripe for it. It never occurred to me that someone of Burke's vintage would have the strength to lug corpses around, but he'd been in the Territorials and was much tougher than you'd imagine from the prissy exterior.'

'Poor Loretta Davenport, never realising the danger she was in.'

'She picked up on *something* hinky, just not the whole picture. Something about Suzanne Mackie bothered her and she probably felt the woman needed professional help. She may also have noticed the unwholesome dynamic between Mackie and Burke without being able to put her finger on what was wrong. Unfortunately, given Mackie's paranoia and persecution complex, by deciding to confront her, Loretta tripped the switch and sealed her fate. Once again, Burke was there waiting in the wings to help with the aftermath.' Another gulp of wine as though he was trying to rinse away something foul. 'I think Mackie got a taste for killing and egged Burke on to join her. He most likely didn't need too much persuasion given the sense of omnipotence he felt after dispatching Pardoe — and their twisted sexuality found an outlet in the quasi-erotic display of Davenport's body.'

'Would they have gone on to kill again, d'you think?'

'Who can say?' Markham rejoined sombrely. 'At any rate, Burke knew the game was up and took himself out of the equation.' He tried not to recall the image of those mangled remains and the pathetic spectacle of that toupee spattered with blood and brain matter.

'You reckon *she* was the dominant one?'

'Don't forget, she'd killed many years before when Mary Priddy had the misfortune to encounter her in that greenhouse.'

'I'd forgotten about your cold case. How did it come about that she attacked the child?'

Markham's face was grim as he recalled the briefing he had received from the local special hospital where the woman was currently confined.

'Going on what Mackie told her psych team at the Newman, it appears the little girl wandered away from the play area and somehow found her way to the Palm House where Mackie was doing "antiquarian research". According to Mackie, the child was cheeky, asking if she had permission to be there. It was when Mackie realised this was the daughter of Helen Priddy, the woman John Sinnott preferred to her, that the red mist descended. She shook Mary violently and then panicked when the child started screaming . . . one vicious shove was all it took, and next minute the child lay dead at the bottom of that slurry pit with a broken neck. It seems likely the episode was sufficiently traumatic that her violent streak lay dormant for decades after that.'

'Until a combination of circumstances, together with proximity to someone who shared her neuroses, reactivated it,' Eleanor Shaughnessy said sadly.

'There *were* red flags,' Markham said in a tone of infinite regret. 'Sr Renata and Fr Flynn sensed that Suzanne Mackie was potentially big trouble, but it wasn't until that chance sighting of her arguing with Loretta Davenport that anyone made the leap from thinking her a tiresome busybody to imagining she was capable of murder.'

He sat silently for some minutes after that, absent-mindedly running his fingers up and down the stem of his wine glass. The psychologist didn't interrupt his reverie, displaying the same soothing empathy as Kate Burton.

'The woman's medical records indicated she'd had a horrendous menopause,' he went on, 'so maybe with the right kind of therapeutic intervention, things would never have spiralled out of control.'

She was struck by the compassion in his voice.

'John Sinnott's proved himself a true friend,' Markham concluded. 'Going to visit Mackie in the Newman and standing by her. Makes me feel guilty for having imagined the man could ever have been a cold-blooded killer.'

'Will she be fit to stand trial?'

'Eventually, yes. But my bet is she'll be given a hospital order.'

'What about Cathy Price? Did she confess to attacking her?'

'The woman's so disturbed that the Newman team think it could be months before they're able to figure out exactly how it all came about. As things stand, piecing it together from her rantings, it sounds like she got it into her head that Cathy had mocked her to staff at the park, imitated her or made a joke about her being a pathetic old witch.'

'Did that really happen,' Eleanor asked, 'or was it just advanced paranoia?'

'Probably a mixture of the two,' he replied sombrely. 'Being a teenager, Cathy might well have poked fun, said something disparaging or been overheard impersonating her—'

'And then she magnified it all in her mind, to the point where she wasn't reacting rationally.'

'Exactly. Trawling back through her past, it appears there's a history of her blowing minor workplace spats out of all proportion. Then, fresh from taking revenge on Pardoe, the impulse to attack Cathy was suddenly irresistible. She'd developed a taste for it, you see . . .'

'That murder confirms her as a child killer, which might be why she can't face up to it.'

Markham's gaze was clouded, remote. 'I'm not sure we'll ever know, which means no closure for the family.'

Even as he said this, the DI knew he wouldn't rest until he had come up with some sort of coherent narrative to explain Cathy Price's murder. Appalling as it was to think that the teenager's fate was determined by Suzanne Mackie's delusional paranoia, he owed it to her parents and brother to resolve the mystery.

At that minute, Noakes came slouching towards them in what was presumably his idea of appropriate attire for a late-afternoon drink on a pleasantly warm day — baggy matelot jumper teamed with bright green cords, socks of the same hue and Jesus sandals (the beloved George boots having been honourably retired).

'Been telling the doc how it all panned out then, have you?' he demanded, plonking down a pint of Ruddles together with a large bag of pork scratchings.

'Something like that,' Markham replied easily.

'Mackie's never going to be fit to stand trial,' his friend said cheerily. 'Word is she's ranting an' raving away in the Newman . . . prob'ly imagines she's a Druid Queen or Boudicca. Next thing you know, she'll be putting a hex on the trick cyclists.'

Dr Shaughnessy's sea-blue eyes were full of merriment and her beautiful laughter echoed round the beer garden causing heads to turn and fellow drinkers to smile indulgently.

Noakes appraised the psychologist out of the corner of his eye while appearing not to do so.

Markham tried to imagine what his friend was thinking.

No doubt, he reflected, Noakes was telling himself that the guvnor had managed to land a real looker; very striking with her wonderful blonde hair, creamy complexion and blue eyes . . . Scandinavian looking too and blessed with a great figure.

It was certainly true that Eleanor possessed all of those attributes in full measure, along with a statuesque stateliness that was somewhat reminiscent of Penny Mordaunt, the

MP who did such a great job holding up the sword at King Charles's coronation. Added to which, she was a nice woman — or, as Noakes would undoubtedly put it, 'not totally up herself like some of that snotty lot at the university.' Now she and his friend were chatting away happily about how the country was going to the dogs and they needed to bring back national service and tell all the spotty herberts to 'Stand by your beds'.

Of course, relaxed camaraderie was one thing, but Markham was willing to bet Noakes wouldn't be pleased if he took things further with the psychologist. When all was said and done, the other regarded himself as Olivia Mullen's man through and through. He would undoubtedly take the attitude that whatever had gone wrong between her and the guvnor surely wasn't so bad that it couldn't be fixed and any Norse goddess should jolly well butt out.

Markham decided that Noakes's fears were groundless. While he liked Eleanor Shaughnessy, his deepest feelings were engaged elsewhere. For the time being, it was a case of patching over the loneliness inside . . .

'No sign of Burton?' Noakes grunted.

'Kate's headed off to a wellness retreat for Easter,' Markham replied casually.

Noakes's wink in response suggested that he took this to mean Burton was off practising being a nun or doing her "time out" thing at Maryvale. No doubt he would be counting on 'the boss woman, Mother Wotsit' to straighten her out, Markham thought with an amused inner eye roll. He imagined his friend's logic: Burton could just as easily do her dad proud in CID as in a convent saying rosaries and trying to get people time off Purgatory. And of course there was the additional bonus that with Burton tucked out of sight at Maryvale, the way was clear for Markham and Olivia to get back together.

The DI's voice interrupted these ruminations.

'Will Doyle and Carruthers be joining us?'

'It's Bromgrove Rovers against Aston Villa tonight, boss,' this in a tone of mild reproach, 'so I'll be heading off to Doyle's once I've had my pint.'

'How's the private investigation work going, Mr Noakes?' Eleanor Shaughnessy asked politely.

'The estate manager down at the park reckons his next-door neighbour has been having a go at the hedge in his front garden, hacking bits off on the sly . . . wants me to sort it.'

*Secateurs at dawn*, Markham thought, stifling a grin.

'An' then I'm doing a job for this bloke out in Old Carton who reckons one of his lot are on the fiddle.' The proprietor (and sole operative) of *Medway Investigations* self-consciously smoothed down his wayward thatch. 'Could get me into company fraud, mebbe *industrial espionage*, provided I play my cards right.'

'But you'll be ready, willing and able whenever the call comes from CID, eh Noakesy?' Markham said lightly, with an undercurrent of deep meaning behind his words.

*'Jus' you try and stop me.'*

And with that, George Noakes put down his glass, stuffed the remainder of his snack into the dreadful trousers (waste not want not) and, with a parting wave, departed.

Shadows crept across the beer garden, but the inspector and psychologist lingered on, chatting easily about investigations past and present.

After they had gone their separate ways and Markham was back in his empty flat, he told himself that maybe the split with Olivia was for the best. Once Kate Burton emerged from her self-imposed purdah, he was going to do something about the unresolved sexual tension between them. What was the worst that could happen?

In the meantime, whatever happened in his personal life, he still had his work and the gang.

*Onwards* to whatever the morrow might bring.

### THE END

# THE JOFFE BOOKS STORY

We began in 2014 when Jasper agreed to publish his mum's much-rejected romance novel and it became a bestseller.

Since then we've grown into the largest independent publisher in the UK. We're extremely proud to publish some of the very best writers in the world, including Joy Ellis, Faith Martin, Caro Ramsay, Helen Forrester, Simon Brett and Robert Goddard. Everyone at Joffe Books loves reading and we never forget that it all begins with the magic of an author telling a story.

We are proud to publish talented first-time authors, as well as established writers whose books we love introducing to a new generation of readers.

We won Trade Publisher of the Year at the Independent Publishing Awards in 2023 and Best Publisher Award in 2024 at the People's Book Prize. We have been shortlisted for Independent Publisher of the Year at the British Book Awards for the last five years, and were shortlisted for the Diversity and Inclusivity Award at the 2022 Independent Publishing Awards. In 2023 we were shortlisted for Publisher of the Year at the RNA Industry Awards, and in 2024 we were shortlisted at the CWA Daggers for the Best Crime and Mystery Publisher.

We built this company with your help, and we love to hear from you, so please email us about absolutely anything bookish at feedback@joffebooks.com.

If you want to receive free books every Friday and hear about all our new releases, join our mailing list here: www.joffe-books.com/freebooks

And when you tell your friends about us, just remember: it's pronounced Joffe as in coffee or toffee!